Mack Bolan stepped across the gunman's body

Flattening himself against the wall, he listened for the sound of footsteps, but the corridor remained quiet. He risked a glance around the corner and found no one there.

Suddenly he heard pounding boot heels drawing nearer and unclipped a thermite grenade from his web belt. He depressed the safety spoon, listening, gauging the distance of his enemies. On a count of three, he reached around the corner and pitched the grenade uprange.

A fireball blossomed in the corridor, its superheated shock wave roiling up the hall. Men began to scream, tearing at the thermite coals that ate at their flesh.

Bolan emerged from cover in a combat crouch, Uzi up and tracking, stuttering death. In ten seconds it was all over, and he was alone with the dead.

Or so he thought.

MACK BOLAN

The Executioner

DON PENDLETON's EXECUTIONER

MACK BOLAN

Time to Kill

A GOLD EAGLE BOOK FROM
WORLDWIDE

TORONTO • NEW YORK • LONDON • PARIS
AMSTERDAM • STOCKHOLM • HAMBURG
ATHENS • MILAN • TOKYO • SYDNEY

First edition December 1987

ISBN 0-373-61108-0

Special thanks and acknowledgment to
Mike Newton for his contribution to this work.

Printed in Canada

You cannot throw words like heroism and sacrifice
and nobility and honor away without abandoning
the qualities they express.

—Marya Mannes

A hero is a man who does what he can.

—Romain Rolland

Heroism doesn't enter into the equation, this time.
I'm a soldier, doing everything I can to stop the
savages from destroying our world. If that entails a
sacrifice, I'm ready.

—Mack Bolan

To the 700-plus members of the United Nations peacekeeping forces who have given their lives in the cause of world peace.

PROLOGUE

"C'mon, then, lass. It's nae much farther."

Rebecca Rafferty glanced back in the direction of Cairnaben, where the scattered lights looked warm and welcoming. Too far, she thought, but kept it to herself and reached for Tommy Cullen's hand. He helped her up the slope and led her toward the hulking shadow of the castle, still a hundred meters distant.

"Are you sure nobody's there?" she asked again.

"Of course I'm sure," he told her reassuringly. "The laird's gone inta Glasgow, as I told ye. D'ye think I'd bring ye up here for a public show?"

Rebecca shook her head and gave his hand a little squeeze. He wanted her too much to court the risk of serious embarrassment for both of them, and understanding how he wanted her, the passion that was hidden just behind his gentle eyes, had caused her to agree when he suggested that they pay a visit to the castle. Still, the place *did* have an evil reputation, if you listened to the village gossip. If Rebecca had been superstitious, she would have insisted that they try her father's barn, and damn the risk of possible discovery.

Aside from furtive gropings in the darkness when he took her to the cinema or drove her home, she had not "been" with Tommy—or with any boy. The time had come to change all that, however, and she was determined that the first time should be special, unforgettable. If making love inside a ruined castle heightened the experience for both of them, then she was willing to suppress her childish fears and play along.

Tommy Cullen was so persuasive. It was not so much what he said, as how he used his hands when he was whispering his sweet words to her in the dark. She could refuse him nothing when he touched her, and it was only due to circumstance, the lack of decent opportunity, that she had put him off this long. She always seemed to be on curfew, or her father was at home. Lately she had come to understand the raw frustration he must be feeling, and she had decided that the situation must be put to rights.

It had involved deception of her parent, but Rebecca thought he would forgive her, if he only understood the depth of her devotion to Tommy. He must have felt the same about her mother once, but there was no way on God's earth she could discuss her choice with him. Thankfully the plan was foolproof. Barring some disaster that might wake her father before his usual time, she would be safely back at home, in bed, without his ever knowing she had left the house.

The lights of Cairnaben were going out and mist was rolling in from the sea, but Rebecca knew that they would have no problem getting home. The narrow road would be impossible to miss, and once you found it, there was no place you could go other than the village. Getting home was simple. It was still the castle that unnerved her.

Looming over them, no more than fifty meters distant now, the place was more a shell than a ruin. Rebecca had occasionally played here as a child, and despite the intervening years, she still remembered most of it. The outer walls were sound enough—or had been ten years ago. She could recall the massive, curving staircase that led to the tower. In some bygone age the roof had fallen in, and most of the interior walls had been demolished and the stone carted away. There would still be a basement, but she had no wish to see it or discover what was living there in constant darkness.

She did not believe the stories of a ghost who prowled the castle, carrying its severed head beneath one arm and searching for its long-dead adversaries from the olden days. Such tales were for children and old men in their cups; they had no place beneath the light of day.

But Lord, it was so dark tonight.

"This way."

Tommy led her up a path constructed out of crumbling stones, Rebecca slowing him as she tried to watch her footing in the wan moonlight. They reached an archway, formerly a doorway from all appearances, and Tommy hesitated, turning to face her in the shadows.

"Here's your last chance to escape," he told her, smiling. As he spoke he slipped one arm around her waist and bent his head to nuzzle her neck. Rebecca shivered, felt a warm glow spread throughout her body as Tommy's lips trailed across her skin.

"Inside with you," she told him breathlessly. "We haven't got all night."

Reluctantly he pulled away and led her through the Gothic arch and into the deeper shadows of the castle proper. Though the roof was gone, the massive walls prohibited the moonlight from invading darkened corners, and Rebecca clung to Tommy's hand, uncertain of her footing. She hoped there were no rats in residence and was incredibly relieved when Tommy pulled a flashlight from the pocket of his coat and turned it on.

The staircase rose before them, lost in shadow at the top where the beam from Tommy's flashlight failed to reach. He led the way, alert for steps that might have loosened over time, or stones that might have fallen from above. Rebecca started counting the steps to take her mind off the darkness that surrounded them. Then she switched her thoughts to Tommy Cullen and the pleasure they were about to share. She knew it was right.

"Your chamber, ma'am."

The flashlight revealed a room with seamless walls that looked as if they had been etched from living stone. The ceiling here was more or less intact, and there were open windows facing the sea. Rebecca knew that they had reached the summit of the western tower, something she had never risked in childhood. But the games were different now, and it was only right that they should find the castle's highest point, above the hollow shell that lay below.

Tommy killed the flash, but the windows provided enough light to see by. Rebecca moved to stand before the nearest portal, studying the restless sea. Tommy stepped up close behind her, strong hands circling her waist, then rising to cup her breasts. She covered his hands with her own and pulled him tight against her, feeling his excitement as he moved against her, again nuzzling her soft nape.

A sound from below intruded on Rebecca's consciousness. She heard it quite distinctly.

"What's that noise?" she asked.

"Noise?" She heard confusion and frustration in Tommy's voice. "What noise?"

"Downstairs."

"It's your imagination, Becky."

"No, it isn't. Listen!"

Eerie silence, broken seconds later by another shuffling sound.

"A rat."

"How do you know?"

"What else? Nobody lives here, do they, now?"

She turned to face him. "Somebody might have followed us." It was illogical, at best, but she was trying not to think about the castle's reputation, all the stories.

"Like who?"

"I don't *know* who. Your brother, maybe."

"Ryan? Nae, he wouldna have the nerve." But she had set him thinking. "If I caught him spyin' after us, I'd whip him."

The scuffling sound was closer. Rebecca's hand was trembling involuntarily as she reached out for Tommy.

"I'm afraid," she whispered. "It's no good this way. If you could find out what it is . . ."

"What? *Now?*"

She forced a smile. "Please?"

"Aye," he grumbled, pouting as he turned away.

"Hurry, Tom."

"I'm goin', blast it."

"Please be careful."

"It's a rat, I'm tellin' ye."

He left the chamber, padding down the stairs in darkness, and Rebecca thought he must have turned the flashlight off to keep from giving himself away. If someone *was* below—his brother or the constable, for instance—Tommy would have an opportunity to spot him first without giving himself away.

Rebecca moved to the doorway of the chamber and listened as Tommy made his cautious way downstairs. He would protect her, she was sure of that, no matter what might happen. It was probably a rat, as he suspected, but the opportunity to act as her defender would not hurt his ego any, come to think of it.

She heard his voice. "Is anybody there?"

A flash of light was visible below, immediately lost as Tommy cried out in surprise. Or was it fright? She heard a kind of slither-scraping sound before the mocking silence reasserted dominance below her in the shadows.

"Tommy?"

Frightened by the silent darkness, she was afraid to raise
her voice above a whisper.

"Tommy? Can you hear me?"

Nothing.

She forced herself across the threshold, knowing that she
had to navigate the darkened stairs. He must have fallen,
hurt himself, and he would need her. If he had been seriously hurt, it would be her responsibility to summon help,
and never mind her father's anger or the damage to her
precious reputation for being at the castle alone with a man.
It was such an unimportant thing compared to Tommy's
safety.

Stretching out one hand to guide herself along the wall,
Rebecca cautiously descended, testing every step before she
trusted it with her weight. She could not stop the trembling
in her limbs, but she was able to negotiate the stairs with
caution, taking longer than she might have if there had been
moonlight to assist her. At the bottom of the staircase she
called his name again, a little louder this time.

There was no answer from the darkness.

Her foot struck something round, cylindrical, and in the
heartbeat left before she cried out in surprise, Rebecca realized that it must be the flashlight. She went to her hands
and knees, her fingers scrabbling across the rocky floor until she found it, and clasped it to her breast in sweet relief.

She turned the flashlight on and played its beam around
the rugged, lichen-covered walls, immediately sweeping
lower, toward the floor, where Tommy must have fallen if
he tripped or tumbled from the stairs. It took a moment for
her to identify the twisted bundle lying almost at her feet,
but then Rebecca recognized his denim shirt, the shock of
reddish hair. It was a wonder that she had not laid her hand
upon him while she scrambled for the flashlight.

"Tommy?"

There was something strange, unnatural, about his posture. One arm was twisted backward underneath him, his face averted at an angle. Sudden panic gripped Rebecca, and she was about to reach for Tommy when a grating sound behind her stopped her short.

She whirled around and raised the flashlight, froze as she saw the hulking figure revealed in its beam. The face was pale, cadaverous, with yellow eyes and crooked, rotting teeth.

She screamed—or would have, if a giant hand had not reached out to pinch off the sound in her throat. She swung the flashlight toward the lifeless face and felt it batted casually away as she was lifted off the floor. Rebecca could not breathe, and motes of light were swimming on the inside of her eyelids as she kicked and struggled, weakening with every heartbeat. There was a roaring sound in her ears, but it was fading as consciousness slipped away and was lost.

Long moments later, when she was released, Rebecca Rafferty felt nothing as her body hit the floor.

1

The tall man stood in darkness, scanning the city lights below. Then he moved along the roof's perimeter until he faced the River Clyde, whose docks had given birth to countless oceangoing liners, not least among them the *Queen Mary* and the *Queen Elizabeth II*. By night you could not tell the river was polluted and discolored with industrial effluvium. In darkness it was merely swift and powerful, an elemental force of nature.

Glasgow, the commercial capital of Scotland and home of half the country's citizens, is the third largest city in the British Isles. Her contributions to the arts and history are numerous, but none of those had drawn the tall man to a rooftop on the riverfront this warm spring night. Despite her galleries and parks, museums and grand cathedrals, Glasgow was a city that—like every other great metropolis—had different faces, visible in different circumstances and at different times. The face that drew Mack Bolan to the Glasgow riverfront that evening was a mask of violence, etched in blood.

As with the other major cities of the world, Glasgow was not without her slums—the Gorbals—wherein life had been reduced to brute survival, jungle rules for urban hunting grounds. Ranked among the worst of Western Europe's slums, the Gorbals bred disease and violent discontent with an apparently unfeeling status quo. By slow degrees the district was surrendering to urban redevelopment, but years might pass—or decades—before the salvage operation was successful. If it *ever* was.

Meanwhile the streets bred discontent, and discontent bred violence with a revolutionary twist. As in a hundred other cities, petty criminals with grand delusions made an effort to politicize their crimes, selecting slogans, choosing scapegoats, martyrs. In the stews of Glasgow, voices had been raised for independence, violent severing of ties with London, "Scotland for the Scots." If British rule was overthrown, the voices cried, there would be tax reductions, cash enough to go around and jobs for every able-bodied Scotsman. Tyranny had built the slums, and it would take a violent countertyranny to bring them down.

A guiding force behind the revolutionary movement was the so-called Tartan Army, based in Glasgow. With a membership composed of Gorbal thugs and wild-eyed true believers, the group had launched a small but earnest war against the British in Glasgow, lately branching out into the Scottish countryside. There had been bombings, an assassination and several abductions that had fattened the coffers with ransom money. Rumors had begun to circulate of Tartan links with the IRA, the Basques and remnants of the Baader-Meinhof gang. With such connections, analysts suggested, aid from Moscow and the KGB could not be far behind. Some thought it had arrived already in the form of smuggled AK-47s, rocket launchers and grenades.

Mack Bolan made no effort to dismiss the grievances that fueled the Tartan Army's revolutionary fire. The Executioner was no historian, but he was cognizant of certain basic truths. He knew that random violence, aimed at innocent civilians, never had and never would accomplish anything of substance. Mindless violence led to chaos, not Utopia, and terrorism, left unchecked, inevitably grew to feed upon itself, with carnage proving to be both means *and* end. Sometimes strategic counterviolence was required to stem the bloody tide, and Bolan was as proficient as a surgeon when it came to coping with the dark malignancy of terrorism.

He had been pursuing traffickers in heroin, along a brand-new pipeline from the Middle East, through London, to America. The Tartan Army situation had interrupted him, and now the chase would have to wait, the job half-finished while he dealt with more immediate concerns.

The Tartan Army, it seemed, was growing up. It was about to graduate from local small-scale mayhem to the major leagues. In two days' time the British prime minister was scheduled to visit Glasgow in the company of cabinet members and the American undersecretary of state. According to a late strategic leak, the Tartan Army was preparing a reception for the visitors that would, quite literally, knock them dead. If they succeeded, members of the clique would instantly surpass the score of Northern Ireland's finest and secure for themselves a foothold in the headlines. Britain—and the world—would be forced to take them seriously.

Maggie Thatcher and the queen had ample troops at their disposal, but the Scottish terrorists' selection of an American target, as well as Bolan's presence in the general neighborhood, had motivated Washington to make an extraordinary move. Instead of passing information from the recent leak to Downing Street, the Oval Office decided on a brisk, preemptive strike against the Tartan Army in their own hometown. A thrust that if not ending the danger outright would at least retard the serpent's growth. If there were diplomatic repercussions afterward, let the undersecretary earn his pay while he was on the scene.

It had been relatively easy to locate the Tartan Army's base of operations in the Gorbals. One of its financial angels owned an ancient, run-down tenement that overlooked the River Clyde and had been recently condemned. Though unfit for human occupation, it fit the needs of the terrorists precisely, and a spate of secret renovations had assured that it would not collapse around their heads while they were plotting treason in their seventh-floor stronghold. Tonight the Tartan Army's high command had been assembled to discuss their latest hit. The revolutionary thugs were looking forward to a brighter day, but they had reckoned without Mack Bolan.

He was clad in a blacksuit, face and hands masked by combat cosmetics. The sleek Beretta 93-R nestled in side-leather beneath one arm, already fitted with it s custom silencer. The silver AutoMag was in its place of honor, riding military webbing on the soldier's hip, while canvas pouches circling his waist held extra magazines for both side arms. The warrior's combat harness carried a heavy K-Bar fighting knife, and flash and frag grenades, which were designed to stun or slaughter in accordance with the circumstances.

Bolan's head weapon for the Glasgow strike was a mini-Uzi submachine gun, chambered for 9 mm parabellums. With its cyclic rate of 1200 rounds per minute, the stubby weapon was a man-shredder, built to work up close and personal. Measuring barely ten inches overall, the machine pistol merged impressive firepower with concealability in a single, very lethal package. Bolan wore his mini-Uzi on a shoulder strap, with extra 32-round magazines secured in a bandolier across his chest.

The rusty fire escape would be his means of access to the Tartan Army's drab command post. He had discreetly checked out the building that afternoon and discovered that the three street-level entrances were manned around the clock. He could have taken out the guards—and probably without a fuss—but there was still the chance of setting off alarms and scattering his prey before he had a chance to seal off their retreat. The roof was carelessly unguarded, telling

Bolan that while his opponents might be ready to elude police detectives, they were not prepared for a surprise attack delivered by professionals.

The fire escape was ancient and heavily corroded, but it held Bolan's weight as he scrambled down to crouch outside a window on the seventh floor. The windows had been painted over, here and on the next two floors below, ensuring privacy from prying eyes along the waterfront. Inside, the leaders of the Tartan Army could conduct their business in as much security as they could hope to find in Glasgow. They were gathered here tonight, and Bolan meant to teach them just how very *in*secure they had become.

He unclipped two flash grenades from his harness, pulling the pins free on both, holding the safety spoons in place. The move he had in mind would be a matter of precision timing if he was to pull it off. If there was a fumble or delay, Bolan stood a decent chance of being incapacitated with his human targets when the eggs went off.

He started counting down, already braced to scramble up the fire escape as soon as he released the grenades. On *three*, he pitched the first one through the nearest painted window, following a fraction of a second later with the second thrown through a different blacked-out pane. A startled curse was audible from the interior, but Bolan was already up and moving, climbing, as the doomsday numbers ran down in his mind.

Despite the cover of a wall and intervening distance, the concussion of the two grenades was staggering. A blinding flash of light would keep the Tartan warriors from responding with effective fire, while the explosive shock wave perforated eardrums and spewed shattered window glass into the alley below. Not waiting for the smoke to clear, he hit the seventh-story landing in a combat crouch and vaulted through the smoking window frame, his mini-Uzi probing out ahead of him to answer any challenge.

Men were writhing on the floor and staggering through drifting clouds of acrid smoke, hands clasped against their eyes and ears. A few appeared to be unconscious; most were merely shaken, momentarily blinded and deafened by the antipersonnel explosives. Bolan knew that he could not allow them to recover from their shock if he intended to survive.

The Uzi made a sound like ripping canvas as he stroked off short, precision bursts. His targets toppled, awkward in the attitudes of death, some of them fumbling for weapons as their ringing ears picked up the sound of hostile fire. Four straw men. Five. A sixth. He cut them down in turn, then fed the Uzi another magazine and went to work on the unconscious soldiers, making certain that they would not rise again.

A rising clatter shook the stairs and Bolan moved to meet the sentries who had been outside the range of his grenades. He caught the first two on the landing just below him, swept them with a blazing figure eight of parabellum rounds that blew them both away before they realized they were dying on their feet. Others hung back out of sight and pumped reflexive fire along the stairwell, riddling the walls to no effect.

Bolan lobbed a frag grenade, heard desperate curses as the lethal egg was recognized, its blast devouring the swift tattoo of running feet. It was illogical to think that he had killed them all, but it would have to do. He did not have the time or inclination to pursue them through the streets, and they were soldiers of the line, in any case. His war was with the Tartan Army's brass.

A hasty head count made it nine men down, and Bolan spent a moment scooping up the documents and memoranda that had been unceremoniously scattered by the blast of his grenades. Some of the papers had been singed, others bore a speckling of blood, but they would serve. Delivered to Scotland Yard or the SIS, they might provide the key to mopping up surviving members of the Tartan Army in the field.

Concentrating on picking up the scattered documents, Bolan almost missed the sound of a door opening cautiously behind him. Almost. As it was, he had a heartbeat to respond, reflexes taking over as a bullet sliced the air beside his face.

Perhaps the drifting smoke had saved him, or perhaps the gunner had been overanxious. Just emerging from a tiny, squalid bathroom with his pants around his knees, he had been protected from the worst of the concussion. He had heard the others die and decided to take the armed intruder by surprise. The fact that he had never paid attention in his life to squeaky hinges would come back to haunt him now, in spades.

Bolan held the Uzi's trigger down and let the little weapon wander, spewing parabellum manglers in a ragged arc. Enough of them struck home to lift the gunner off his feet and hurl him backward through the open doorway of the bathroom. He rebounded from the filthy sink, collapsing in a limp, untidy heap against the bowl of the commode. Bolan jettisoned the empty magazine and snapped a fresh one in its place.

"For Christ's sake, don't shoot *me*!"

The voice appeared to emanate from everywhere, and nowhere. Bolan scanned the killing ground again and settled on a closet set beside the tiny bathroom. Several of his parabellum rounds had pierced the flimsy door, around chest-level, splintering the panel in an abstract pattern.

"Show yourself!" he barked, the stutter gun unwaveringly locked on target ow.

"I wish I could."

The voice was weaker now, without the strident urgency of life and death. Aware that it could be a trap, Bolan sidled toward the closet, ready to respond with scathing fire to any hostile overture. He stood to one side, gripped the knob and threw the door wide open, ready for the half-expected blast.

"I trust you'll pardon me if I don't stand."

He found a battered figure huddled on the closet floor, wrists bound behind his back in such a way that they were also tethered to his ankles. Despite the darkness of the closet, it was obvious that he had suffered brutal punishment; his eyes were swollen almost shut, his face discolored from the beatings he had absorbed. The captive's tattered shirt bore many bloodstains.

The K-Bar slit his bonds, but the man made no immediate attempt to rise. As Bolan helped him to his feet, the prisoner kept one hand pressed against his ribs, and he could not suppress a painful groan.

"I think I'll have to sit the next one out," he quipped, and cracked the semblance of a smile, grotesque on his misshapen features.

"No can do," the soldier told him. "We're already running out of numbers, and I don't have time to chat with the police."

"You fellows do a bang-up job, I'll give you that, but I must still insist that interagency cooperation is the key to ultimate success."

The guy was rambling, perhaps as the result of a concussion, but Bolan did not have the time to sort it out just now. The hostage needed urgent medical attention, and a riot squad would be en route by now, alerted to reports of gunfire and explosions in the Gorbals. With the current atmosphere of tension, they might be inclined to let their weapons do the talking, sorting out the pieces later, but it didn't really matter. Bolan was a foreign national who had committed several homicides and other felonies on British soil. The

White House would be forced to disavow him if he let himself be taken, and he was not ready for another murder trial.

"This way," he instructed, helping to support the battered captive as they crossed the smoky killing ground.

"A bang-up job," the stranger said again. "I have to hand it to you chaps at SAS."

The Executioner suppressed an urge to laugh, already concentrating on the crossing from their building to the next line. His bruised companion did not seem to notice.

"A trifle flashy, I suppose," he said, "but never mind. I mean to sing your praises dutifully when I get back to MI-5."

2

"A damned good thing for me you dropped in when you did," the newly liberated hostage said when they had reached the street. "Those bastards would have had me in the Clyde tonight, and no mistake."

"My pleasure," Bolan told him, still uncertain how to treat the man's assumption that he worked for SAS, Britain's elite Special Air Service team of antiterrorist commandos. He had enough to cope with at the moment, just sorting out the fact that his companion was an operative of MI-5, the covert security service responsible for internal security and domestic counterintelligence activities.

It stood to reason that the Tartan Army would be under scrutiny by MI-5, but Bolan was surprised to find one of their agents trussed up like a Christmas turkey in a closet of the terrorists' command post, ready for the slaughter. The guy had been through some sincere interrogation, doubtless as the Tartans tried to find out his identity and the names of his employers. He was hurting, still unsteady on his feet, and there had been a time or two when Bolan thought that he would lose him as they scrambled down another fire escape a half block from the terrorist HQ.

Another fifty meters and they were at the rental car that Bolan had sequestered in a narrow alley, safe from prying eyes. The soldier bundled his companion into the passenger's seat, then stowed his mini-Uzi in the trunk, slipped on a trench coat and slid in behind the wheel.

"I really ought to thank you," the agent said.

"You have."

"No, properly, I mean."

Before he shook the hand that was extended, Bolan noted that a couple of the fingernails were missing, crudely ripped away as if with pliers. His companion winced a little as they shook, but smiled around the pain.

"Harry Wilson. But, of course, you know that."

"Do I?"

"Certainly. I mean, you *were* dispatched to find me... weren't you?"

Bolan did not need to answer that one. He saw realization dawning in Wilson's eyes as the man from MI-5 reassessed his narrow brush with death.

"Good Lord. How extraordinary."

Bolan put the rental car in motion, wheeling onto Clyde Street. In his rearview mirror he observed a crowd assembled on the sidewalk near his recent target. Smoke was pouring from the topmost windows in a volume that was not consistent with the usual effect of stun grenades.

Someone had set the place on fire.

He thought about the possibilities and swiftly settled on the Tartan sentries. He had taken out two of them, at least, and might have bagged another one or two with his grenade, but he could not assume that there were no survivors. Lacking time and the ability to transport any gear or papers that were still inside the terrorist command post, fire would be the logical alternative for cleaning house. A decent conflagration would destroy all documents and incriminating lists, as well as delay positive ID on any of the dead. With any luck, police might be confounded for a period of days, while the surviving terrorists regrouped and found themselves another sanctuary. By the time their late, lamented leaders were identified, replacements would be issuing new orders, plotting new campaigns.

When viewed from that light, Bolan's effort might seem wasted, futile. But the documents he had gathered from the terrorist command post would provide police and MI-5 with a directory of Tartan Army backers, the financial angels and covert supporters who had kept the terrorists in money, guns and ammunition. Once that basis of support was swept away, the self-appointed "freedom fighters" would be easy pickings, vulnerable even on their own home ground.

As for the Executioner, his own most urgent errand at the moment was the delivery of Harry Wilson to the nearest hospital. The man from MI-5 sat hunched in pain, arms cradling his rib cage, breathing shallowly, and Bolan noted crusts of blood around his ears. He had absorbed hellacious punishment, perhaps for days on end, and Bolan would not be inclined to bet against the presence of internal injuries. For all of that, the guy was still intent on talking as they drove.

"Good thing you happened by just now," he said, still managing a smile despite the pain he must be suffering. "We haven't got much time."

"I know about the PM's visit," Bolan answered, hoping it would calm him down. "Relax, the meet's secure."

Beside him, Wilson stiffened in the bucket seat, eyes widening in evident surprise.

"The PM's visit? Damn it, man, I don't care anything about the PM's visit! I've been feeding intel back to MI-5 on that for days. Security's so tight, the boys had fairly given up on trying anything."

"So, what's the problem?"

"It's the *shipment*! Don't you understand that? Don't you understand *anything*?"

Bolan was making a left onto Saltmarket, which would become High Street a few blocks farther on and take him straight into emergency receiving at the nearest hospital, but something in Wilson's tone alerted him to danger, and he swerved the rental off into a side street, pulling up against the curb with engine idling.

He turned to Wilson, pinned the guy with eyes of tempered steel.

"What shipment?"

"Arms from Redland, coming through Cairnaben. Off the trawlers, near as I can tell. I put out one dispatch before they figured I was grassing and they started playing Twenty Questions. I was hoping my report had gotten through."

"Cairnaben?"

"Right. That's west, not far from Mallaig. We've been watching trawlers, and—"

A sudden coughing fit seized Wilson, doubling him over in his seat. He coughed dark blood onto the dash, his rumpled slacks, the carpeting. Without a moment's hesitation Bolan cranked the rental car around in a tight U-turn and nosed into the flow on Saltmarket, heading north. It was less than a mile to the hospital now, and he wondered if his passenger would make it. A police car passed them, headed in the opposite direction, flashing lights and whooping siren emptying the lanes ahead as officers responded to the shooting call. Too late.

As Bolan drove, his mind was occupied with sorting out the pieces of the puzzle the man from MI-5 had laid before him. It had long been documented that the IRA had access to Soviet weapons, and of late a similar arrangement with the Tartan Army had been generally assumed, but the pipeline hadn't been exposed. The capture of a load in transit, preferably while still aboard—or just off-loading from—a Russian trawler, would embarrass Moscow and provide the Western powers with a hefty propaganda weapon. Not that Soviet support for terrorists around the world was any kind of secret, but the KGB had never been precisely interrupted in the act of arming murderers before. If Bolan could disrupt a standing operation and humiliate his adversaries in the process, the opportunity might be too good to miss.

On the other hand, if Wilson had already passed the information on to his superiors, then Bolan might be stumbling into a cross fire with the Soviets and MI-5. Involvement of a wild card like himself might blow the British play and inadvertently assist the Russians; it would certainly increase the odds against survival for a solitary man, outnumbered and outgunned on every side.

And if the message had not been received by MI-5, what then?

"When was the shipment due to land?" he asked when Wilson seemed to have recovered from his coughing fit.

"Tonight, tomorrow morning... it depends. Whichever, plan another day or two for transport. After that, there won't be a hope in hell of finding anything until the guns start turning up in Belfast... or in London, for that matter."

The pain struck again, low and hard, forcing out Wilson's breath from between clenched teeth. Beneath the mottled bruises and the drying blood, he was as pale as death.

"I think the bastards may have done for me," he said. Incredibly he smiled.

"We're almost there. Hang on."

The hospital parking lot was crowded with vehicles and pedestrians weaving their way between ranks of cars as visiting hours got under way. Bolan followed the signs for emergency receiving, circling around to the rear of the building, parking his rental in a space designated For Ambulance Only.

Wilson was a deadweight in his arms as Bolan helped him from the car. The man from MI-5 could barely stand, but Bolan draped one arm across his shoulders, serving as a human crutch as they proceeded toward the double doors of the emergency receiving room. A startled nurse glanced up as Bolan entered, taking in his blackened face and hands in wonderment, proceeding to a brisk, professional assessment of his maimed companion.

"This way, quickly!"

Bolan followed her through swinging doors, and other nurses suddenly appeared as if from nowhere, taking Wilson off his hands. They helped him climb onto a linen-draped examination table, plumped pillows underneath his head, one of the women racing off to find the resident on duty. Bolan wished the man all the best, dropped the sheaf of captured Tartan Army documents on an empty bed beside the door and took himself away from there.

It was still early yet for the parade of casualties who were Emergency Receiving's stock in trade. The doctors should have ample time with Wilson, provided that the guy had any time to spare. There was a chance that Bolan had arrived too late to help him, but he could not let the thought prey on his mind. The man from MI-5 had been an unexpected bonus, and his information just might prove to be the jackpot.

Firing up the rental, Bolan wheeled across the crowded parking lot and found himself a corner on the far perimeter. He left the engine running as he wiped the battlefield cosmetic from his face and hands, already running down the odds and angles of a makeshift operation in his mind.

For openers, destruction of the narcotics pipeline would have to wait. Bolan didn't like leaving a job half done, but there appeared to be no viable alternative. If Wilson's information on the weapons shipment was correct, the soldier had a deadline he could not afford to miss. He might already be too late, but there was still a chance, and while that chance remained, he felt compelled to seize the time.

Possible entanglement with MI-5, that worried Bolan. Walking into an operation cold and unprepared was bad enough, but risks were multiplied tenfold when there were friendly players on the field along with hostiles, unidentified as such. Uniforms were not standard issue in the MI-5, Bolan knew, and he had no desire to take out any friendlies by mistake. Throughout his private war, the Executioner had never fired upon a soldier of the same side, and he didn't like the thought of starting now as a result of ignorance.

It would be simpler to just forget about this lead and put his faith in British state security, go on about his business and forget the whole damned thing. Except that turning off his mind to challenges had never been a strong point with the Executioner. If Russian arms were coming into Scotland from the sea and Bolan had an opportunity to staunch the flow, he could not walk away and leave his duty unfulfilled.

If nothing else, he could detour through Cairnaben, have a look around, and scrub the mission if it looked like MI-5 or SAS had matters well in hand. If he should stumble on an arms consignment in the process, incidental to his visit, so much the better. Let the Russians know their moves were being monitored, observed. Prepare them for the fact of opposition each and every time they planted unclean feet on foreign soil.

So much for hesitation. He would turn the rental in, acquire another, and declare himself a short "vacation" in Cairnaben. If he came up empty, then he would have lost a day or two at most.

The Executioner was primed and ready. Either way it played, the lead from Harry Wilson was an opportunity he could not afford to pass. But he was going in with eyes wide open, conscious of the risks involved, anticipating trouble. Any other angle of approach would have been tantamount to suicide.

And Bolan had too much to live for to throw his life away.

He had war everlasting, hell on earth, to keep him warm. From Vietnam, through his encounters with the Mafia, to Glasgow's killing ground, it was the life that Bolan had chosen for himself.

And he would not have had it any other way.

3

The new car was a BMW two-door, painted a nondescript gray. A more expensive car than Bolan's former compact rental, it would give him greater speed in the event of a pursuit, and it was heavier, more solidly constructed, in case he had to ram some obstacle along the way. The back seat held his luggage, while the bulk of Bolan's gear and weapons were concealed beneath a blanket in the trunk. He wore the sleek Beretta 93-R in its custom shoulder rigging and had found the silver AutoMag a handy place beneath the driver's seat.

He was not sorry to be leaving Glasgow for the west. The city was a bustling, vital part of Scotland, but the nation's heart was in her countryside, among the lochs and moors, the mountains and the gently rolling meadows that supported herds of woolly sheep with painted brands upon their flanks. The country roads were narrow, winding, flanked by waist-high walls of stone, with gravel lay-bys to alleviate congestion in the tighter spots. As Bolan headed northwest out of Glasgow toward Dumbarton, the traffic thinned appreciably and he was free to concentrate on his mission.

For the most part he was flying blind. He knew his destination, was aware of Harry Wilson's dark suspicion that the Soviets were landing arms, but otherwise the operation was a total blank. If there was more than one Russian trawler at Cairnaben, he would have to find a means of checking every one without a clear idea of his objective. "Arms" could range from rifles and grenades to RPGs and field artillery, or even baby nukes. Depending on the item, there were various disguises readily available, and Bolan would be on his own.

Against what odds?

That was the problem in a nutshell. No Soviet ship left port without a resident political officer appointed from Dzerzhinsky Square. The KGB would be on hand, but the questions would be *who* and, more importantly, *how many?* One or two observers would not be a problem; on the other hand, a crew of crack commandos from the Spetsnaz naval unit might turn out to be a major headache. Even fatal.

The Spetsnaz troops were Moscow's rough equivalent of Green Berets or Rangers, with a twist. Instead of simply being trained for combat, they could double, in a pinch, as terrorists, assassins, spies. They were the Soviet elite and they deserved their reputation for ferocity and cunning. In Afghanistan, the Spetsnaz soldiers were responsible for all of Russia's narrow gains, and they were known to man the long-disputed Chinese border. Bolan had encountered them on one or two occasions, and he had survived, but he would never take the outcome of a clash with hostile troops for granted. Even the clumsiest soldier might get lucky, and it only took a single round to drop the most proficient combat expert in the world. One round, and all of Bolan's work might be for nothing.

He had already done his job in Scotland, scattering the Tartan Army, wiping out its leadership and gathering sufficient documentary evidence for MI-5 and SAS to finish mopping up. If he accomplished nothing else, he had achieved his purpose, and the salvaging of Harry Wilson was a bonus he could not ignore. Distracted for a moment by an image of the agent's battered face, Bolan wondered if he had survived the night. In any case, that portion of his mission was behind him, finished. That which lay ahead demanded full attention to the present, concentration on his every move.

He passed through Dumbarton, compelled to wait outside town for several moments while a shepherd drove his flock across the narrow road. There seemed to be no urgency about the stockman's task; he waved at Bolan, smiling easily as several bleating stragglers cleared the pavement, waddling along behind their fellows toward the nearest meadow and their next meal.

From Dumbarton, the soldier traveled northward to Crianlarich. All along the route, the heather was in bloom, surrounding country cottages and turning velvet hills to works of art. The scenery reminded him at times of Ireland, and another hellfire visit to the British Isles he had undertaken on his own, against the odds.

Reconnaissance and preparation were the watchwords of a cautious warrior, and this time Bolan was going in blind. Readiness could make the difference when the odds were stacked against you and there seemed to be no hope of victory. If you were ready, if you did your homework and preserved the slim advantage of surprise, you had a chance. The soldier who responded blindly, playing every set by ear, was normally the first to fall. It was impossible to plan for every possible contingency, but you could damn well try, and trying could make all the difference in the world.

He was entering the Trossachs now—the "bristled country," so-called for its luxuriant vegetation, boasting some of Scotland's finest scenery in moor, mountain and loch. The narrow road was winding ever upward, but the BMW responded instantly to Bolan's touch upon the gearshift, clinging to the curves and climbing steadily with power in reserve. There was a minimum of traffic here, and misty rain began to fall as Bolan neared the Pass of Glencoe. Stretched below him lay the "weeping glen," where Campbells and MacDonalds once had carried out vendettas to the death, the hallowed ground all green and peaceful now. For just a moment, Bolan half imagined he could hear the pipers rallying the clans for one more battle on the mountainside.

The BMW took another curve, and Bolan realized that he was not imagining the sound. There was a scenic turnout just ahead, providing a magnificent, commanding view of the surrounding peaks, and on the grassy verge, a piper dressed in full regalia was playing "Sons of Glencoe" for an audience of stone.

Bolan parked his rental on the shoulder, nodding to the piper, who responded with a twinkling eye. A blanket had been spread beside him, to receive donations if a tourist chanced to stop, and Bolan dropped a pound note atop the scattering of coins. With reedy music ringing in his ears, he scanned the mountains with their crowns of mist and let the gentle rain caress his face. Those crags had witnessed generations of familial conflict, brutal feuds and internecine carnage, but their faces were composed and tranquil now, as if no hand had ever been upraised in anger here. The mountains could forgive, but Bolan wondered if they ever managed to forget.

He listened to two long laments, returning to his rental as the piper launched into "Amazing Grace." Despite the rain, he rolled down the driver's window and drove that way for half a mile, until the final strains were lost among the mountain peaks. Reluctantly he rolled the window up again and shut himself inside the hurtling cocoon.

The pipes had touched him in a way that music seldom did, and Bolan wondered whether it had been the setting and the season, or the fact that he was driving into danger, facing unknown odds for an ill-defined objective. Part of Bolan was tired of everlasting war, the struggle to survive from one day to the next, the pursuit of enemies who seemed to have an inexhaustible supply of fresh replacements. Part of him was sick of death, and longed for all the killing to be over, done with. Finished.

On the flip side Bolan realized that everlasting war meant never-ending sacrifice—of time and energy, of family and friends, of peace and solitude. There would be time enough to rest when he was done, and in the meantime there were battles waiting to be fought, a host of adversaries bent on eating up the gentle builders of the world. One man *could* make a difference, if he tried, and Bolan was a man who tried his hardest all the time.

Someday he might return to Glencoe in a time of peace, to stop awhile and cherish all the beauty of the weeping glen. Someday.

But not *this* day.

The everlasting war was waiting for him, still, and Bolan would not let his duty slide. While life and strength remained, he owed the effort to a world that, by and large, had seemingly forgotten how to stand and fight for decency, the values of a bygone era. Bolan did not see himself as a reactionary force, but neither was he perfectly in tune with modern mores, the departure from established values that had built America from scratch. A patriot who recognized his country's foibles, acting to correct them when and where he could, the Executioner was unashamed of his devotion to the national ideal. An anti-Communist for reasons that transcended ideology, he recognized the demarcation line between dissent and treason, having had firsthand experience with both. He had no interest in personal beliefs, except where they intruded on the rights of other men to live in peace. When that occurred, and the authorities appeared unable or unwilling to respond, the Executioner was ready with a rough solution of his own.

He motored through Fort William, the capital of Lochaber and a major touring center for the western Highlands, crossing the Caledonian Canal at Corpach. Stopping there to eat, the soldier checked his map and found that he would have to travel thirty more kilometers to reach Cairnaben. Most of that turned out to be a winding, one-lane track with overhanging trees and rocky walls set close on either side.

Cairnaben was a tiny coastal town with lovely cobbled streets, a few klicks south of Mallaig, on the Sound of Arisaig. A kilometer or less northward, Loch Morar preserved her secrets in the style of her more famous sister, Ness. The village made its living from the sea, and always had. The local herdsmen, with their sheep and cattle, played a distant second fiddle to able-bodied seamen in the local pecking order, though the rivalry had never blossomed into open animosity.

As Bolan made his way to the hotel, he spied the hulking ruins of a castle set upon a hilltop above the town. From a distance it conjured images of knights and damsels in distress. Up close, he thought, it was more likely to resemble something out of *Frankenstein*.

The small town's one and only functioning hotel was the Cairnaben Arms. Bolan had phoned ahead for a reservation, and the fresh-faced girl behind the registration desk was ready with his key when he arrived. She showed him to a third-floor room with private bath and a breathtaking view of the sound, refusing the tip that he offered and closing the door on a smile sweet enough to break hearts.

Bolan left his luggage on the bed and stood in front of the window, staring down at water and the docks a hundred yards away. It was impossible to miss the Russian trawler, half again as large as any of the local fishing boats in port, the hammer and sickle hanging limp along the flagstaff. The foredeck was deserted and Bolan scanned the docks to either side, examining the shacks that might provide him cover for a visit after nightfall.

Supper was announced for seven, and it would be hours after that before full dark descended on the western Highlands. Bolan thought that midnight should be adequate for an examination of the ship, and that left time to kill. He showered, dressed, slipped a windbreaker over the Beretta's shoulder rig and took a walking tour of the village, dawdling past shops that offered groceries, clothing, souvenirs. He was surprised to find a merchant on the docks who carried diving gear, and even more surprised to find a wet suit in his size. With North Atlantic temperatures in mind, he purchased it and locked the brown-wrapped parcel in the BMW's trunk before returning in his hotel room.

An hour before he had to dress for dinner, the Executioner lay down to take a nap, the 93-R tucked beneath his pillow, fingers curled around the weapon's grip. Bolan hovered on the brink of sleep and tried to recollect the last time he had truly rested. Living on the edge had taught the Executioner to sleep "with one eye open," and to wake in combat readiness the moment that his senses registered potential danger. He had often gone for days on end without sleep, and there had rarely been a time since he returned from Vietnam when Bolan had been free to rest in peace. A few times, yes, at Stony Man, before the roof fell in....

That part of Bolan's life was dead and buried; his affiliation with the government these days was more a marriage of convenience than any firm commitment one side to the other. Bolan took assignments from the Oval Office, like the Tartan Army strike in Glasgow, when he recognized their urgency and had no other pressing actions under way. At other times he played the cards he was dealt by chance or Fate, as with his unexpected visit to Cairnaben. Either way, his life was on the line each time he took the field, and Bolan took each mission as it came, devoting all his skill and energy to the destruction of his enemies at hand.

In his heart he hoped Cairnaben and her people would not suffer from his presence. He had no desire to visit hellfire on the tiny coastal village, but he knew how easily a quiet probe could turn to something loud and deadly, all unplanned. There were so many unknown quantities, the name and number of his current opposition chief among them.

Bolan thought that some discreet inquiries might enlighten him in that regard, and he possessed a fair idea of where the questions should be asked. But there was a time, and now the weight of sleep was bearing Bolan down below the conscious level to a dreamscape where an altogether different battle was conducted. Here the warrior fought against himself as much as any enemy, reviewing failures from his past, anticipating risks and dangers to the innocent who crossed his path. Sometimes, in dreams, he weighed the human costs of everlasting war and wondered if it might not be a better, more humane alternative to leave the savages alone and mind his own damned business for a change.

But he knew the answer going in, and he had never been a casual observer, comfortable on the sidelines. From the moment Bolan realized that he could make a difference, he had recognized a positive responsibility to stand against the jackals, to resist them each and every time they showed themselves, destroy them where he could. It was a task he had welcomed in his youth, before he realized that it would be forever, and he could not shirk the burden now when he had come so far and given up so much in its pursuit. Surrender was a damned sight worse than failure; it was abdication to the enemy, and Bolan could no more allow the cannibals to have their way without a fight than he could voluntarily stop breathing.

When the end came, when they cut him down as Bolan knew they must, someday, he would be satisfied that he had done his best with every moment he was given, seizing every opportunity to stand and make a difference in the world. When he was gone, the job would not be done by any means, but Bolan would have given it a decent start. And underneath the callous layer of conditioned cynicism, he believed with all his heart that there would always be another warrior, somewhere, to continue where the battle had left off.

It was the closest thing to faith the Executioner possessed, and for the moment, it would have to be enough.

4

Bolan joined his fellow lodgers in the lounge of the Cairnaben Arms at 7:00 p.m. Menus were distributed and cocktail orders taken by the same young woman who had shown him to his room that afternoon. He ordered a pint of Guinness and sipped the stout, dark ale while waiting for the summons to the dining room.

He was impressed, as always, by the leisured pace, the sheer civility of British dining. Orders seemed to be invariably taken in the lounge, with book-lined walls, a fire in season, while the guests enjoyed a drink, perused the latest news, or simply passed the time in pleasant conversation. Ushered to the tables when their food was ready, diners were relieved of sitting stiffly at attention for a quarter hour, longing for the waitress to arrive and end their misery. There was no trace of greasy, fast-food dining, and Mack Bolan did not miss it in the least.

He ate a leisurely meal of Highland beef and smoked salmon, which were preceded by a luscious garden salad. Everything was perfect, and Bolan left a healthy tip for the waitress who had served him. Foregoing coffee in the lounge, he was outside and on the street by 8:15, as tardy dusk began to fall across Cairnaben.

Bolan headed for the docks, a brisk five-minute walk from his hotel. The Russian trawler still seemed deserted, and he wondered where the crew was. Assuming an eight- to ten-man crew—excluding KGB "observers"—there could be a problem if all the men were belowdecks, waiting for him when he went aboard. There seemed to be no real alternative, however, and it was a problem the soldier would be forced to deal with if, and when, it came to pass.

The western ports of Scotland had been long suspected as a target for the Soviets. Their trawlers were accepted into port with minimal restrictions, despite the fact that some of them were fitted out more for spying than for netting fish. It was an open secret that the Russians favored fishing off the Scottish coast as much for information as for salmon and the other native species. With the right equipment, NATO movements in the north of Britain could be comfortably monitored by ships at sea, the latest codes, descriptions of maneuvers relayed by satellite to Moscow in the twinkling of an eye. It was a natural, and short of barring Russia from the shipping lanes, there seemed to be no ready-made solution to the problem.

A supply route for the terrorists was something relatively new, however. IRA guerillas had been getting arms from the United States for over sixty years; more recently, a secondary source had been discovered in Dzerzhinsky Square. But new security procedures made a one-stop shipment to the Provos risky business, and while arms kept flowing into urban combat zones, supply lines had been hastily rerouted, improvised. In retrospect, the tiny coastal towns of western Scotland seemed so perfect for the purpose that it was incredible no one had thought of it before.

The Tartan Army was a recent twist, but provost marshals for the KGB had never been discriminating in their choice of terrorists selected for material assistance. From the Baader-Meinhof gang and Red Brigades to SWAPO and the African National Congress, any group that had an ax to grind might gain assistance from the Soviets, and it was no particular concern of Moscow if the ax was carried in the right or left hand—just as long as it cut deep against society. Disruption was the goal, and random violence served the purposes of the KGB quite nicely, whether bombs were planted by the looney left or fascist right. If all else failed, the Russians had been known to kill their friends, thereby creating instant martyrs for whichever cause they might be funding at the moment.

Bolan knew the ins and outs of power politics, the rules to live and die by in a world where men—and even countries—were employed as pawns in global games of terror. He was well acquainted with the facts of life—and sudden death—on secret battlefields where wins and losses never made it to the headlines or the history books. He recognized the names and faces of the secret rulers, men behind the scenes who twisted truth and lives until it was impossible to tell the guilty from the innocent without a program.

Bolan knew all that, and he was still disgusted by the depths of callous inhumanity to which his enemies descended. Studying the Scottish coast, so tranquil in the early dusk, he wished that everlasting war had brought him anywhere but here. It was obscene to violate this gentle land with fire and blood, but he might have no choice. The course of Bolan's war might be predetermined by the Universe. For all he knew, inevitable Death might overtake him here and ring the curtain down on one man's never-ending quest. If so, he was prepared, but Bolan would not stoically accept defeat. While life remained, he would keep fighting to let the jackals feel the heat of cleansing fire.

His gaze turned inland for a moment, focused on the castle overlooking Cairnaben. In the purple light of dusk, its battlements looked ominous, forbidding. For an instant Bolan thought he saw a light wink on and off behind a window in the nearest tower, but he paid it no attention: tourists scouring the ruins, or a trick of fading light. Whichever, it had no connection with his private war against the savages.

Retreating past the trawler, Bolan met a pair of Russian seamen disembarking, walking swiftly with their heads bent, eyes downcast, as if they were conditioned to expect hostility from strangers. Bolan followed them along the cobbled street until they ducked into a tiny pub, The Anchor, situated near the docks. A shout of greeting as the door swung shut behind them told him where the other Soviets had gone to ground, and he continued on, secure in the knowledge that the trawler's crew would be engaged for several hours yet.

The soldier's destination was a larger public house, The Piper's Rest, which was a few doors down from his hotel. From what he had been able to observe, it catered less to seamen than to people of the town, and Bolan knew that pubs were gold mines of intelligence, if you could only separate the precious ore from worthless slag.

The Piper's Rest was filling up already, but he found a solitary table near the door and ordered Guinness when the barmaid came around. He scrutinized the other patrons casually, picking out a face or two from the Cairnaben Arms before he settled on a group of locals at a nearby table. One of them, a burly laborer, was grousing to the other four, who alternately sympathized and tried to quiet him. From where he sat Bolan was not able to discern the man's complaint, except that it appeared to center on someone or something that was lost.

Approaching strangers in a bar was hazardous at best, and doubly so on unfamiliar ground where enemies had yet to be identified. If Russian arms were moving through Cairnaben, there was better than an even chance that someone in the village was collaborating with the smugglers, eliminating the necessity of the KGB implanting an illegal sleeper on the scene. Bolan knew that he could lose it with a careless word to hostile ears, a question that aroused suspicion and provoked some unexpected hostile action from the opposition. Flushing out the enemy was one thing, but bringing down a hit against yourself was something else entirely.

Bolan was prepared to run a casual inquiry past the barmaid when the door swung open to admit a tall, distinguished-looking gentleman. The new arrival scrutinized his fellow patrons briefly, nodding here and there to an acquaintance, and then found himself a place at the bar. He ordered whiskey, drank it down, and seemed intent on carrying his refill to an empty table when the grumbler near Bolan staggered to his feet and shook a trembling finger at the taller, younger man.

"Yoor fault it is," he hissed. "Wha's come of my Rebecca, then?"

"Allow me to assure you, Mr. Rafferty—"

"Ashoor me, is it? Aye, ye can ashoor me she'll be comin' home, an' Tommy Cullen wi' her. Ain't ol' Rob Cullen crippled up wi' grief so bad that he could nae be here tonight. Ye can ashoor me them two kids is safe an' sound, MacAllister."

"I've told you that I have no knowledge of your children, Rafferty. Perhaps, if you had supervised them properly, they would be safe at home tonight."

"You bloody bastard!"

With a snarl, the drunken man broke free of clutching hands and rushed the object of his anger, hands outstretched as if to catch his adversary by the throat. Instead of falling back from the assault, the young man stood his ground. When his attacker was within arm's reach, he dashed his whiskey in the drunkard's eyes and followed with a looping blow that caught his adversary underneath the chin and drove him sideways, draping him across a nearby table.

There was silence for a moment while the fallen man's companions sized up the situation, with muttered consultations passed among themselves, and as they lumbered to their feet, there was no doubt that they were bent upon continuing the fight. Mack Bolan was prepared to intervene if things got nasty, but it did not come to that. The barkeep, brandishing a cudgel, interposed himself between the stoic one and the angry four, prepared to meet all comers.

"We'll have naught of that," he growled. "All those o' ye who want a brawl besides can take your bi'ness t' The Anchor, an' good riddance."

"Steady, Ben," the oldest of the would-be brawlers said, his tone apologetic. "There's nae call for bannin' anyone."

"My house, my rules," the barman answered flatly. "Them 'at doesn't like it needn't come again."

"Ye can't blame Rafferty for frettin', Ben, not wi' Rebecca gone an' all."

"I'm layin' blame for naught, but I su'gest ye take yon scarecrow home before he finds himself in jail."

"We'll do tha', Ben."

And suiting words to action, two of them collected their companion from the floor. Between whiskey and the solid uppercut delivered by his young opponent, Rafferty was out of it, a deadweight on the shoulders of the men who carried him outside. His two unburdened comrades gave the barkeep a wide berth, following the others into outer darkness. After they were safely gone, the heavyset proprietor turned back to face MacAllister.

"I'm sorry 'bout the row, sir."

"Nonsense. No harm done."

"I run a decent house."

"I know that, Ben. I'll have another whiskey for the road, before I go."

"Yes, sir, an' this one's on the piper."

Bolan nursed his Guinness, watched the young man down his whiskey and depart, with thanks to the proprietor for his assistance. If MacAllister was worried by the prospect of his recent adversaries waiting for him on the street outside, it didn't show.

Whatever might be happening around Cairnaben, there was tension in the air, with a potential for explosion into sudden violence. The reference to missing children tantalized, and Bolan made his mind up to pursue the matter cautiously, with circumspection. When the barmaid came around with seconds on the Guinness, he detained her with a question, hoping that it sounded casual.

"That Rafferty? He's summat of a troublemaker, that one. Mind ye, he's got reason to be worried, with his daughter gone an' all."

"A runaway?"

"The constable would like to say so, an' especially since young Tommy Cullen turned up missin' at the same time. They were sweet on each other, they were, and the constable, he reckons they've eloped."

"Her father doesn't think so?"

"Nay. Ol' Rafferty believes there's been foul play or summat like. He reckons Becky an' her Tom ha' been abducted, though there's naught to say so."

"There's no evidence?"

"Nay, not a fig...unless ye count the findin' of Rebecca's scarf up near the castle. Tha's what sets Ol' Rafferty snappin' every time he sees Shane MacAllister these days."

"Why's that?"

"I reckoned ye were new around Cairnaben." There was more than casual interest in the barmaid's smile as she continued. "Young MacAllister, he owns the castle, don't he? E'ryone knows *that*. Been in his family forever, as they say. The constable was up there quick, once Becky's scarf was foun', but there was nary sign of her or Tommy in the place."

"Apparently her father wasn't satisfied."

"Not 'alf, that one. He blames MacAllister, for fair, but can't prove naught against 'im."

"What do *you* think?"

That evoked a smile that lit the woman's face.

"*I* think they've run to Glasgow, maybe all the way to London. Yowuns like their privacy, the same as you or me, but there's naught for it in Cairnaben, if ye follow me. A town this size, ye mostly tell yoor secrets to the wall on Sunday night an' hear 'em back again come Monday mornin', from the postman."

He joined her in a smile. "No secrets in Cairnaben?"

A trace of deeper color crept into the barmaid's cheeks. "I wouldna go so far as that," she said. "I might ha' one or two myself, but what's the good o' secrets if you never get to share 'em out?"

"You've got a point."

"Will you be stayin' long?"

He shrugged. "That's hard to say."

"Might be we'll see each other yet again."

"I wouldn't be surprised."

"I'm Sarah Taggart."

"Mike Belasko," Bolan answered, giving her the name he had used to register at the hotel.

"I'm pleased to know you, Michael."

Bolan smiled. "The pleasure's mine."

"Could be, at that."

He watched her beat a slow and sinuous retreat in the direction of the bar. She was attractive, and she had been informative, but Bolan had no reason to believe she had more information on the feud between MacAllister and Rafferty. In any case, a pair of teenage runaways could have no bearing on his mission in Cairnaben. This was not America, with its ubiquitous display of billboards seeking missing children, and the KGB was not engaged, so far as

Bolan knew, in snatching youthful lovers from the Scottish Highlands.

The soldier checked his watch and found that it was getting on toward ten o'clock. The ale in front of him would be his last, but he could nurse it for a while yet, flirt a little with the barmaid if the opportunity arose. It would not do for him to try the Russian trawler too early; better if he let the crewmen have another hour at The Anchor, putting down their liquor at a rate that would be bound to leave them less than alert should they return while he was still aboard.

It would be risky, but Bolan knew it was the only way to gather the intelligence he required. Whatever might be happening around Cairnaben, he would find the answer—or a part of it—inside the Russian trawler's hold. From there he had no idea of where the trail might lead him. He would have to wait and see.

Meanwhile he was safe and warm inside The Piper's Rest. As safe as he could hope to be while waging everlasting war against the cannibals.

5

Emerging from The Piper's Rest, Bolan detoured to his rented BMW and retrieved the newly purchased wet suit from the trunk. The streets of Cairnaben were dark and empty at this hour, innocent of modern streetlights. Leaving nothing to chance, he scanned the windows of surrounding structures and his own hotel, a number of them showing lights, but he could find no evidence that he was under hostile scrutiny.

The soldier took no chances. Tiny as it was, the village boasted several other streets, and Bolan struck off to the east from the Cairnaben Arms, moving resolutely uphill, away from the waterfront. As he walked he was alert for any sound of footsteps on his trail, but there was none. Apart from muted sounds of radio or television in a couple of the houses that he passed and a whisper from the sea that would be audible throughout the village, Bolan's walk was cloaked in silence.

On reflection, there was nothing ominous about the darkness or the quiet of Cairnaben. The little seaside town was settling into sleep, and any connotations of the sinister were drawn from Bolan's own imagination. Except that Harry Wilson had suspected Russian arms were passing through the village, bound for ultimate delivery to terrorists throughout the British Isles, and that was sinister enough for Bolan.

When Bolan realized that he was running out of town, he took a right and traveled in the direction of the docks. There were no shops around him, rather simple, honest homes of working men and mariners, their small yard tidy to perfection, windows generally dark and silent. Here and there the watchdogs of Cairnaben stared as he passed, dark shapes on ropes or chains behind their low-slung fences, but they made no sound as Bolan left their private turf inviolate. He was a passing shadow in the night, and nothing more.

The temperature at dockside seemed a chilling ten degrees or more below the normal average for the town, and Bolan was immediately thankful for the wet suit. He did not relish stripping down and changing on the pier, exposed to wind and any casual passerby, but he was spared by the discovery of a fishing shack that had been left unlocked. The shed was dark and cramped inside, malodorous from years of storing bait and unwashed fishing gear, but it was all he had, and Bolan was not one to look a gift horse in the mouth.

A penlight helped him to get his bearings, and he rapidly undressed, the butcher's paper serving to protect his neatly folded suit. The wet suit fit him snugly, and it came complete with clinging, moccasinlike rubber boots. He had not purchased flippers or a face mask, since his swim would be no more than thirty yards. Bolan's head and hands would be exposed, but he did not intend to linger in the water any longer than was absolutely necessary. Going in, his only weapon was the Army K-Bar in a sheath secured to his leg with black electrician's tape.

Bolan entered the water between two local fishing boats, downrange from the Soviet trawler. It was colder than he had imagined, but he swam with long, determined strokes, ignoring the numbness that was creeping rapidly into his face and fingers. Twenty yards. Ten. He reached the hawser line and clung there for a moment, catching his breath and blowing on his fingers to restore a semblance of circulation. When a measure of feeling had returned, he scrambled up the line, hand over hand.

Bolan climbed to the railing in darkness, his wet suit blending with the night, the hawser rough against his palms despite their relative insensitivity from cold. He hung suspended from the rail, prepared to free-fall if the need arose, until he had convinced himself no sentries were on duty at the stern. After a moment he hit the afterdeck, immediately dropping to a combat crouch.

From this point on his every move was critical. For all intents and purposes, the soldier was unarmed. If he was spotted by a lookout, speed would be his only refuge, and odds would be against him all the way.

Like always.

He crossed the deck with loping strides and found a shadowed niche beneath the companionway leading to the bridge. Each step that Bolan traveled from the railing shaved the odds of ultimate survival if he was discovered. He could not outrun a bullet, and he had no doubt that several members of the crew, at least, would be armed while they were docked in port. The Soviets were always jealous of their sovereign rights, and paranoia would be geometrically increased if there was contraband on board.

The hold was forward, with an access hatch amidships, offset from the larger loading bays that would receive the daily catch. Bolan was surprised to find it both unguarded and unlocked, a lapse that might have indicated that the Russians felt secure, or that they simply had nothing to hide. Whichever way it played, the Executioner would have to find out for himself, and that meant checking out the hold.

He tried the hatch, prepared to bolt at the first indication of an ambush, thankful that the rusty-looking hinges did not squeal in protest. The odor from the hold assaulted Bolan's nostrils, strong and fishy from a hundred past catches. His penlight cut a sliver from the darkness and revealed that there were no fish currently on board. Instead the hold contained assorted crates in different sizes that were lashed together in a pyramid of sorts.

He killed the flash and scrambled down a ladder that was mounted on the bulkhead, closing the access hatch behind him. Here, belowdecks, the inevitable smell of fish was stifling, inescapable. Breathing through his mouth, Bolan let the luminescent finger of his penlight sweep the hold, searching for the corners, finding them empty.

He was alone.

The markings on the crates defied immediate translation, and these crates bore no English labels. Several of the smaller crates appeared to be the proper size for small arms, but the larger ones were baffling. Unless the Soviets were moving disassembled light artillery, there must be something else inside the crates that formed the bottom level of the makeshift pyramid.

No closer to the solution of the riddle than he had been on arrival in Cairnaben, Bolan scanned the hold for a tool that might enable him to open up the crates and scrutinize their contents. It was risky, granted; if the Soviets discovered that their cargo had been tampered with, there was no way of gauging their reaction. If they had the guns available, Cairnaben might be scoured for intruders, but the search would have to be discreet. The KGB could not afford to flex their muscles too obviously in the British Isles, but that would not prevent elimination of an interloper, if he could be singled out, identified and isolated.

It would *definitely* not protect Mack Bolan if the old men of Dzerzhinsky Square discovered his involvement in the matter.

The soldier's war with Moscow dated from his early days as Colonel John Phoenix, when he had been less than startled to discover Russian fingers in the pie of international assassination, terrorism, revolution and extortion. Moscow had a stake in any movement that destabilized the Western powers, and it mattered little, in the final analysis, if they were funding radicals or neo-fascists, just as long as chaos, loss of life and counterviolence were the end results. With several dozen "liberation armies" taking to the field on any given day, there was no need for Moscow to devise a grand conspiracy. The Russians merely had to play the field, supplying friends and enemies alike with all the deadly toys they could handle, leaving them to do their homicidal thing, and letting all the lethal chips fall where they may.

If Shiites murdered Christians in Beirut or Catholics ambushed Protestants in Belfast, if a synagogue was bombed by Palestinians in Tel Aviv or burned by Klansmen in the Mississippi delta, it was all the same. The Russians came up winners all around. Just as some celebrities believed there was no such thing as bad publicity, so leaders of the KGB had learned that every violent act, no matter how bizarre, could benefit the revolution in the end. If a sadistic psychopath was killing women in New York or children in L.A., the animal became a symbol of "capitalist American decadence." If a cop was forced to fire on vicious thugs in self-defense, the propaganda mill transformed his action into "neo-Nazi-style repression of the masses." Moscow couldn't lose, in any case, and rigid censorship at home prevented any leaks of "counterrevolutionary aberrant behavior" in the Russian populace itself.

Support from Moscow for the terrorists in Northern Ireland was not news. The IRA had long accepted weapons from the KGB, and there were indications that their Protestant opponents, the Ulster Defense Association, had begun to ask for foreign aid as well. No one would seriously claim that gunmen of the IRA or UDA were raving socialists, but the abiding strength of Moscow's plan revolved around the fact that ideology made not the slightest bit of difference. There would be no winners in Belfast, but the endemic violence might require a British military presence in the north of Ireland for another generation, draining strength from other fronts, while endless negative publicity eroded faith in parliament and in democracy itself.

As Colonel Phoenix, Bolan had done everything within his power to turn the creeping tide of terrorism. From the outset he had recognized the fact that he was taking on another hopeless, everlasting war, but he had not prepared himself for tragedy and treason in his own backyard. His manhunt for the murderers of April Rose had taken Bolan from the Blue Ridge Mountains of Virginia to the Oval Office, and eventually to the streets of Moscow. His identity was not a secret to the Russians anymore, and Bolan knew that they would spare no effort, no expense, to capture him or kill him if the opportunity arose.

He knew the risks involved, and still the soldier had no working options. Dedicated to the struggle rather than to the elusive thought of victory, he fought because he *could*. He had it in his power to make a difference. It was an obligation that the Executioner could not ignore.

There was the possibility, of course, that Harry Wilson's information had been wrong. Intelligence from MI-5 had no more built-in guarantees than information gathered by the CIA, Mossad, or the KGB itself. His sources might have been mistaken, or he might have been the target for deliberate disinformation—from the Soviets, the Tartan Army or some third player yet unrecognized.

But there was only one way to be certain. He retrieved a crowbar from a wall hook near the ladder he had descended. Curious about the larger crates, he chose the nearest one and wedged the tip of his crowbar between two slats on the side, prepared to wrench them out and take a look inside. The method was impossible to cover, but he dared not waste the time required for disassembling the pyramid. Presented with a choice of evils, Bolan took the quick way out and damned the risk.

He was about to throw his weight against the crowbar when a latch was thrown above him and the loading bays were trundled back to offer him an unexpected view of velvet sky and twinkling stars. Retreating swiftly to the shadows of a vat designed for holding fish on ice, he crawled back into the tightest corner that his body could accommodate.

Voices spoke Russian above him, calling back and forth like workmen anywhere until a softer, sterner voice demanded silence. Bolan heard the creaking of a power winch and risked a glance, which only served to verify the nightmare. They were coming down, no less than half a dozen of them, riding on a platform hung from cables. He was trapped inside the hold.

The K-Bar might as well have been a toothpick for all the good that it would do him. He was strong and fast, but Bolan cherished no illusions of his own ability to tackle six men virtually empty-handed and destroy them all. And there had to be a seventh man on deck to operate the winch. He could scarcely fail to notice the commotion if the Executioner attacked his comrades in the hold.

His only hope lay in the fine art of invisibility. If they were coming for the crates, his enemies would not be likely to conduct a close examination of the hold. If he remained precisely where he was and made no sound, there was a chance that they might overlook him. The alternative would be a virtually hopeless last-ditch stand, and while the soldier had no abstract fear of death, he did not relish the idea of dying here without a purpose or an opportunity of striking hard against the enemy.

If he had been successful in his effort to discover what was in the larger crates, he would have been doomed. The Russians would have been alerted, and they would have scoured the hold until they found him, cornered in his secret niche. Instead of one chance in a thousand, Bolan would have had no chance at all. He would be dead.

He watched and listened as the pyramid of crates was broken down and then reloaded on the mobile platform, large crates on the bottom, smaller ones on top. It took the best part of an hour, five men working while the sixth—undoubtedly a spotter for the KGB—stood by and supervised. When all the crates were loaded and lashed down, the watchdog climbed on board the platform with the cargo, and the seamen scrambled up the ladder, exiting by way of the same access hatch that had admitted Bolan to the hold. He waited as the platform rose and gradually disappeared from sight. The crewmen were on deck again, and in another moment they were cranking shut the loading bays, eliminating Bolan's view of stars and sky. The darkness of the hold seemed absolute but Bolan did not use the pencil flash. Not yet. Instead he waited for the sounds above to die away by slow degrees, aware that he was swiftly running out of time.

The moving crew's arrival had prevented Bolan from achieving his objective, but he was not beaten yet. If he could not immediately scrutinize the contents of the crates, there was a chance that he could make out their destination. If he could escape the trawler soon enough, he could retrieve his car and overtake the vehicles that must be waiting to receive the cargo at the dockside.

And if he muffed it, let himself be seen as he emerged from the hold, he would be dead. It was that simple. There would be no second chances, no reprieves. Crossing to the ladder mounted on the bulkhead, Bolan grasped a metal rung and started climbing toward the deck. Perhaps toward Death.

6

Departing from the trawler was more perilous than boarding. Crewmen were on deck and on the pier, engaged in loading heavy crates aboard a pair of canvas-covered trucks. Their watchdog stood against the rail, content to observe for now, and Bolan was impressed with how the sailors worked in silence, straining at the larger crates but never slowing down.

It was a meager fifteen feet between his hideout and the fantail, but it felt like miles. One slip, one inadvertent sound, and Bolan would be dancing on his own, at center stage, for a most unappreciative audience. But there was no alternative, and he could not afford to let the cargo slip away without at least attempting to pursue it.

Edging out from cover, Bolan crossed the open deck with even measured strides. He was prepared to bolt and try to vault the rail if he was spotted, but until that moment came, discretion was the better path. The crew was otherwise engaged, their hawk-faced supervisor totally intent on watching every move they made below him on the pier.

He reached the railing at the stern and stepped across it, slithered down the hawser line. It seemed as if the water had grown colder in his absence, but he reckoned that his own imagination was to blame for any seeming difference in temperature. From surface level, he had lost sight of the trucks, but Bolan had not heard their engines yet. He still had time.

Emerging from the water near the shack that had served him as a dressing room, he ducked inside to retrieve his clothes. The cobblestones were hard beneath his rubber moccasins as Bolan sprinted for his car, arriving as the truck engines coughed to life downrange. He dropped the suit on the empty seat beside him, rummaging through pockets for an agitated moment till he found his car keys.

They were rolling, and the Executioner did not intend to lose them now.

The BMW's engine caught first time and Bolan put the car in motion, leaving off the headlights. It was bright enough to see by moonlight for a hundred yards or so, and in a sleepy village such as Cairnaben, lights would be an instant warning that a tail had been acquired.

Bolan knew he'd be seen if he cruised along the waterfront, so he took the first street west of the Cairnaben Arms, immediately turning right and following a loop that hugged the natural contour of the land, meeting the dockside road two hundred yards beyond the Russian trawler. The second truck had rumbled through the intersection moments earlier, and Bolan turned the BMW northward in pursuit.

The drivers were not running dark or bothering about concealment. They were confident of having the highway to themselves this time of night, and Bolan counted his blessings, hanging back, being guided by the cherry taillights up ahead.

The road was narrow, dark and winding as it hugged the coastline, but the Executioner had little difficulty following the trucks, and he did not have far to go in any case. The point vehicle started slowing after they had traveled little more than a mile, its follow-up decelerating seconds later. Bolan dropped the BMW into neutral, coasting to a halt along the grassy shoulder, scanning the terrain ahead and studying the chain link fence that started on the verge and ran downslope in the direction of the sea.

He pulled the car off the road and found a shelter for it in a stand of twisted, weathered trees. Bolan got out and took the sleek Beretta with him, slipping into shoulder harness as he broke from cover. He moved cautiously in a combat crouch along the gently rolling hillside. By the time he reached the fence, a gate with concertina wire on top had closed behind the trucks, they were grumbling along a sloping driveway toward a clutch of buildings set beside the water. A sentry trailed them, ambling along the drive and taking his own sweet time, a shotgun tucked beneath his arm.

Bolan did not need his pencil flash to read the sign suspended from the gate.

MacAllister Enterprises, Ltd.
Cannery Division

The name brought back to mind an image of the cultured gentleman who had been confronted by angry drunks at The Piper's Rest. Of course, the name was hardly an unusual one in Scotland but the Executioner was no believer in coincidence.

He moved along the fence, downslope, and kept the trucks in sight as they pulled up outside the cannery. From Bolan's vantage point he had a sweeping view of piers and loading docks, and the plant itself with half a dozen good-sized buildings clustered on the water, ready to receive the catch from waiting boats and ship it out again on trucks to markets scattered through the British Isles and Western Europe. If the fish were running, Shane MacAllister would have himself a decent business here, and Bolan wondered what his tie-in with the Soviets might be.

He was not buying fish from Russian trawlers; that much was a certainty. The same applied to equipment for the cannery. The Soviets did not export industrial machines to

Britain, and the pickup system would have been unorthodox. That narrowed Bolan's options to contraband, but it did not resolve the nagging points of "what" and "why."

He watched as the truck drivers dropped their tailgates and a team of burly stevedores appeared as if from nowhere, hauling out the heavy crates and lugging them inside the cannery. Another sentry joined the first and lingered on the sidelines, watching. Once again the soldier wondered what might be inside the larger boxes. In his own experience, the kind of hardware used by terrorists around the world came wrapped in smaller packages, and Bolan wondered if the lead from Harry Wilson might be taking him in an entirely new direction.

Clearly MI-5's man in the Tartan Army had believed that he was tracking arms for terrorists, but had he been mistaken? Might the Soviets be backing an entirely different sort of action in Cairnaben? And if so, what was their play?

A look inside the cannery might answer some of those important questions, but he had not come prepared for such a probe tonight. The warrior had already stretched his luck beyond the breaking point, examining the Russian trawler and escaping underneath the very nose of the KGB. It would be pushing things to try the cannery, and Bolan had no way of knowing if there might be other guards inside or prowling on the grounds. MacAllister was clearly interested in preserving whatever was contained within those crates or hidden in the cannery from prying eyes—at any cost. A midnight transfer, guards with shotguns, fences topped with razor wire. The portrait of a man with something to conceal was inescapable, but Bolan was no closer to solution of the mystery than he had been in Glasgow when he first met Harry Wilson.

No. Correction. Twenty-four short hours earlier, he had not known MacAllister existed, had known nothing of his tie-in with the Soviets. His knowledge might be little greater at the present, but at least he knew that some connection *did* exist, apparently of benefit to both sides since they took such pains to keep it secret.

It was Bolan's task to crack that riddle, fit the pieces of the puzzle into place, but he could only do so much tonight. There must be other angles of attack that would supply him with the answers he sought, and if a recon of the plant was necessary, he could check it out tomorrow night, come back with all the tools and hardware he would need to do a first-rate job.

Delay had never been the soldier's style, but he had witnessed the results of hasty actions in the field a thousand times. Invariably the results were unexpected, often ugly, sometimes fatal.

The final crates were being hoisted to the loading dock, and Bolan watched them disappear inside the cannery. A steel door rumbled down to block his view of the machinery inside. Retreating from the chain link fence, the Executioner retraced his steps until he reached the BMW.

The trucks would be departing soon, and Bolan did not want to meet them on the highway. There was no point in arousing suspicions prematurely, and he needed time to think. Secure from prying eyes, he stripped the wet suit off and changed back into his street clothes. There were wrinkles in his suit, but that would be the least of Bolan's problems if he could not pierce the veil of secrecy surrounding MacAllister Enterprises. Something sinister was happening around Cairnaben, he was sure of that, but without some solid leads, the Executioner was blowing smoke.

Sounds of heavy engines rumbled on the highway, and Bolan watched as the trucks lumbered past. He let them have a good head start, in case they had picked a tail up at the cannery. When fifteen minutes had elapsed, he gunned the BMW's engine into life, switched on the lights and motored slowly back to the Cairnaben Arms.

En route, his mind was sorting through the pieces of the puzzle he had in hand. An undercover man from MI-5, convinced that arms were being smuggled through Cairnaben by the KGB. A local laird and businessman whose dealings with the Soviets were carried out in darkness, under guard. A pair of missing lovers, one of whom, at least, had passed MacAllister's ancestral home the night she disappeared.

And had she gone inside? Might there be something in the ruined castle worth a closer look?

He filed the thought away for future reference and concentrated on the winding road. Ahead of him the taillights of the trucks had vanished, and he had no fear of running into them again before he reached Cairnaben. He was free and clear.

The Piper's Rest was dark and shuttered as Bolan passed, and stragglers from the Russian boat were ambling from The Anchor toward the docks. He wondered if the crewmen might be privy to the contents of the crates they had carried from their port of embarkation, and as quickly put it out of mind. The common seamen would not be informed of such details, nor would they be inclined to speak with an American, provided he could find a sailor who spoke English well enough to understand his questions.

Bolan knew that there would be no easy answers this time out, no handy oracle to point him in the right direction if he went astray. At this point MacAllister was all he had, and while he was not willing to call the man a traitor, it seemed obvious that he was dealing with the enemy in ways that would have interested MI-5.

It crossed the soldier's mind that he could wash his hands of the Cairnaben mystery by picking up a phone. A call to London would suffice, a reference to Harry Wilson and the Tartan Army, followed up by details of what Bolan had observed so far. He would be free to pick up his pursuit of the heroin traffickers before the latest shipment of their poison hit the streets of Manhattan.

It would be simple, but Bolan could not bring himself to seriously contemplate the thought.

It smacked of cheap surrender, and he did not like the taste it left behind. The Executioner had never been a quitter, and he was not starting now. Surrender was not a part of his vocabulary or his plans.

If the MacAllister equation took a bit more time to crack, then he would count the necessary time well spent, provided that it led to a solution of the riddle. Once committed to the chase, he would not break it off until his prey was run to earth and captured or destroyed.

He drove through the dark streets of Cairnaben, passing homes and shops with shutters drawn against the night, lights extinguished, families asleep. It was a simple village, out of time and rather out of style, but Bolan hoped that his arrival would not wreak some catastrophic change. He did not wish to touch these simple lives with fire and steel, except perhaps for one or two exceptions who might be deserving of the Executioner's attention.

Shane MacAllister was not on Bolan's hit list. Yet. The man was clearly not aboveboard in his dealings with the Soviets, but Bolan had not driven halfway across Scotland to pin the mark of the beast on a black marketeer. In the event MacAllister's affiliation with the Russians proved to be a routine criminal concern, the Executioner would be content to drop a dime to Scotland Yard or MI-5 and let the wheels of justice roll. However, if Cairnaben's laird turned out to be collaborating with the KGB in moving arms to terrorists, then he would have judged himself, and nothing would be left beyond the execution of his sentence.

Death.

It was the only recourse left to Bolan in an everlasting war where prisoners were neither sought nor taken. He was not a therapist or jailer, and the savages who were his enemies had never benefitted from the countless rehabilitation programs organized on their behalf throughout the course of modern history. The cure for evil was obliteration, cleansing fire, and Bolan had no time for pondering ''the man within the man.'' There might be some degree of abstract good in every human being, but the savages had let that portion of themselves become atrophic from neglect, and it was lost beyond recall. A mad dog might have been the family pet in brighter days, but there was still no cure for the burning poison in his veins. The good old days were dead and gone; Mack Bolan waged his everlasting conflict here and now, against the enemies who made themselves available, employing any tool that came to hand.

Bolan backed the BMW into a parking space, switched off the lights and killed the engine. He folded the wet suit, stashed it in the trunk and spread out an army blanket to cover both the suit and his accumulated hardware. He was packing enough heat to bring down a major portion of the village, but Bolan hoped it would not come to that, and none of it was any good without a solid target in the first place.

If MacAllister was working with the Soviets—and everything suggested that he was—then he would have to have a contact or control. The truck drivers and the stevedores were merely beasts of burden; none of them would be entrusted with authority to close a deal or issue orders on behalf of the KGB. Aside from that, it had appeared that most or all of them were locals, which precluded any ranking position within the Soviet apparatus. Bolan was not ready to begin a search for sleeper agents when the trawlers had apparent unrestricted access to the port, with seamen—and potential spies—at leave to come ashore.

He was surprised that MI-5 had taken no more visible precautions on the coast. Undoubtedly the radio transmissions from all Russian ships were regularly monitored, but Bolan would have thought an agent on the scene appropriate, considering the various potentials for abuse of diplomatic "understandings." Still, he was not here to second-guess the British or tell them how to do their jobs in countering subversion. If he found a flagrant case this time, the Executioner would deal with it himself, and let them pick the pieces up as best they could when he was done.

The door to the Cairnaben Arms was locked, but Bolan, like the other guests, had been entrusted with a key for his convenience. The custom was another measure of the antiquated charm one found in villages throughout the British Isles, a touch of yesteryear that Bolan hoped might somehow manage to endure the modern age of inhumanity and violence.

He locked the door behind him and crossed the vacant lobby where a single light was burning to accommodate late guests. There was no elevator and fatigue was creeping over Bolan as he climbed the stairs, reminding him that he had slept a total of three hours in the past two days. How many savages had he destroyed since last he settled on a pillow and allowed himself to dream in peace?

Not enough. Not yet.

Bolan unlocked his door, stepped across the threshold, closed and locked it again. The room was dark, except where moonlight filtered through the curtains, pooling on the carpet near the window. Reaching for the light switch, Bolan flicked it on... and froze.

A woman stood before him, in the center of the room, and she was leveling a pistol at his chest.

"I'd be obliged if you would stand completely still," she said calmly. "If not, I am afraid I may be forced to shoot you."

7

"Michael Belasko?"

She was cool and collected, and the Walther automatic in her hand was steady as she held it trained on Bolan. There was just a trace of whitening around the knuckle on her trigger finger, and the soldier knew it would require a miracle for him to beat her play at point-blank range.

"You've got me," he replied, acknowledging the name he had used to register at the Cairnaben Arms.

"It seems I have." Her smile was ice. "I hope you won't mind answering some questions."

"Do I have an option?"

"There are always options, Mr. Belasko."

"Call me Mike."

"No, thank you."

She was a honey-blonde, five-eight and put together like an athlete. Bolan took her measure in a glance, and then allowed his eyes to linger out of interest. He was looking at a cool professional, but there was fire inside, if anyone could crack the outer shell of ice.

"You have me at a disadvantage."

"And I mean to keep it that way. What is your connection with the Tartan Army, Mr. Belasko?"

Bolan raised an eyebrow. "None at all."

"Do you deny that you have visited the Tartan Army's offices in Glasgow?"

"If you want to call that dump an office, be my guest. It looked more like a going-out-of-business sale."

She frowned. "We think the Tartans may be going out of business, thanks to you, in part."

"I'm glad to hear it. Who is 'we'?"

She did not seem to hear the question, but it scarcely mattered. If she knew that much about the Glasgow raid, the odds were ten to one that she was MI-5.

"You are familiar with a man named Harry Wilson?"

"We met, briefly."

"I believe you saved his life, in fact."

So, Wilson had survived...or was the woman merely saying that to draw him out, elicit some reaction?

"He was in a bit of trouble. I was handy."

"Which returns us to the question of your tie-in with the Tartan Army."

"Does it?"

"Mr. Belasko, I have no more time for parlor games." She cocked the Walther, held it leveled at his chest. "I wish to know precisely whom you represent."

"I'm self-employed."

"A contract agent? And for whom? The CIA?"

"I'm more or less an independent," Bolan said. It was a truthful answer, more or less.

"We are expected to believe that you selected Tartan central on your own initiative, expending energy and ordnance without a sponsor? It really won't wash, Mr. Belasko."

"Frankly, I don't give a damn what 'we' believe," he told her, picking out a chair and settling into it. "If you don't plan to use that thing, why don't you put it down?"

She hesitated, but the Walther finally dropped as far as Bolan's groin. He was not altogether certain that he liked the change.

"Who *are* you?" she demanded, anger cracking the veneer of cool detachment.

"Let's just say I'm a troubleshooter."

"We don't need a Yank to do our shooting for us, thank you."

"Well, your Mr. Wilson needed *someone*, and we weren't exactly overrun by eager agents from MI-5."

The flicker in her eyes told Bolan he had scored. The woman was an operative, all right, and she had traced him here by chasing Wilson's lead on smuggled arms. Selection of her target should have been a relatively simple task, considering the fact that there was only one hotel in town, and it was scarcely overcrowded with Americans.

"What brings you to Cairnaben?"

"I like fishing."

"Oh, yes? Go on and pull the other, while you're at it."

Bolan smiled. "All right, let's say I'm interested in hardware, shall we?"

"Russian hardware?"

"Possibly."

"And what's your interest, Mr. Belasko?"

"Personal."

"That won't do, I'm afraid. You're out of bounds. It isn't open season here, the way it seems to be in the United States. There are procedures to be followed."

"I can see they're working well."

The woman stiffened, stung by Bolan's tone. "We get results," she snapped. "We just don't feel the need to blaze away at everything that moves."

"The gradual approach."

"Where necessary, yes."

"And meanwhile, weapons keep flowing to the terrorists, unchecked." He fixed her with a steady gaze. "How many dead in Belfast while you follow your procedures?"

"I suppose you have a quick solution to the problem?"

"I've been known to get results."

"Like Glasgow?"

"When it's called for."

"I could have you up on charges."

"But you won't. If you intended to arrest me, I'd be in the lock-up now."

The Walther slipped again, until its muzzle was directed toward the floor.

"Touché. I didn't come to lock you up."

"Why, then?"

"To find out who the hell you are and what you're up to." Something softened in her eyes. "To thank you for my partner's life."

"I'm glad he made it."

"It was touch and go. The Tartans worked him over rather badly."

"I was there, remember?"

"Yes. Were you . . . alone?"

He understood the woman's question. She was wondering if one man had inflicted all the damage done in Glasgow.

"I told you I'm an independent. But I can't take all the credit. One of the survivors set the place on fire."

"I see."

"What now?"

"I'm not quite sure. Officially, I'm checking on a lead from Harry. Vague reports of weapons moving through Cairnaben. What I do depends on what I find."

"Sounds fair enough."

"And you?"

"I don't exist, officially. Until I know the players, I don't have a game plan."

"Sports analogies. Why is it that for every illustration you Yanks fall back to the football field?"

"You mean it isn't cricket?"

When she laughed, the sound was natural, almost relaxed.

"I'm still at something of a disadvantage," Bolan said.

She eased down the Walther's hammer and slipped the weapon inside her purse. "I don't suppose I'll have to shoot you, after all."

"I meant your name."

The woman blushed. "It's Rachel. Rachel Hunter. I wonder, Mr. Belasko, if I might suggest a proposition."

"You can always ask."

"If you are, as you say, an independent, you might benefit from access to our network. Background information, technical support, that sort of thing. Conversely I believe that you could help us—help *me*—crack this riddle and eliminate a nasty situation."

Bolan frowned. He hesitated to accept an ally in his lonely struggle, for a multitude of reasons. Technical support was not a problem in the kind of war he fought against the savages, and there was every chance that he would get this woman whacked if he allowed her to accompany him into the killing grounds.

"An interesting proposal. And if I decline?"

"There is the matter of a shooting fray in Glasgow. The police are anxious to discuss a dozen homicides or so."

"That wouldn't get you anywhere."

"I realize that, Mr. Belasko. On the whole, however, I believe we have a great deal less to lose."

"Correction. Your superiors in London may have less to lose. With me, *you* stand a decent chance of losing everything."

"I know the risks involved. I'm a professional, remember? It's no good trying to scare me off."

"I wouldn't dream of it," he told her. "But remember, you're no use to anybody if you're dead."

"I'm touched by your concern."

"We're both professionals, remember?"

"Yes. All right, then shall we say a marriage of convenience?"

Bolan nodded slowly. He could see no clear-cut benefits from working hand-in-glove with MI-5, but neither did he need the kind of interference the Brits could throw his way if he rebuffed the offer. There would be enough hard opposition from the Russians, if and when his hunch proved out, and Bolan did not need to find his path obstructed by soldiers of the same side.

"Ground rules?"

It was the lady's turn to frown. "I'd like to leave that open for the moment. There are various procedures to be recognized, of course, but no point worrying about that until we know exactly what we're up against."

It was a sensible response, and Bolan took the woman at her word. Quickly, economically, he told her of the stories he had heard at The Piper's Rest, his visit to the trawler and his run up-country to MacAllister's cannery.

"You've been busy," Rachel said. "What's your reading on the cargo?"

"Could be weapons," Bolan answered, "but it really doesn't play. Too bulky, for the most part. Not enough munitions boxes, crates of rifles, things like that. Right now I'm flying blind."

"MacAllister?"

The solder shrugged. "He's obviously working with the Russians, but in what capacity? For all I know, he's just a crooked businessman who's cutting trade agreements of his own to turn a dollar."

"That would be a pound, but you're correct, of course. It isn't half enough."

"I'll want a look inside the cannery, ASAP."

"I beg your pardon?"

Bolan smiled. "As soon as possible. It wouldn't hurt to check the castle while we're at it. If those two teenagers really ran away to find a justice of the peace, all well and good. But if they stumbled onto something that they weren't supposed to see, it could be another handle on our problem."

"Right. I'll take the castle."

"Whoa. Let's think about this for a second."

Rachel Hunter bristled. "I suppose you have an antiquated American notion that a woman cannot do the job?"

"I know a few who could," he told her flatly. "But I don't know you from Adam."

"I believe it should be Eve."

"Combat experience?"

"I beg your pardon?"

"Do you have experience in combat? Have you ever killed a man?"

"What difference does it make?"

"I'll take that as a negative. The *difference* is that we're dealing with a high-risk situation here. If my suspicions are correct, MacAllister or one of his associates may be a murderer. The KGB is almost certainly involved, and they aren't known for taking prisoners. Before you put it on the line, I want to know if you can pull your weight."

"I'm trained in a variety of weapons, and in unarmed self-defense," she told him stiffly.

"Very nice. But paper targets don't shoot back."

"Believe me, I can take care of myself."

"I hope so. If you fumble on the firing line, there isn't any second chance."

"I'm touched by your concern."

The temperature in Bolan's room had dropped appreciably, but he forged ahead. "I'll scout the castle tomorrow," he said, "Provided you can find a way to keep MacAllister distracted."

"I'll come up with something."

"If I hit on something at the castle, we can move. If not, we'll have to wait and run a recon on the cannery."

"All right."

The woman obviously did not relish playing second string, but she would have to prove herself before the Executioner relied upon her, with his life at stake. Too much was riding on the play for Bolan to entrust his mission to a wild card, even one who looked as competent as Rachel Hunter.

"I'll make my run tomorrow morning," Bolan told her. "Call at ten o'clock. That gives you time enough to reach MacAllister?"

"I'll reach him," she replied, already moving toward the door. He caught her there and briefly blocked her way.

"It might be better all around if London didn't know about our deal."

"No worries. They would never have approved it anyway."

She closed the door behind her and Bolan was alone, to grapple with the doubts she had left behind. Would her "assistance" be a boon or a detriment to his campaign? Would he be forced to shepherd her across the rough spots, looking out for her at every turn? When they were finished, would there be another bleeding turkey on his soul?

Whichever way it played, the woman had herself to thank for anything that came her way from that point on. A self-invited visitor to Bolan's world, she had to realize that there could be no turning back. She was committed to a one-way journey through the hellgrounds, and her ticket had been punched through to the end of the line.

The Executioner could only hope that she would make it there alive.

RACHEL HUNTER LOCKED THE DOOR behind her, crossed the room and dropped her handbag on the bed. Her room was one floor down from Michael Belasko's, and she felt the anger simmering inside as she imagined him, so smug, self-satisfied, dictating terms as if she were his secretary rather than a duly constituted officer with the authority to lock him up on murder charges.

Not that she could make the charges stick without a great deal more in terms of solid evidence. Thus far, she had been acting on a tip from Harry Wilson, following her partner's lead in the pursuit of Russian arms, assuming that the tall American from Glasgow would be close at hand. She had been lucky, finding him so quickly, but she wondered now if she had bitten off too much.

His attitude had been infuriating, chauvinism thinly veiled by false concern, but Rachel realized there might be something to his estimation of the risks involved. She had no real idea of what they might be up against, but after hearing Belasko out, it seemed that there was more at stake than a cache of smuggled Russian arms. Perhaps a great deal more.

As she undressed for bed, she thought about the brash American. He was attractive in a rugged sort of way. His movements were precise and economical, devoid of wasted energy, but Rachel sensed that he would be a holy terror if his anger was released, left unchecked. There was a hint of violence in his posture, in his words, and Glasgow proved that he was capable of killing.

Still, if asked, she could not have selected Belasko from a lineup as the man who had machine-gunned something like a dozen members of the Tartan Army, making off with Harry Wilson and a satchel of important documents, including lists of members in the area of London. Roundups were already under way, and if they broke the Tartans this time, it would certainly be due, in no small measure, to the bloody work of Michael Belasko.

Scowling, Rachel realized that she had never learned precisely who he was, who his employers were. She would have bet her life that he was not employed with the CIA. The Company was prone to shallow, xenophobic agents in the field, and Belasko struck her as a rather more enlightened sort, despite his attitudes on dealing with the outlaw class. He placed the usual American reliance on a dose of blood and thunder, always good to put things right, but there was nothing of the casual swashbuckler in his attitude. He was a man, she sensed, who had experienced the very worst life had to offer, and he was engaged in handing back the bloody worst to those who seemed deserving.

It occurred to her that he might be a mercenary, and she put the notion out of mind immediately. There was nothing to be earned from gunning down the leaders of the Tartan Army, less to gain—and everything to lose—by clashing with the KGB around Cairnaben. His commitment to the mission was impressive, even though it brought him onto foreign soil, beyond his legal jurisdiction.

Granted that he had any legal jurisdiction to begin with.

A disturbing thought had entered Rachel's mind, an inkling that Mike Belasko might not name his boss because there *was* no boss. He might be acting on his own, without a sponsor, living out some personal vendetta that would bring them both to grief before the final act played out. The notion seemed preposterous.

She showered quickly, dried herself and slipped into a nightgown, pulling sheets and blanket up around her chin before she killed the bedside lamp. The western Highlands boasted chilly nights regardless of the season, and the air outside had learned to bite already. Rachel lay awake, eyes open, staring at the ceiling, and she wondered what she might have gotten into with the stranger from America.

He had been right about the crates. Assuming he had told the truth, they did not sound like weapons. But if arms were not the cargo, what was? The Russians would not take such pains to smuggle machinery in the dead of night and under guard. There must be something else....

Shane MacAllister would hold the key, and Rachel would confront him in the morning. She would need a cover, something simple but effective that would dupe her mark without creating endless complications for herself. It took her fifteen minutes to devise a story that was perfect for Rachel's purposes.

The cover would suffice, and if she blew it, then she would take care of herself.

"Have you ever killed a man?"

She had not, and until this evening she had taken pride in having served nine years without encountering a situation where she might be forced to take a human life. There had been one or two near misses, but Rachel had been lucky.

Why then did she suddenly feel so inadequate, outmatched? What did it matter if her hands had never been responsible for spilling blood? Was homicide some badge of honor, to be worn with pardonable pride?

She realized the difference in values permeating every phase of British and American society. Police in Britain still patrolled their beats unarmed, although increasingly detectives carried weapons and the growth of "special squads" had signaled a reliance on the strength of arms against particularly violent felons. Incidents like the assassination of a female constable outside the Libyan embassy in London had produced a subtle change in British attitudes toward violence. Never prone to suffer insults lightly, Britons had begun to speak of fighting back in kind, and they were not just speaking in whispers, either.

Still, it was a far cry from America, John Wayne and Dirty Harry. There were fundamental differences that Britons, Rachel hoped, would never overcome. Civility was part of it; a quiet dignity that permeated every level of society to some extent. Until the past few years, the bloody *gangsters* had not even carried firearms as a rule, and those who did were often weeded out by members of their own fraternity as renegades, unfit to live with others of their kind. If that civility was changing, disappearing, Rachel viewed it as a sign of devolution, rather than a mark of progress.

But she had not made the world in which she lived. It was her job to deal with criminals and traitors on a daily basis, but she did not have to emulate their tactics in the process. She believed that there was still a solid line between enforcement of the law and violation of that law in order's name. When lawmen stooped to lawlessness, they were no better than the animals they struggled to control.

Rachel was determined not to cross that line, no matter how she might be tempted in the course of her assignment. Neither would she let the brash American force her into compromising that which she believed in. She was taking risks enough already, holding out on her superiors at MI-5, cooperating with a stranger in pursuit of goals that were not clear by any means. If anything went wrong, she was prepared to shoulder full responsibility.

Provided that she was still alive.

The possibility of death had crossed her mind before, but after listening to Belasko, it was weighing on her now, oppressive in the darkness of her bedroom. Could she really do her job, when lives were on the line and it was do-or-die? Would some inadequacy in her character result in absolute disaster for herself? For Belasko? For the mission they were undertaking?

Rachel closed her eyes and concentrated on the goal of sleep. Her final thoughts were images of Michael Belasko, leveling a pistol at her face. And smiling.

8

Tim Rafferty was drunk, but it was not enough. The Highlands did not hold enough ale and whiskey to anesthetize him now. The pain he felt was too intense for liquor to alleviate the burning in his gut, the hollow ache inside his chest where once a healthy heart had beaten strong and sound. He could have drowned himself in alcohol without securing relief.

He did not mind the headache. Tim was used to those, from drink and being bashed around in different pubs. He knew that it would pass, but he would not forget the fact that Shane MacAllister had struck him, and he didn't have a chance to fight back. His lordship was probably above bare-knuckle sparring with the likes of Rafferty, but there would come a day—and soon, sweet Jesus—when the bastard would not have a chance to run away.

The pain tormenting Rafferty was psychological in origin, comprised of loneliness and guilt, the impotence of stifled, pent-up rage. Tonight he felt as if he might explode, and God help any man or beast in the vicinity when he erupted into screaming violence.

Shane MacAllister had gotten off too easy at The Piper's Rest. His day was coming, though, and Rafferty could wait a while for that one, let his fury simmer while he wore out every other channel of investigation in an effort to retrieve his daughter. Since his wife's abrupt and unexpected death two years ago, Rebecca was the only thing worth holding on to in his life, and Rafferty would not give up on her without a fight.

He was not buying that malarkey from the constables about his Becky running off with Tommy Cullen. They were sweet on each other, right enough, and he would not have been surprised to learn that they had passed the stage of holding hands in their relationship. Rebecca's mother had been quick that way, but faithful as the summer day was long, and the Lord knew that Rebecca had attained the age where she could do a bit of thinking for herself. It was the eloping part he couldn't buy, no matter how he tried.

He had not always been the kind of father that Rebecca might have wanted for herself. He could be rough around the edges at times, and he was not shy about unloading chores upon his only child. But it was always done with love, and he believed Rebecca knew that in her heart. She also knew he liked the Cullen boy, and while he would have kicked the randy bastard's ass if he had ever caught them at it, you couldn't blame the young for *being* young. If Becky had it in her mind to settle down with Tommy Cullen, there would certainly have been no need to run away. Tim Rafferty would have given the bride away with a smile. He would have danced at their wedding till the bloody cows came home.

MacAllister had done away with them, somehow, for reasons Rafferty could not begin to comprehend. He might not know the "why" or "how" of it, but he was certain, all the same. Rebecca's scarf had been the kicker, found no more than forty meters from the ruins of his lordship's tumble-down ancestral home. The constables suggested that she might have dropped it there as she was passing by on the way to somewhere else, but they could never name a likely destination. They were fuzzy-headed men, but they could not have failed to notice that MacAllister's estate was off the beaten track. You didn't pass that way en route to Mallaig in the north, nor on your way to any other town, either. Not by choice.

There was a road, of course, that led up to the castle, but it was a dead-end track that petered out amid the ruins. No one in Cairnaben would attempt to use that road for going anywhere but up and back again; it was a fact of life the bloody constables had thus far chosen to ignore.

No question there was something queer about the castle. All the stories Rafferty had heard since childhood must have *something* to them, even if they were exaggerated in the telling. Where there were clouds of smoke, you should expect to find at least a little flame, and Rafferty had spent a lifetime steering clear of the MacAllister estate, his caution overriding curiosity.

Until tonight.

He had to know about Rebecca, had to find some clue, and if the bloody constables were good for nothing, he would do the job himself. They told him they had "looked around" the ruins, and he knew that might mean anything—or nothing. Lazy at the best of times, the local bulls, once having made their minds up that the case was an elopement, had expended precious little energy in searching for his child. The fact that Tommy Cullen had gone missing proved the case, in their official minds, but it meant something else again to Rafferty.

It meant MacAllister had claimed two victims for the price of one.

Three weeks had passed since Becky disappeared with Tommy Cullen, and in that time Rafferty had come to grips with the realization that his daughter was dead. If she had run away to marry, she would certainly have been in touch by now to smooth things over and receive her father's blessing. As a living hostage, she was worthless; Rafferty possessed no worldly goods of any value, and he would have heard from kidnappers by now in any case. He *knew* Rebecca must be dead, as well as Tommy Cullen, and the certain knowledge only deepened his resolve to see the matter through.

Tim Rafferty could not begin to guess at motives Mac-Allister might have for murdering his daughter. A rich man had no need of force and violence, while a pervert—rich or otherwise—would probably have looked for simpler game, a girl alone, without an escort. Tommy Cullen had been a burly lad, and he could have given a fair accounting of himself when called upon. Whatever else he might have done with Becky in the secret hours of the night, he would have fought for her, no matter what the odds. Of that Tim Rafferty was certain.

He had attempted to discuss the bloody business with Tommy's father, but Rob Cullen had withdrawn into a shell, refusing to admit the possibility that Tommy might have come to grief. They had not spoken in the past two weeks, Rob sitting at home and waiting for a call or letter that would never come, attempting to convince himself that Tommy was alive and well. He would prefer to think his youngest son had run away, abandoned him without a word, forever, than to face the truth.

Whatever might have motivated the destruction of his world, Tim Rafferty was certain that the answer—or a portion of it—lay within the ruins of MacAllister's ancestral castle. Standing on a windswept slope above Cairnaben, hands tucked deep within the pockets of his threadbare coat for warmth, he thought that there was no time like the present.

Rafferty had gone back to retrieve a flashlight from his dark and empty house—a home no longer now that Becky had been snatched away from him. He would not need the light until he reached the castle proper; on the moor above the village there was ample moonlight to permit negotiation of the narrow path. He took no pains to hide himself, prepared to stand and fight if he was challenged, and be damned to anyone who tried to turn him from his course.

Ten minutes of steady hiking brought him to the ruins, and he spent another quarter hour studying the outer wall from different angles. There were half a dozen separate ways of gaining entrance, only two of them intended by the architects, and after circling the ruins like a hunter stalking prey, the grizzled Scotsman chose his angle of attack. The northern wall was breached at one point, where the stone and mortar had collapsed long generations hence, and Rafferty was able to negotiate the rockfall with a minimum of effort, stumbling only once as the effects of drink caught him. Another moment and he was inside the castle of the clan MacAllister, dark, jagged walls surrounding him on every side like dragon's teeth.

He hauled the flashlight out and turned it on. He found himself inside a courtyard, flanked by chambers lacking roofs and portions of their walls. At one time, he supposed, they had been storage rooms or sleeping quarters for the castle guards. These days a rat or two might be in residence, but he was otherwise alone, the ruins seemingly deserted.

Rafferty set off across the courtyard toward the sole surviving tower with its winding flight of stairs. A bird's-eye view would let him scan the yard and open rooms below to best advantage, spotting any sections that appeared to warrant further scrutiny. And there was yet another motive, dating back to childhood, that he would not readily acknowledge, even to himself.

From boyhood he had longed to see Cairnaben and the seashore from those lofty tower windows. Several of his playmates claimed that they had made the trek, by night or day, but he had always doubted their veracity. As for himself, Tim Rafferty had never found the courage...until now, when he had nothing more to lose.

He thought about the stories that had made his hair stand on end, of restless ghosts and things no man could rightly name, of witches dancing through the ruins in the blackest hours of All Saints' Eve.

There had been Tad McCarran, who had shot himself to death outside the castle walls in 1943. The village wags allowed the blame for that one rested squarely on the shoulders of McCarran's wife, who had absconded with the family savings and a fancy man a few days previous, but suicide and scandal sparked a whole new round of stories dealing with the castle's "evil atmosphere."

And there was Arny Cole, who had tried to climb the tower on a dare in 1965 and plummeted a hundred feet to his death instead of picking up the tenner he was promised by his mates if he could make it to the top. No matter that he had been drinking steadily beforehand, and the stunt was foolish to begin with. Never mind that ancient stones are apt to break away without a by-your-leave just when you need them most for handholds. There were those who saw a mystery in Arny's fall, and brand-new stories made the rounds, together with a few that had been hauled out of mothballs and dusted off for the occasion.

The McAllisters were cursed, according to the stories. Rather, their estate was cursed, and anyone who set a foot therein without protection from the saints was flirting with disaster, not to mention probable damnation. There was disagreement in the legends as to whether one or other of the early lairds had dabbled in Satanic lore or had offended Lucifer by shunning his advances. Historians were in agreement that the clan MacAllister had suffered rare misfortune spanning several generations while their leaders occupied the castle on the hill above Cairnaben. When they finally had the sense to settle elsewhere, in the middle 1840s, the Homeric run of sad misfortune had evaporated overnight, and Lady Luck had smiled upon the family to the present day, endowing them with newfound wealth, prestige and healthy sons.

Tim Rafferty was not a superstitious man, but he could not suppress a shudder as he reached the tower steps, his flashlight beam devoured by the inky shadows lurking in the stairwell. Gooseflesh prickled on his arms, and for a moment he was eight years old again and terrified about facing down the bogeyman.

Except that now he had a deep, abiding rage to melt the fear away. The bogeyman, or someone acting in his stead, had claimed a life he held most dear, and Rafferty was not about to let the bastard get away with it. If he was dealing with a man or beast or something in between, he meant to have his pound of flesh this night. And if he had to pay a late call by MacAllister's when he was finished at the castle to collect the debt that he was owed, so be it.

Climbing slowly, legs a bit unsteady from all the ale and whiskey he had consumed, Tim Rafferty eventually reached the topmost chamber of the ruined tower. Standing in the open window, leaning on his hands, he scanned the moonlit coast for a kilometer in each direction. A second window to his left would offer him a new perspective on Cairnaben village, and he was about to take it in when he was suddenly distracted by a sound downstairs.

He hesitated on the topmost stair and listened, scarcely breathing. He heard shuffling footsteps, heavy, plodding, in the darkness far below. There could be no mistake.

He drew the clasp knife from his pocket, flicked it open with an easy, practiced gesture, smiling as the long, curved blade reflected pallid moonlight. Rafferty had honed the blade to razor sharpness, kept it there with weekly stroppings, whether it was used meantime or not. The handle, heavy bone and brass, felt like an old friend in his hand.

He meant to find the bloody sod who did his strolling after midnight in the castle ruins, have a word or two in private, and discover if he might know anything about a pair of missing children from the village. With any luck the bastard might try something funny, giving Rafferty the chance to pare him down a bit before they got around to their discussion. If the creeper was involved in Becky's disappearance, he was dead already, wandering around the castle grounds on borrowed time. The pains of hell would be as nothing in comparison with what an outraged father could deliver, given half a chance.

He took his time about descending, moving with exaggerated caution, feeling his way, not relying on the flashlight. The light would be his secret ace, a way to blind his prey when he was close enough to strike, but he could not afford to give the enemy advance warning of his presence. The claustrophobic stairwell seemed about to smother him, but Rafferty went slowly, took his time, the knife held ready, just in case an ambush might be waiting for him in the shadows.

The courtyard was shrouded in darkness, scarcely broken by the moonlight, with looming walls on every side. He hesitated, listening, until the sound of shuffling footsteps was repeated somewhere on his flank, no more than twenty meters away. He set off with determined strides, avoiding obstacles by instinct, homing in on the telltale sounds of someone who was disinclined to travel quietly. Amazed at his ability to pick his way amid the rubble silently, Tim was congratulating himself on his achievement when he stumbled, fell headlong and skinned his forehead on the stones. The clasp knife skittered from his fingers and was lost in darkness.

Somewhere up ahead of Rafferty, the shuffling footsteps halted, hesitated, then reversed themselves. He wasted precious moments searching for his weapon, still afraid to turn on the flashlight in case it drew his enemy to where he lay. The footsteps were almost on top of him when he panicked, scrambled to his feet and bolted back in the direction of the stairs.

Without a light to guide him, Rafferty collided with the wall and skinned his hands. Reeling, he succeeded on his second try and started up the stairs, half crawling after he had missed a step and came down painfully on hands and knees. He could hear the sounds of an almost leisurely pursuit behind him. His enemy, whoever it might be, appeared to have no difficulty with the darkness.

Something in his mind demanded that he stand and fight, but Rafferty was running on survival instincts now. Thus far, the sounds that emanated from the darkness had not been particularly threatening, but he was overpowered by a sense of menace and evil that were almost palpable. A hundred different tales and legends of the "haunted" castle came to mind, and while he knew that all of them were fantasies, the knowledge gave him precious little comfort now.

He reached the midpoint of the staircase, hesitated, heard the heavy, awkward feet below him as they climbed. Driven on to greater speed, Rafferty staggered to his feet with arms outstretched, palms braced against the walls on either side. He started to climb faster, stumbling more frequently along the way, and twice fell forward onto his face before he had a chance to catch himself. The second time he chipped a tooth against the rugged stonework of the stairs, and blinding pain lanced upward through his skull. A bleat of pain escaped from bloody lips before he caught himself and bit it off abruptly.

Frozen on the stairs, he heard the enemy stop dead below him. This would be the time for a legitimate night watchman to communicate, call out a warning that the stairs were treacherous in darkness, offer to negotiate a simple trespass charge if nothing had been stolen from the ruins. Deathly silence filled the stairwell, almost physical in its intensity, and Rafferty was certain now that his pursuer meant to do him harm.

There might be ways to mitigate the damage, yet. Evacuation of the tower while the stairs were held would be impossible; poor Arny Cole had fairly proved that fact, and he had lost it climbing *up* the wall, in God's own daylight. Scrambling down the rugged face in darkness, with his hands all trembly from the booze—and fear—was nothing short of suicidal.

He could fight, of course, although he still felt more like running at the moment. He could lay an ambush on the threshold of the topmost chamber, spring upon the bastard when he least expected it and knock him down the stairs. That ought to slow the bastard down a bit, and once he took the fall, then Rafferty could use his flashlight to hurry down the stairs and finish off the job if need be.

It could work. If necessary, he might even shine the flashlight in the bloody bugger's eyes before he knocked him backward, down the steps. It wouldn't hurt to blind him for an instant, gain an extra, small advantage for himself while he was at it. God knew he needed all the help that he could get.

He missed his footing on the top step, almost fell again, but caught himself and reeled across the threshold. Ever-open windows stared unblinkingly across Cairnaben toward the sea. He risked the flashlight for a moment, scanning till he found himself a brick and seized it, hefting it for weight and balance in his palm. He had a weapon now, and Rafferty no longer felt defenseless, like a child afraid of shadows in the night.

He waited, standing in the middle of the room, off center so that he would not be caught in silhouette by moonlight from the windows. With the flashlight poised and ready, jagged stonework heavy in his hand, he waited, listening to heavy, dragging footsteps on the stairs. It would be another moment before the enemy appeared, and Rafferty was conscious of a sudden, burning need to urinate. He clenched his teeth and concentrated on the outline of the doorway, deeper shadows of the stairwell just beyond.

In childhood he had played hide and seek with siblings, friends, and there had always been a tingling of anticipation as the hunter tracked him down, a trace of fear, despite the fact that nothing would be done to him when he was found. That feeling had returned tonight, but multiplied a hundred times, a thousand, by the knowledge that he would badly injured, very likely killed, if he was captured. For reasons he could not explain, he knew his life was hanging by a thread, and that abysmal knowledge gave him new determination to survive.

A sound, beyond the threshold. Movement in the doorway, as a shadow, hulking, powerful, prepared to enter. Rafferty stepped forward, switched the flashlight on—

And screamed.

The face was something from an alcoholic's nightmare, twisted and discolored, with protruding teeth like fangs and hollow, lifeless eyes. The worst part, though, for Rafferty, was that it hovered nearly two full feet above his own blanched countenance. One glance, and he knew he was dealing with a giant. He felt his bladder go in a steaming rush.

Tim Rafferty was sobbing as the creature turned to face him, but he stood his ground and launched the brick with all of his remaining strength. The giant sidestepped, took it on the shoulder with a snarl of anger, seemingly impervious to pain. Rafferty threw the flashlight next, and he was thankful when it struck the stone and shattered, bringing back the darkness to obscure his vision of the enemy.

There was no exit, save the one behind the growling apparition, and no weapon left to use against his enemy. He bolted for the nearest window, desperate, convinced that

Arny Cole had never felt such inspiration in his wild, abbreviated life.

Without a backward glance he swung one leg across the windowsill and thrust his head out, trying not to concentrate on stones and sloping fields below. The ground was at least a hundred feet away, now that he thought of it in concrete terms, but it was better than a dead-end wrestling match with Frankenstein, and all of it for nothing when the thing threw him out the bloody window, anyway. This road, at least, gave him some kind of chance, however slim, to make it home alive.

But he was having trouble with his other leg, twisted as it was, the heel of his old shoe jammed tight against the windowsill, his knee against his chest. He hammered at the stubborn foot with angry fists, but it refused to budge an inch.

Until the big hands closed around his throat.

That broke the log jam, right enough, but he was moving in the wrong direction as his adversary yanked him back inside and held him at arm's length so his feet were dangling inches from the floor. Tim seized the opportunity to plant a solid kick or two against the giant's ribs, but for the good it did him, he might just as well have saved his effort.

Bony thumbs were pressing on his larynx, shutting off his wind, and Rafferty saw colored pinwheels spinning on the insides of his eyelids. He knew that he was dying, but the magnitude of what was happening escaped him, and he did not recognize the moment when it came. One instant, he was thrashing in the giant's grip; the next, his form hung slack, a broken puppet waiting for repairs.

The creature held him for another moment, making certain that the job was done before he let the body drop. It stooped to grasp the dead man by his heels, dragged him from the chamber and down the stairs. Tim's skull struck every step along the way.

There would be traces left behind. The creature knew that much, but it was not concerned. The cleanup was for others. It had done the job for which it was responsible, and now it could be fed.

9

"Lord MacAllister will see you now."

The receptionist smiled with apparent sincerity, leading the way to a stout oaken door with a polished brass plate that read Private. The door opened into an oak-paneled office with rich, deep pile carpeting and walls of built-in bookcases that were jammed with texts on animal husbandry, maritime law and procedures, ichthyology and a wide variety of other subjects. Picture windows on the west admitted dazzling sunlight, offering a spectacular view of the coastline below Cairnaben.

Shane MacAllister was turning from the window as Rachel Hunter entered. For a moment, with the light behind him, she could not see his face; for that brief instant he was totally anonymous, a cipher. The illusion vanished as he moved to greet her, stretching out one hand to clasp her own.

"Miss Scribner, good of you to come."

The name had seemed to fit her cover, but it sounded strange to Rachel now, pronounced in MacAllister's mellow tones.

"On the contrary, Your Lordship. It was generous of you to make your time available."

"I hope you'll do me a tremendous favor and forget about this 'lordship' business, altogether. It's a purely honorary title, I assure you. Comes with the genes, I'm afraid."

"Very well, er..."

"Shane," he suggested.

"Thank you, Shane." She let him show her to a comfortable chair and waited as he settled in behind his massive desk. "As I informed your secretary, the *Daily Mirror* is doing a series of articles on Britain's 'unknown' businessmen, entrepreneurs who are not generally in the public eye."

"I read the *Mirror* regularly," he informed her, "and I haven't seen your series. Must have overlooked it, I suppose."

"It's still in preparation."

"Ah. Well, that explains it, then."

"I rather hoped that you could take my readers on a walking tour of your life, within the limits of propriety, of course. A survey of your several businesses and how they operate, a family history—that sort of thing."

"It all sounds rather tedious to me," he said, and smiled.

"It won't be, I assure you."

"Well, then, if you'll give me some idea of where you wish to start, perhaps ask questions?"

"Certainly. Do you object to my recording this?"

He smiled. "No, not at all . . . unless you plan to use the lot in evidence against me."

Rachel felt her own smile stretching toward the point of no return. Was he suspicious of her now, this early in the game? Had he been warned, somehow? Or was he merely being playful, making points, perhaps considering the possibility of conquest?

He was certainly attractive; Rachel had to give him that. A charmer from the outset, this MacAllister. The local women would be falling over him, and so, she thought, would many of the more sophisticated types in Glasgow, Edinburgh, even London. He had a certain boyish charm, but there was steel inside, beneath the bluff exterior. A trace of it shone through around the eyes.

"I wouldn't think of it," she said, and set her small recorder on the desk between them, double-checking it before she settled back into her chair.

"Where shall we start?"

"A bit of background first, I think. We have your bio at the *Mirror*, but I do so want to take a fresh approach."

"There isn't much spectacular about the family, I'm afraid. We were a lot of landed gentry in the old times, rather badly gone to seed around the time of George I and the disturbance in the colonies. I might be on the dole right now, if old Anson MacAllister—my great-great-grandfather—hadn't put the remnants of the family fortune in a fishing boat. I'm told that he worked like a slave with his men for a number of years building up what the family had lost. And, of course, there was always the land."

"And the castle."

"Yes, now that you mention it."

"What was it like, growing up as a lord?"

"Rather tedious, actually. Private schools, that sort of thing. There were always appearances to be preserved."

"No peccadilloes?"

"Nothing comes to mind, but even if it did…ah, well, I'm sure you understand."

"Of course. Your business is primarily in fishing?"

"We're a good deal more diverse, these days. We have a cartage firm in Edinburgh that serves about two-thirds of Scotland. There are sheep and cattle in the western Highlands, various investments down in London."

"And the cannery?"

"Of course."

Had she imagined it, or had a flicker of uneasiness been visible in his eyes?

"When you say 'we'—"

"I'm being damned pretentious, I suppose. In fact, it's *me*. There are no more MacAllisters. For good or ill, I'm the end of the line."

"Never married?"

"Once, briefly. An awful mistake of my youth."

"And no children?"

"For that I'm eternally grateful."

"I take it your interests don't run toward preserving the line."

"It's a matter of total indifference to me. If I marry again someday, maybe... And if not, *c'est la vie*."

"I think my readers would enjoy a glimpse inside the public man, if I maybe so bold. A hobby, for example, or a favorite sport?"

"I do some shooting, and I like to ride, although I shy away from competitions. Too damned old to break my neck pursuing trophies, I suppose."

She made a show of thumbing through her pocket notebook, as if refreshing her memory on important questions. In fact the pages were completely blank, but Rachel had the questions firmly planted in her mind, and she was very close to running out of small talk.

"I observed a Russian trawler moored in port this morning. Have you any business dealings with the Soviets?"

MacAllister shook his head. "None whatsoever. Trade with ComBloc countries is completely regulated by the government, as I'm sure you're aware. The Russian trawlers are allowed to berth at several points along the coast—Cairnaben, Mallaig, other places—for supplies and fuel, emergencies, that sort of thing."

"The seamen are allowed to come ashore?"

He nodded, smiling. "And I gather that they spend a pretty ruble at The Anchor, swilling grog. From all accounts, the Russians are a thirsty lot."

"I hate to bring this next bit up."

His frown revealed more curiosity than apprehension. "Come now, don't be bashful. If I have a family skeleton, I'd like to shake the old boy's hand."

"Oh, very well. For some time, there have been...*stories* told about your family's estate."

"The eyesore on the hill? Is that all?" MacAllister threw his head back and laughed out loud. "I thought for a moment that you'd traced the family tree to Jack the Ripper— or worse yet, the Labour Party."

Rachel smiled. "About the stories..."

"Yes, of course. I don't recall the lot, but most of them are pretty standard spooks-and-goblins fare. We haven't got a headless horseman, I'm afraid, but if memory serves, there was some sort of mutilated maiden, said to traipse around the battlements on moonlit nights. It never seemed quite worth the cost and bother of an exorcism."

"Recently there were reports of disappearances."

"I beg your pardon?"

"Thomas Cullen and Rebecca Rafferty, young people from the village. Rumor has it that they disappeared close by your castle, if not actually from the grounds."

His frown took on the makings of a scowl. "Pure rubbish. Someone has been letting their imagination run, at your expense. The local constable has carried out his own investigation of the case, and he has classified the so-called missing persons as a pair of runaways. From all accounts, they seem to have eloped."

"And yet there is the matter of a scarf that was discovered at the castle."

"No, I really must take issue with you there. A very common woolen scarf was found some distance from the grounds. I am aware of nothing, other than some idle rumors, to connect the scarf with either of the runaways. If truth be told, there must be hundreds like it in the district."

"Be that as it may, some of the locals seem to blame you for the disappearances."

"Cairnaben has its share of superstitious fools. I really can't be held responsible for what they think."

"Of course not." Smiling sweetly, Rachel changed her angle of attack. "Would it be possible to have a look inside your cannery? Perhaps take photographs?"

"Oh, I imagine that could be arranged."

"As for the castle—"

"I'm afraid I'll have to disappoint your readers, there. The grounds are quite unsafe, with unexpected rockfalls and the cellars caving in. I have some older photographs that might be suitable for reproduction in your paper, and you're welcome to them, but we really can't have people wandering around the place and getting into dutch."

"Well, then, about that tour of the cannery—"

"I'll make arrangements with the overseer for tomorrow or the next day. Are you staying locally?"

"I have a room at the Cairnaben Arms."

"Delightful." He stood up and moved around the desk. "I'll be in touch, then."

Rachel smiled. "And I'll be looking forward to it."

MacAllister saw her to the door then closed it firmly behind her. Outside, while walking back to her car, she resisted the urge to glance back at his office, convinced that he—or someone—was watching her, studying her like a bug under glass.

He was glib, that one, but he had not been especially convincing. As yet, she had no idea what MacAllister might be attempting to hide on the family estate, but his lame recitation of hazards had failed to persuade her. There might well be dangers inside those crumbling walls, Rachel thought, but she doubted that rockfalls and drops into basements were all of the risk.

Mike Belasko might have something for her when they met again that afternoon. She hoped he would be careful, scouting out the ruins, but she sensed that he could take care of himself. A heavy who crossed that one would be well advised to pay up on his life insurance first, and no mistake.

She wondered if it was the smell of danger that made Belasko so attractive, finally deciding that it did not matter in the least. They were professionals, and private feelings had no place in the performance of their duty. The assignment must come first, and never mind that she was skating on thin ice already, flirting with a charge of negligence and insubordination through her failure to advise the brass at MI-5 of her alliance with the tall American. With Harry sidelined, gravely injured, she would take her allies as they came, as long as they produced results.

And Belasko, she believed, was definitely one to get results.

MACALLISTER STOOD WATCHING through the blinds as Rachel Scribner drove away in the direction of Cairnaben. Situated half a mile from town, on property that had been family owned for generations, the nerve center of MacAllister Enterprises occupied a commanding rise of ground, equidistant from Cairnaben and the ruins of the family castle. Moving now toward windows facing that direction, Shane MacAllister spent several moments staring at the source of all his problems, studying the tower that thrust upward like a rude, contemptuous finger.

It was totally irrational, of course, for him to blame the castle. It was nothing more than ancient stone and rotting mortar, mindless and inanimate. The problem lay within himself, in his avarice and weakness. If he had been able to rely upon his principles, resist temptation of the easy profit, tax-free pounds in numbered Swiss accounts, he would have been entirely bettcr off.

If he had been stronger.

And now, of course, it was too late.

The woman had seen through him, he was certain of it. Worse, he was convinced that she had lied to him from the beginning, that she had no more connection with the *Daily Mirror* than he did. She was a spy of some sort, almost certainly, but who had put her on his track? And why?

He had his secretary dial the *Daily Mirror* offices in London and he asked for Rachel Scribner, acting suitably chagrined when he was told that no one by that name was presently on staff. It was a clumsy error on the opposition's part, but he experienced no sense of triumph. Knowing who the enemy was *not* put him no closer to discovery of who she *was*.

Reluctantly MacAllister admitted that he ought to call Andreiovitch. It was the only logical recourse available, and if they were about to be exposed, each moment wasted was a critical error. His control would have the answers, the solutions to their problem. Something permanent and nasty could be planned for Rachel Scribner, or whomever she might be behind the smiling mask. She was available and ripe for picking, waiting for his call.

There was the possibility that she was not alone. If there were others, then the risks were geometrically increased. Andreiovitch might not be able to arrange so many accidents and disappearances. The Russian's confidence was boundless, like his ego, but he was a human being, after all, with human foibles, human failings.

Still, while there was any chance at all, he had to trust Andreiovitch. His choice was made, the devil's bargain signed and sealed in blood. He could no more recant his understanding with the Soviets than he could change the color of his skin. Whatever happened to him now was preordained, perhaps determined from the moment of his birth. He might be able to alleviate the outcome, cut his

losses in the end, but for the moment his best hope lay with
the Russian. If they hung together, showed the enemy a
firm, united front, they still might pull it off.

He cursed Tom Cullen and his girlfriend. If they had not
been randy, looking for a place to tease each other at the
wrong damned moment, he would not have had a problem
in the world. Their deaths had been unfortunate, albeit
necessary, and he felt a twinge of sadness when he thought
about the youngsters, even though the two of them had
brought disaster on themselves. It had been clever, causing
them to disappear with rumors of elopement in the air, and
everything had been fine...until the blasted scarf was found.

He cursed the garment. Nothing but a colored handful of
wool, and it might bring MacAllister's whole world crash-
ing down around his ears. The very idea was preposterous,
but there it was. The straw that broke the bloody camel's
back.

But done was done, and it was no good worrying about
the past. The present counted now, and his manipulation of
the present would determine what the future held in store.
Assuming that he *had* a future.

He would not go to prison, he had made his mind up on
that score. No bars and stout gray walls to box him in for
twenty years or life. It was a nuisance that the government
had done away with hanging. The former penalty for treason had been death, and he believed that it was only fit-
ting, in the circumstances. There was no damned good in
living if you had to do it in a cage, and Shane MacAllister
had known from the beginning that he would not stand for
trial if he was finally exposed. It was unthinkable, a trav-
esty of life he could never bear.

The simple fact, concealed from everyone since childhood, was that he had always suffered from particularly
savage claustrophobia. With time—and secret therapy—he
had controlled his weakness to the point where he could

function in a crowded room, step into closets if the need arose and ride on elevators with the best of them. But at the very thought of spending years inside a cell, his stomach tied itself in knots and he began to sweat.

Before he served a day in prison, he would kill himself. It would be preferable to escape, of course, but he had no illusions of his own ability to survive on the run, living like a hunted animal from one taut moment to the next. Andreiovitch might manage to arrange a sanctuary for him with the Soviets, but it was doubtful. He was not an ace of spies, like Philby or a covert warrior of the revolution. If there was a modern-day society with smaller tolerance for traitors than his homeland, it would have to be the Soviet regime. At best, he would be shuffled to the side and soon forgotten, viewed—when he was viewed at all—with thinly veiled contempt. In time they would be tempted to dispose of him entirely, and that brought him back to thoughts of prison, always granting that they did not kill him outright.

No. His hopes lay with Andreiovitch, and while they might be slim, at least some hope remained. The Russian might devise a workable solution for their mutual predicament, provided there was time to save the play.

Disgusted with himself, he sat down in the swivel chair behind his desk and reached out for the telephone.

Andreiovitch would know precisely what to do. It was his job.

And, more importantly, his life was riding on the line, beside MacAllister's.

10

He took the high road from Cairnaben, driving slowly, every inch the tourist in his shiny BMW, examining the moors. There was a feeling here of altitude, of climbing to the summit of the earth. Rich greens and browns were broken here and there by purple stands of heather, splashed across the land like paint across an artist's palette. The sky above was gunmetal, threatening rain, but its overcast only served to make the striking colors of the moors that much more vivid.

Ahead of Bolan, on his left, Castle MacAllister stood like a piece of living history, battlements thrusting up from the earth as if it had sprouted from bedrock. Driving past, he half expected knights in rusty armor to emerge from the ruins and issue a challenge, demand that he answer their call for invading their territory. Yet nothing stirred except a pair of sea gulls that rose briefly from the tower's apex, settling again as Bolan passed.

The place appeared to be deserted, but he would not know for certain until he had a look inside. If there were guards, he would be courting death by visiting the place in daylight, but he felt a mounting sense of urgency, the need to move, do something. If he was careful this time, he might be able to preserve the image of a tourist checking out the local sights. Broad daylight was an awkward time for murder, after all. And if there were no guards, then there was likely nothing in the place worth guarding.

He had prepared himself for disappointment, knowing that there were a dozen different reasons why young lovers might have vanished from Cairnaben. There was every possibility that they had actually eloped, regardless of the scarf. They might be miles away by now, and laughing up their sleeves...but Bolan didn't think so. As he pulled the BMW over on the grassy shoulder and killed its engine, Bolan spent another moment studying the ruined keep. This was a place of violence, he could feel it. And if Bolan's instincts were correct, the bloodshed was not totally confined to ancient history.

He left the car and locked it. Dressed in sheepskin jacket, shirt and slacks, the Executioner might easily have passed inspection as a tourist, just as long as the examination was superficial. Underneath the jacket, Bolan wore the sleek Beretta in its custom shoulder rigging snug beneath his left arm, with two spare magazines in pouches underneath his right. The other hardware was secure inside the BMW's trunk, and would remain there. This would be a soft probe, feeling out the ground, collecting available intelligence.

Except that Bolan knew the soft probes had a way of going hard without a moment's warning, fire and thunder coming out of nowhere to surprise the best prepared warrior. It could happen in a heartbeat, and he always made an effort to anticipate the unexpected, where he could.

He hoped that Rachel Hunter did the same. Her interview with Shane MacAllister appeared to be a milk run, but there were a dozen ways it could go sour. If MacAllister became suspicious, if the woman said too much, her cover could be blown and she could wind up dead. It would be simple for a stranger and a phony journalist to disappear, presumably departing from Cairnaben, headed back for London. By the time her pals from MI-5 could mount a search, there would be nothing left to find. MacAllister would have his alibi in place, complete with witnesses who saw the woman leave his office safe and sound.

He put the problem out of mind. The woman was a professional, and she could take care of herself. It did not matter if she gathered any useful information from Mac-Allister this time around, as long as she distracted him and kept him at his office while the soldier made his recon of the ruined castle. Any hard intelligence she managed to collect would just be frosting on the cake.

The soil was spongy under Bolan's feet as he began to climb the slope, approaching from the castle's southern flank. There was a breach in the crumbling wall, and if his luck held out, it would provide him with a means of access to the grounds. He scanned the property with wary eyes, alert for any sign of danger as he closed the distance.

He reached the outer castle wall and hesitated, listening. Aside from sea gulls calling in the tower overhead, the ruins were completely silent, seemingly devoid of life. Scrambling over fallen stones, the soldier found himself inside a ruined chamber, open to the sky above. It might have been a storeroom at one time or even quarters for the castle guards, but any furniture or other artifacts had long since disappeared, removed by looters or dissolved by Mother Nature over time. The earthen floor was bare, worn down almost to bedrock by erosion, and the inner walls were thick with lichen sprouting mushrooms in the shadowed corners of the room.

There was a narrow door directly opposite, and Bolan hesitated on the threshold, listening again in case his entry had provoked some audible reaction.

Nothing.

Bolan made his way with cautious strides through the doorway and out into the courtyard proper. If Shane MacAllister's ancestral keep ran true to form, there would be basements under foot, and Bolan's plans did not include a sudden plunge through darkness onto jagged stones. An accident on unfamiliar ground could be as lethal as a bullet in the brain, and he had no desire to jeopardize his life through foolish negligence.

The courtyard was a littered wasteland, heaped with rubble where the walls and roofs of inner chambers had collapsed. Apparently no one was interested in cleaning up the place and making it presentable. Where others might have seen the castle as a money-maker, Shane MacAllister seemed perfectly content to leave it undisturbed.

As Bolan advanced on the tower steps, he swept his eyes around the interior, ready to respond to the first sign of danger. His jacket was unbuttoned, granting easy access to the pistol in its shoulder rigging, but he hoped he would be able to avoid a confrontation. It did not serve his purposes to warn MacAllister that someone was onto him.

A glint of polished metal caught his eye. He veered in that direction, stooped, retrieved a wicked-looking clasp knife from the earthen floor. Reflectively he turned the weapon over in his hands, examining the workmanship, evaluating its condition.

Little could be estimated from the blade of stainless steel, but the polished wooden handle had not been long exposed to wind and rain. The pommel was of shiny brass, untarnished, and a quarter-inch of blade had recently been broken off—so recently, in fact, that rust had not yet formed along the line of fracture.

Bolan turned the clasp knife over in his hands, examining the blade. The owner's name had been engraved there, etched in lines of flowing script, perhaps at the behest of friends or relatives who had originally presented the knife as a gift: Tim Rafferty.

Bolan folded the knife and slipped it into his pocket, returning his attention to the tower steps. Rafferty had been here, some time after his removal from The Piper's Rest, and he had come prepared for trouble. Whether he had simply dropped the knife and failed to find it in the dark or whether he had been disarmed remained for Bolan to determine when he got back to Cairnaben. If the elder Rafferty was missing, he had evidence to link the vanished man with Shane MacAllister's estate. On the other hand, if Rafferty was still around, then he could put the castle out of mind and concentrate upon the cannery, where crates of Russian hardware had been unloaded in the middle of the night.

He had reached the stairs, had one foot on the bottom step, when he was suddenly distracted by a shuffling sound from somewhere amid the ruins. Turning, Bolan thought he caught a hint of movement on the far side of the courtyard, barely glimpsed and quickly covered as his eyes came into perfect focus.

Sentries? He was not about to take a chance. Retreating, Bolan made his way along the wide perimeter until he reached the threshold of the chamber through which he first gained entry. With a final glance behind him, he stepped through—and found a double-barreled shotgun aimed directly at his face.

"There, now. Where d'ye think ye're goin', laddie?"

He spent a moment studying the gunner: ruddy face and graying hair above the double hammers of the shotgun, rounded chest and belly set on slender legs below. He did not raise his hands, aware that any sudden movement might surprise the gunner, prompting him to fire.

"Can ye not answer, then?"

A different voice, and Bolan slowly turned his head to find a second 12-gauge covering him on his left. Its owner was a younger man, less heavyset, with sandy hair and crooked, yellow teeth.

"Speak up!" the first man growled, and thrust the muzzle of his piece in Bolan's face for emphasis. "I'm gettin' itchy."

Bolan risked a cautious smile. "Hey, take it easy, will ya? No one told me that the place was posted, or I never would've stopped. You really oughta have a sign outside."

"A sign be damned," the younger man snapped. "Ye 'ave no business 'ere."

"Well, since you put it that way, I'll be glad to leave."

"I bet ye would." The older man grinned. "An' jus' suppose we're of a mind to keep ye 'ere?"

"Now wait a sec—"

"Be that yer car below, on the road?"

"The BMW? Yes, it is."

"A BMW, is it? Ain't we fancy, 'ere."

"It's rented, actually."

"What say we jus' check it out?"

"If you insist."

"We do, indeed."

He knew that there might never be a better chance, and Bolan made his move without a second thought. The younger of his adversaries had the muzzle of his shotgun elevated now, to let him pass, and Bolan took advantage of the moment, stepping toward the gray-haired man, one hand encircling the barrels of his shotgun, twisting it off target as the sentry started to react. He shot a straight-armed jab at his opponent's face, the heel of Bolan's hand impacting on the gunner's nose and snapping cartilage, releasing jets of blood.

The shotgun detonated twice in his fist, and Bolan felt its breath against his side as buckshot sprayed the open door behind him. Flash heat scorched his palm as Bolan wrenched the weapon free and spun to face his second enemy.

The younger man had flinched from the explosion of his partner's weapon, hunching back against the wall, and now, too late, he struggled to recover, to bring his gun around in time to save himself. The stock of Bolan's liberated shotgun caught the man just above one eye and cracked his skull against the mossy stones behind him. He was folding, eyes rolled back into his head, when Bolan let him have another butt stroke, dropping him on the spot.

The older man was out of it, scrabbling around on knees and elbows, hands locked around his shattered face. Refusing to take chances, Bolan hit him with a solid stroke behind one ear and put him temporarily to sleep, facedown upon the bloodstained earthen floor.

It would be no great task to kill them now, but it would serve no purpose, either. Bolan dropped the empty piece beside its owner and evacuated in the same way he had entered, through a fissure in the southern wall. The moors stretched off on every side, obscured by mist on the horizon. Bolan noticed that a gentle rain was falling, pattering against the castle walls and whispering around him on the spongy grass.

Behind him, from the general direction of the castle courtyard, Bolan heard a growling, drawing closer by the moment. Someone, some*thing*, was reacting to the sounds of combat, closing fast, and Bolan was not in the mood to hang around for introductions. Time enough to get acquainted with the castle's other denizens when he returned.

And there was no doubt in the soldier's mind that he was coming back. No doubt at all.

He jogged downslope to reach the BMW, quickly opened the driver's door and slid behind the wheel. He had the car in motion when a hulking figure burst into the open, waving long, ungainly arms and bellowing his rage.

The backup sentry was a giant, close to seven feet in height, and Bolan was relieved that he had not been forced to spar with *that* one. He would almost certainly have had to shoot him and his soft probe had gone hard enough, without stray corpses littering the countryside.

So much for quiet recons. If Shane MacAllister was not aware that he was being shadowed, he would damned sure know it soon enough. He would not know precisely *who* was looking into his activities, but there could not be more than half a dozen strangers in Cairnaben at the moment, counting Rachel and himself. MacAllister was sharp enough to make the obvious connection, when he thought about it, and the threat of imminent exposure only added urgency to Bolan's mission.

Still, for all of that, he would be forced to wait for nightfall. He could hardly penetrate the cannery in daylight, risking violent confrontation with the workers present. It was not his goal to spark a slaughter in Cairnaben, and he would not endanger neutral residents.

A covered truck was approaching, burning up the narrow highway as its driver shifted through the gears. Unquestionably it was headed for the castle, and he edged the BMW over toward the shoulder, leaving room for it to pass. The truck was past him in an instant, but he still had time to read the logo on its door: MacAllister Enterprises, Ltd.

The soldier frowned, accelerating down the narrow track, the truck dwindling in his rearview mirror. It was one of those that he had followed to the cannery last night, and Bolan did not doubt that it was carrying a portion of the Russian trawler's cargo.

Why would MacAllister ship hardware to the ruined castle? For concealment? Or, he wondered, might there be some other reason?

Bolan let the question travel with him. He would definitely have to pay a second visit to the castle, going in with fire and thunder this time if he was opposed. The very fact that it was under guard meant *something* must be hidden there, and Bolan had no doubt the hulking giant and his clumsy sidekicks had disposed of Rafferty last night. In all probability, the missing teenagers had stumbled onto something they were not supposed to see, and Bolan would have bet that they were buried somewhere on the castle grounds or on the lonely moors that stretched for miles beyond.

Anything worth killing to conceal was also worth exposing, and before the Executioner was finished in Cairnaben, he would solve the riddle of MacAllister's connection with the Soviets. In light of what had happened at the castle, he hoped that Rachel Hunter had gathered some intelligence that would assist him in his search for a solution to the puzzle. More immediately, he hoped that she had made it through her interview with Shane MacAllister intact, without a hitch that might destroy her cover and alert him prematurely to her double role.

The laird would be alerted soon enough, once word of the intrusion reached his ears. He might react in a variety of ways, but sheer self-preservation would demand that he respond, to cut his losses, terminate the threat at any cost. If he was under supervision by the KGB, as Bolan thought entirely probable, the obligatory reaction would be swift, decisive, final.

If Shane MacAllister was half as sharp as Bolan thought, it would not take him long to see through Rachel's cover as a journalist. The timing of her interview, on top of the incursion at the castle, would not be accepted as a casual coincidence. When the retaliations started, Rachel might initially be in more pressing danger than the Executioner.

So far, MacAllister was unaware of Bolan's presence in Cairnaben—or, he had been unaware, until this morning. It would take some time for him to put the finger on a suspect, and with any luck at all, by that time Bolan would have pierced the veil of secrecy around the Scotsman's covert links with Moscow.

If Rachel's interview had gone as planned, the lady should be waiting for him at the Cairnaben Arms. He did not wholly trust the feelings the woman had inspired. Emotion had no place in combat, if a soldier was to live and fight another day. Beloved flesh was always vulnerable, and a warrior who involved himself with comrades in arms beyond a professional level made himself vulnerable, as well.

The Executioner had learned that much through grim experience.

There were already too many gentle casualties in Mack Bolan's everlasting war. He did not need another sacrificial lamb to sanctify his struggle, or remind him of the costs inherent in a hopeless war against the odds. If any lives were to be sacrificed around Cairnaben, Bolan and his enemies would bear the weight.

And he could feel it coming down like a yoke across his shoulders. He was still uncertain of the game or the players, but they were approaching overtime. And soon, the Executioner would have to punt or run, with certain disaster waiting for him if he chose the wrong approach.

11

Harry Wilson knew that it was time to look for some excitement. Two days in the hospital, and still the doctors had discovered nothing more than bruises and abrasions. Granted, he still felt as if a rugby team had used his body for a practice ball, but he would live, and based upon the doctors' own admissions, there were no internal injuries of any consequence.

Damned lucky, that. He could have milked it for a few more days without half trying, but it was not Wilson's style to lay around and watch the world go by. He had a job to finish, in Cairnaben, and it would require a great deal more than cuts and bruises to prevent him from continuing the work that he had started.

Rachel would be there already. She had come to see him shortly after he had been admitted to the hospital, and he had told her everything—about the tall American, the Tartan Army, his suspicions of a shipment moving through Cairnaben in the next few days. He'd told her, knowing that she would not hesitate or ask for reinforcements. Knowing she would be in mortal danger. She was a professional, as he was, and it was not Wilson's place to shelter her from the realities of their profession. Rachel knew the risks, and she would do her job in spite of them.

He would not classify her as a reckless agent, but he often got the feeling that she felt a need to prove herself, convince her colleagues she was equal to the task at hand. He sometimes wondered if she suffered feelings of inadequacy based on sex. Despite her training, the proficiency that she had demonstrated on a dozen tough assignments in the past three years, she still deferred to Wilson and her other male associates. Her attitude was not subservient but rather self-effacing, playing down her contributions whenever possible.

He wondered if she might feel a need to make her mark and win the recognition of her superiors, which she had managed to avoid thus far.

It could be a risky business, and while he had the utmost confidence in Rachel, Wilson hoped his partner knew what she was doing. At the very least, he should be there to help her if the job went sour.

As he crawled out of bed, the man from MI-5 was instantly reminded of the beating he had taken two days earlier. A hundred different points of pain cried out at once as Wilson tottered on his feet, protests running all together in an instant, leaving him dizzy and faint. He willed himself to remain upright, moving sluggishly toward the closet on feet that felt as if they were made of lead.

They had saved his clothes, somehow, and while the outfit had seen better days, it would suffice until he reached his apartment and changed. There would be bags to pack, as well, and hardware to secure, but he was taking one step at a time.

It was a simple matter, shrugging off the flimsy robe, and now he felt a draft, as if to emphasize the throbbing of his countless bruises and abrasions. Bending down to pull his shorts and slacks on, Wilson felt as if he might throw up—except that he had eaten nothing more substantial than a cup of broth the past two days, and there was nothing in his stomach.

He dressed slowly, struggling into his shirt and jacket, pulling on his stockings and lacing up his shoes—with difficulty—when the duty nurse surprised him, clucking from the doorway. Gray of hair and square of build, she waddled toward him, scowling.

"And what are we doing out of bed?" she asked imperiously.

"One of us is leaving," Wilson told her, managing a smile.

"I daresay not," she snapped. "We aren't discharged."

"Then you can stay and man the fort."

She vanished, muttering, and reappeared with an orderly in tow.

"I must insist that you get back in bed at once," the dragon lady ordered.

"Must you?" Wilson found new strength as he stood up and moved in the direction of the door. Perhaps the kinks were working out, or maybe it was the adrenaline produced by prospects of a contest. Either way, the giddiness was fading, and a measure of the old resilience was returning to his stride.

The orderly was tall and muscular, an athlete by the look of him. His face was blank, devoid of animosity or any other conscious thought beyond a vestige of amusement in his eyes.

"Why not get back in bed, old son?" The voice was purest cockney, not without a trace of arrogance.

"Your doctor is en route," the nurse declared, as if that settled everything.

"I'm glad to hear it," Wilson answered, smiling. "He'll be needed if Snow White here doesn't stand aside."

"I beg your pardon!"

Wilson shot a warning finger toward the corner.

"Beg from over there," he cautioned. "I don't have the time to deal with idiots."

He watched the angry color rising in his adversary's cheeks. "That's it, then," snapped the orderly. "I'll put the blighter back in bed."

The move was clumsy, and Wilson had no trouble stepping underneath the lunge, despite his stiffness and the squeals of pain from battered muscles. Driving hard with an elbow against the young man's solar plexus, Wilson emptied out his lungs and dropped him to his knees. A chop behind one ear, and the guy was finished, stretched out on the floor. The duty nurse was on her knees beside him in an instant, blubbering.

"You've injured him!"

"A pity. Well, at least he ought to find a qualified physician somewhere in the house."

Once, outside, he hailed a cab and gave the driver his address. Five minutes brought him to his door, and Wilson let himself in. He was not half surprised to find the small apartment ransacked, drawers emptied, the contents of his closets strewn across the floor in rumpled heaps.

It would have been the Tartan Army, he supposed. There had been ample time to toss the place once Wilson's cover had been blown. They would have been attempting to discover evidence of his employers, find out who had sponsored Wilson's infiltration of their ranks before they put him down. They had been wasting time, of course. There had been nothing for the wrecking crew to find, unless . . .

He hurried to the tiny bathroom and raised the lid on the toilet tank, relaxing when he saw that the plastic package was safe and sound. He took it out, removed the Heckler & Koch VP-70 from its waterproof wrapping and checked the automatic's load. There was no sign of tampering with the weapon or its extra magazines, and Wilson slipped the hardware into the pocket of his overcoat as he moved toward the bedroom.

He stripped off his clothes, showered quickly, and then chose a clean, if rumpled, outfit from the items scattered on the floor. His luggage had been examined and hurled across the room, but they had missed the hidden pocket in his suitcase that contained the VP-70's silencer.

He wondered if the American had gone on to Cairnaben. It was comforting to think that Rachel might have someone to fall back on if the play went sour. If she was cornered, blown as he had been in Glasgow.

No more time to waste. He filled the suitcase, paying minimal attention to coordination in the garments he selected from the floor. He was not going to a bloody fashion show, and when the shooting started, it would matter very little what the best-dressed man from MI-5 was wearing. None of it was bulletproof, and he would have to watch himself from this point on, aware that he had stretched his luck beyond the breaking point already.

There was nothing in the fridge but eggs. He scrambled half a dozen, wolfed them down with milk that seemed about to turn, and lingered long enough to brew himself some coffee. He had two stout cups for starters and poured the rest into a thermos, which would keep it warm for hours. He could not afford to doze behind the wheel, and time was of the essence.

They had not searched his car, perhaps because they had not recognized it, parked as it was beside the others in a common lot. In any case, his other piece of hardware was secure inside the trunk, and Wilson shifted it beneath the driver's seat before he turned the key in the ignition, gratified that the engine responded instantly.

The journey would take five hours, maybe six, depending on the traffic and the stops he made. If he could drive straight through, there still might be a chance, however slim, of making it in time to be some use to Rachel. And the American, if he was there. He might be able to repay the tall man's favor yet, although he had a sneaking hunch that the man could take care of himself.

EMERGING FROM THE BATHROOM, Rachel Hunter checked the bedside clock again and frowned. No sign of Michael Belasko, and she was concerned that he had run into some kind of opposition at the castle while she stalled Mac-Allister. If their suspicions were correct, it was entirely possible that sentries would be posted on the site, and with reports of people disappearing in the neighborhood, she knew there was a chance the guards—if they had been posted—might be prone to shooting first and asking questions later.

Of course, he wasn't really late at all. Not yet. But she was anxious all the same. She had already had one partner injured on this job and—

Rachel stopped herself, remembering that the American was not her partner. He was not affiliated with her firm in any way, and if she had been pressed, the woman could not have explained precisely *who* or *what* he was. Theirs was a marriage of convenience, and nothing more.

Her brief encounter with MacAllister had convinced her the Scotsman had something to hide, and Belasko's information on the laird's connection with the Soviets left several possibilities wide open. If MacAllister was dabbling in treason, it would certainly be worth his time to bury any witnesses who might be able to give evidence against him. The scanty evidence suggested he had done precisely that, and very recently. If true, another death would mean no more to him than stepping on a roach. It would be tantamount to pest control.

It worried Rachel that she had not cracked the mystery of Shane MacAllister's covert detente with Moscow. Given time...

But time was the commodity she did not possess. If Harry's estimation of the situation was correct, they might already be too late to stop the Russian shipment, turn it back before the weapons—or whatever—fell into the hands of terrorists.

She hoped that Harry was behaving in the hospital. She knew how he could be when he was sidelined, chafing at the bit and spoiling for a fight. In that way, he was rather like Mike Belasko, but it was the only similarity between them she had been able to discover. Wilson was a quiet man, soft-spoken, while the American impressed her as a blood-and-thunder sort, conditioned to expect a show of violence and respond in kind. She knew that Harry had been forced to kill in line of duty, but he never spoke about it in her presence. He was not averse to mixing with the heavies, cracking heads if necessary, but his British temperament shone through, regardless of the circumstances. Given any sort of chance, he would negotiate for the surrender of his quarry, while Mike Belasko, Rachel felt convinced, would simply kill his man and have it over with.

At bottom, she supposed the tall American was frightening. When she was with him, she felt as if he might explode at any moment, and she knew that the unleashing of his wrath would be an awesome thing to witness. He exuded strength—no, *power*—but she sensed that he was not a reckless warrior. From the evidence in Glasgow, he was fully capable of killing, but he seemed to choose his targets carefully. By contrast, many of the operations carried out by the CIA were clumsy, hit-and-run affairs, with poor results and frequent casualties among the innocent.

At any rate, she knew for certain that Belasko had no close, continuing association with the Company. She had employed one of Cairnaben's three pay telephones to reach her section chief in London. It was not the most secure of lines, but it had served its purpose, and a search of the computer files at MI-5 had turned up nothing under Belasko's name or general description. Agents of the CIA were kept on file by MI-5, as were the personnel of the KGB, Mossad, and every other known clandestine service in the world. There would be gaps, of course, in the available intelligence—no information on the sleepers and illegals, the deep-cover specialists. Some overt contract agents might have slipped the net, as well, but Rachel still had faith enough in MI-5 to realize that if Belasko was receiving orders out of Langley, he was someone new, unknown.

He was not young enough to be a fresh recruit from military service, though his expert training was apparent...in the Glasgow operation, in his every move. He was a pro, and that meant solid field experience. But where? And when?

It as infuriating, this uncertainty and doubt. She yearned to trust the tall American, and yet she did not even know his name. The "Belasko" was an alias, of course; she knew that much, and realizing that, she knew precisely nothing. If the man was operating on his own, he would bear even closer watching, but they were already spread so thin that Rachel wondered whether she could do two jobs at once.

If not, MacAllister would have to take priority. The warning from her partner raised the specter of a clear and present danger from the Soviets. Whatever Michael Belasko might be up to, and whomever he was working for, at least their missions of the moment seemed to coincide. If the man proved to be an adversary somewhere down the road, then she would deal with that when it arose.

Not for the first time, Rachel wondered if she had the will to kill a man with calculation, in cold blood. She had no doubt that she was capable of taking human life in self-defense; her training had been excellent in that regard, providing both the physical and mental preparation necessary for a killing in the line of duty. Straight-off murder would be something else, and Rachel wondered if her partner, Harry, might be capable of bringing off a planned assassination. Normally such tactics were outside the realm of MI-5, more likely to be shouldered by the lads of SIS—the famous "double-O's"—but anything might happen in the course of an assignment. If Mike Belasko proved to be an enemy, she would be forced to take decisive action, and while London would be theoretically in charge, the final life-and-death decisions were invariably made on-site, by agents in the field.

If only Harry had been there, to smile and offer his advice, invariably laced with biting sarcasm. How she missed him, but she recognized dependence on her partner as a sign of weakness, insecurity that was potentially a killer. If she did not trust herself, then she was doomed to fail, no matter who might be on hand to carry her across the rough spots. Inevitably, here or on some other field of battle, Rachel would be forced to stand alone, and her survival would depend upon the strength that she developed on her own. Mike Belasko manifestly had not reached his present state by waiting on advice from others; neither had her partner, and if Rachel missed him now, she could at least draw solace from the knowledge that he would have ordered her to do her best, no matter what the cost.

No question, Belasko was late now, but Rachel would not permit herself to worry. Late was not the same as never coming. It was not the same as blown and killed or captured by the enemy. It simply meant that he was taking time with his examination of the castle. She should be content that he was conscientious, let it go at that. The hard intelligence that he collected might include the information they would need to stay alive as they accelerated their campaign against MacAllister.

She did not know what Belasko had in mind, but Rachel had her mind set on examining the laird's files. She would have to wait for darkness, let the building empty of employees, but she knew that she could pull it off. No problem.

Mike Belasko might have other plans, but she would not allow him to divert her from her quest. He had business of his own in Scotland, and it seemed to be mere happenstance, at best, when their exclusive interests coincided. Both of them had been directed to Cairnaben by the words of Harry Wilson, but their goals, once on the scene, would not be necessarily the same. She served the British Commonwealth, while only God knew who Belasko served.

For years there had been talk about a supersecret action group created by the President of the United States to handle jobs that were too sensitive or too sophisticated for the CIA. All things considered, it appeared that Washington's campaign against world terrorism had been prosecuted more effectively in covert moves and countermoves, than at the diplomatic level where confusion reigned supreme. The brass at MI-5 could never prove that such an action group existed in the U.S. government, although they had built up classified biographies on certain "special" operatives of Uncle Sam.

From all appearances, there was a new breed in the making, trained and totally committed to responding on a level the terrorists could understand without the benefit of an interpreter. She was not privy to the details, but she understood that operations had been carried out in South America and in parts of Africa and Asia that appeared to bear the U.S. stamp without revealing any trace of CIA or military intervention. Clearly, someone was at work, and from the frequency of incidents, one man could not have been responsible for all of them ... but Rachel would not be surprised to find a man like Belasko in the vanguard.

She wiped clean her mental slate and concentrated on MacAllister. Her London call had turned up no new information on her target, either, but she was prepared to buy his link with KGB upon the strength of Belasko's word, together with her own late observations of the man himself. The Scotsman had a secret, and she had no doubts in her mind on that score. She believed that he had killed to keep that secret safe, but his resistance only made her that much more determined to expose him.

Trafficking in weapons, dealing Russian arms to terrorists, was bad enough. But she had a feeling that Mac-Allister was more than just a mercenary middleman. Like Belasko, she had come to wonder whether weapons were involved at all—and if they were, she was convinced that there was something else, some overriding, all-important *something* that was tucked away behind the scenes.

12

Major Pavel Andreiovitch relaxed and lit a fat cigar. Lunch had been excellent, the salmon typically superb, and he was feeling lazy, sated. At such times he often sought the company of an easy woman, but it was too early in the day, and he did not possess the energy.

He savored the cigar, a rich Havana, forming smoke rings on his tongue and blowing them in the direction of the ceiling. Seated on the wide veranda of his holiday retreat, he scanned a scenic vista of the Scottish coastline, watching flocks of sea gulls as they wheeled above the cliff tops. Life was sweet, and he intended to enjoy it to the fullest.

His assignment to the British Isles had been a plum, no doubt about it. He refused to entertain the thought that luck had played a part in his selection for the post, although he might as easily have been assigned to lead the Spetsnaz forces in Afghanistan, or to interrogate defectors from the ranks of Solidarity in Warsaw. He had been assisted by heredity, to some degree—it never hurt to be a hero's son, and Pavel's father, Sergei Andreiovitch, had been a certified hero of the revolution—but the major stubbornly retained some of the credit for himself. If he had not achieved an adequate solution to the covert Balkan prisoner exchange, emerging from the shambles with a rare surprise for his superiors, he might not be in Scotland at the moment, savoring the salmon and the intermittent sun, which seemed to shed its warmth so much more generously here than in Siberia, for instance.

Success was generally rewarded by the Committee for State Security—Komitet Gosudarstvennoi Bezopasnosti—but rewards were sometimes cleverly disguised, ringed all around with pitfalls. An operative who succeeded too well in clandestine work might run the risk of making certain people in Moscow nervous, and he might be sidelined, even sabotaged, by those with cause to fear him. It was not unheard of for a bright young man with the KGB to draw a suicide assignment out of nowhere, when it might have been more logical to spare him, send some dolt to do the butcher's work and take advantage of the new light's talent in a more productive way. Self-interest was the key, of course, and true survivors shunned opinions or activities that might make enemies, while steering clear of any rash alliances with friends who might fall out of favor.

Pavel Andreiovitch believed his current posting was a true reward, devoid of any conscious booby-traps...although it still might blow up in his face if he was careless. Those who overstepped their limitations were destroyed. It was inevitable, a law of nature. The weak and the careless were doomed from the start.

Neither weak nor careless, Pavel Andreiovitch was confident of ultimate success in Scotland. He had worked too long and hard on minor details to be taken by surprise at this late date. The groundwork was complete in every detail, with the second-stage construction under way. They would be harvesting intelligence before much longer, and the steady flow would be a living monument to his success.

Andreiovitch grimaced at the choice of metaphors. Monuments were normally erected to the dead, and he was very much alive. His work in Scotland might win him a posting to Dzerzhinsky Square, but he was not entirely happy with the thought of going home. All things considered, he preferred the Scottish Highlands, Glasgow, even London, to the drudgery of Moscow.

There was nothing in the least disloyal about the major's preference. In almost thirty years of service to the revolution, he had never faltered in performance of his duty, and he never would. But there were creature comforts here that might not be so readily available at home. The food was better, for a start. Despite the frequent gibes and jokes directed at English cooking, he enjoyed the solid fare and found it very palatable in comparison with Moscow's offerings. The liquor was of better quality, as well, but Pavel found his special pleasure in the women. In comparison with Moscow specimens, the average British female was a dazzler, sleek and lovely. In the two years since his posting to the British Isles, Andreiovitch had sampled widely from the charms of women who could not resist a diplomat, a man of influence. They tried so very hard to please, and Pavel made no effort whatsoever to resist them.

He was thinking that a brandy might be nice when his valet appeared on the veranda, cleared his throat discreetly and announced, "Telephone, sir. Lord MacAllister."

He sighed. Damn MacAllister, anyway. There went his brandy, at least for the moment. Some trivial matter, no doubt, that the Scotsman did not have sufficient initiative to deal with on his own. Sometimes, in the face of his contact's timidity, Pavel regretted selecting the man. But he could not undo it, not now, with their plans so very near fruition. Later, perhaps, if MacAllister could not shape up...

"I'll take it here, Ivan."

"Yes, sir. At once."

Ivan Shpakevich brought the telephone, its long extension cord trailed out behind him as he crossed the flagstone patio. When he had placed the instrument at Pavel's elbow, he retreated out of earshot, waiting for the signal that would hail him back to take the phone away. As an employee of the KGB, Ivan Shpakevich recognized his duties and his place. A combination bodyguard and butler, he was one of the most trusted members in the major's entourage, but even he was not privy to the details of Andreiovitch's dealings with MacAllister.

Perhaps a dozen men in Moscow could recite the details of the scheme from memory, and all of them were in agreement that the secret must be carefully preserved at any cost. His mission was too vital, far too sensitive, to gamble on its success or failure lightly. If Andreiovitch succeeded, as he was convinced he must, it would be a tremendous coup for the KGB in Britain and in Western Europe.

He would not fail. The consequence of failure was disgrace, destruction. He would not—*could* not—allow himself the luxury of doubt. Such thoughts were self-destructive, deathwatch beetles in the mind and heart.

"Hello?"

"We have a problem."

Pavel frowned. MacAllister had proved himself a worrier before, but there was more than simple agitation in his voice. He sounded close to panic, and Andreiovitch was worried that his contact might forget that they were on the telephone and say something that he might regret.

"The usual place," he said before MacAllister could launch into a recitation of his troubles. "In one hour."

"Yes."

The line went dead, and Pavel cradled the receiver, beckoning for Ivan Shpakevich to take the telephone away. Another problem. He was growing disillusioned with MacAllister's ability to think for himself. Lately the Scotsman had been weakening, losing his resolve. Andreiovitch suspected that MacAllister regretted their affiliation, but it was too late for him to back out now. The laird of Cairnaben was committed, like it or not, until such time as Pavel chose to set him free.

Soon, perhaps. MacAllister had very nearly served his purpose, and the Russian grew increasingly impatient with the man's apparent weakness. When he had outlived his usefulness, the Scotsman would become expendable, and Pavel would enjoy disposing of the weakling who was rapidly becoming an encumbrance.

Rising from his lounge chair, Andreiovitch spared one last glance for the cliffs, then passed through tall French doors and along a corridor to his bedroom. He dressed quickly and slipped a Walther PP automatic in the pocket of his coat. He doubted that there would be any need for violence this afternoon, but old habits died hard, and it was safer to go armed. In the event of any trouble, he knew ways to cover up his tracks, and if worse came to worst, there was always the shield of diplomatic immunity for him to hide behind.

Andreiovitch still marveled at the way in which supposedly intelligent Western governments permitted agents of the KGB to masquerade as diplomats, cloaking themselves with immunity from arrest and prosecution. They apparently believed that bending over backward to avoid offending Moscow would protect their own envoys in the Soviet Union from detention and interrogation. Dreamers. Someday, when they all woke up and smelled the coffee, it would be too late.

And "someday" would be that much sooner, thanks to Pavel Andreiovitch and his efforts in Scotland. He had accomplished much, for someone who could visit the Highlands only on weekends and designated holidays, reserving the lion's share of his time for spurious diplomatic duties in London and Glasgow. As a cultural attaché to the Soviet embassy, he had seen more museums and concerts in the past two years than most men saw in twenty. Never strong on art or culture for their own sake, Pavel learned to grin and bear it, spouting platitudes about the need for "cultural detente" while scheming, all the while, to bring the British power structure down.

The sleek Mercedes purred to life, and Pavel caught the narrow highway eastward, seeking higher ground amid the moors. He drove alone, secure in the knowledge that he would not be attacked or ambushed on the road. Some of his comrades, in assorted other duty stations, were required to ride in armored limousines, their escorts bristling with automatic weapons, but on the moors, Andreiovitch felt absolutely safe. If anyone attempted to molest him, it was the attacker who should have cause to worry.

He had murdered seven men, two women and a child in the line of duty through the years. None of the killings— which included wiping out a family of three and faking evidence to simulate a burglary in Budapest—had preyed upon what passed for Pavel's conscience. As a creature of the state, he knew that duty came before all else. The individual was unimportant. Life was cheap.

Except, of course, his own. A consummate survivor, Pavel Andreiovitch had taken pains to make himself invincible against his enemies . . . and, more importantly, against the treachery of so-called friends. Throughout his years with the KGB, he had accumulated debts, obliging others when they needed favors, just as long as they were compromised and he was not. At need, he could demand assistance from a wide variety of Soviet officials, and a few surprising sources on the Western side of the iron curtain, as well. In practice, Pavel knew that no man was invulnerable to attack—a lone assassin with a grudge could cancel years of preparation in the time it took to pull a trigger once—but in the prime of life, he felt as reasonably safe as any agent of the KGB could ever hope to feel.

His normal rendezvous with Shane MacAllister was eight miles from his holiday retreat, and equidistant from Cairnaben. He invariably set the meetings far enough ahead so that he could be waiting when the Scotsman finally approached. He used the time to check his backtrack and put his mind at ease concerning tails, and he observed MacAllister with equal care, convinced the Scotsman was incapable of taking adequate precautions on his own.

Thus far there seemed to be no indication that the operation had been blown. He would be known to MI-5, of course. They were not fools, but neither could they link him with MacAllister, and at the moment that was all that mattered. Pavel did not care if they suspected him of plotting to abduct the queen, as long as their attention was diverted from Cairnaben and the western Highlands.

He parked in the middle of nowhere, atop a bleak hilltop commanding the moors in all directions. No one could approach by air or land without being observed, and scattered houses visible on the horizon were too far away for the successful deployment of directional microphones. As for himself, Andreiovitch had his Mercedes screened for listening devices twice a day, and he would not set foot outside the car or roll the insulated windows down while speaking with MacAllister.

Another thirty minutes passed before he saw the Scotsman coming, his Rolls winding its way along the narrow road that crossed the moors from Cairnaben. As always, when they met at his insistence, MacAllister left his driver at home, handling the long car himself—and with considerable difficulty, if appearances were not deceiving. Pavel waited while the laird of Cairnaben brought the Rolls around and killed its engine. He climbed out and moved stiffly toward the Mercedes, sliding in on the passenger's side.

Play "Action Poker" to see if you can get

- ◆ 4 hard-hitting, action-packed Gold Eagle novels just like the one you're reading — FREE
- ◆ PLUS a useful pocket knife — FREE

Peel off the card on the front of this brochure and stick it in the hand opposite. Find out how many gifts you can receive ABSOLUTELY FREE. They're yours to keep even if you never buy another Gold Eagle novel.

Then deal yourself in for more gut-chilling action at deep subscriber savings

Once you have read your free books, we're willing to bet you'll want more of those page-crackling, razor-edge stories. So we'll send you six brand new Gold Eagle books every other month to preview. (Two Mack Bolans and one each of Able Team, Phoenix Force, Vietnam: Ground Zero and SOBs.)

- ◆ Hot-off-the-press novels with the kind of no-holds — barred action you crave.
- ◆ Delivered right to your home.
- ◆ Months before they're available in stores.
- ◆ At hefty savings off the retail price.
- ◆ Always with the right to cancel and owe nothing.

You will pay only $2.49 for each book — 11% less than the retail price — plus 95¢ postage and handling per shipment.

Enjoy special subscriber privileges

- ◆ With every shipment you will receive AUTOMAG, our exciting newsletter FREE.
- ◆ Plus special books to preview free and buy at rock bottom discount.

CLAIM YOUR FREE GIFT! MAIL THIS CARD TODAY.

BUSINESS REPLY CARD

First Class   Permit No. 717   Buffalo, NY

Postage will be paid by addressee

Gold Eagle Reader Service
901 Fuhrmann Blvd.
P.O. Box 1394
Buffalo, NY 14240-9963

NO POSTAGE
NECESSARY
IF MAILED
IN THE
UNITED STATES

"Thank you for seeing me," he said by way of introduction.

"It sounded urgent.

"I'm afraid it is."

"Go on."

MacAllister proceeded to explain about the female journalist, one Rachel Scribner, who was not, in fact, a writer for the *Daily Mirror*. He re_____ _____ _at another local—an adult, this time—had trespa__ _n his castle grounds at night and had been made to disappear. The prowler was related to a teenaged girl who had similarly "vanished" some time earlier with her paramour. The most disturbing news, however, when combined with all the other recent happenings, concerned itself with an intruder at the castle on that very morning. This one had succeeded in escaping from the dolts MacAllister referred to as his guards, humiliating two of them and getting clean away without leaving a clue to his identity. It was, as Shane MacAllister had told him on the telephone, a problem.

If he was not very careful, Pavel knew the problem could become an absolute catastrophe, and in short order, too. This latter business did not point to locals chasing evidence of vanished fools and children. Someone with a modicum of skill had been surprised while checking out MacAllister's estate, and if he had been frightened off before he could learn anything of substance, there was every possibility he might return.

The woman was a different problem, though Andreiovitch was not inclined to see the incidents as unrelated. Coming, as they had, within an hour of each other, it would be stretching the laws of chance beyond endurance to suppose that the events were mere coincidence. A firm believer in conspiracies, as one who had initiated several on his own, Andreiovitch was certain that the woman had been sent to pump MacAllister for information while assuring, at the same time, that he would not leave his office and disturb the more important probe of his ancestral home.

The man had slipped their clutches, but the woman might still be available at the Cairnaben Arms. It might be possible to question her and, failing that, she could be silenced before relaying any further information back to her superiors, whoever they might be.

He spelled out the operation for MacAllister, advising him on what to do and promising material assistance if it should prove necessary. For the moment he preferred to let the locals cope with any difficulties that arose. It would be awkward for Andreiovitch to use his own men because of the obvious attendant risks. If one of them was killed or captured, questions would result, and he was not prepared with answers. Secrecy was paramount, and if the local rabble muffed the operation, got themselves arrested with incriminating evidence, it was no real loss. They had no knowledge of the stakes involved, the master plan, and he could always silence them in custody, if it should come to that.

He would assist if it became imperative, essential. Their cooperative venture in Cairnaben was too critical for interference to be tolerated. In a pinch, Andreiovitch would call upon his backup force of Spetsnaz gunners and eliminate the threat. He would revert to doing that which he did best.

But it would have to be a last resort. His cover had been too well planned and cultivated, too well tended, for Andreiovitch to jeopardize it rashly. And if he should deem it necessary to commit his troops, he would insist on leading them himself. That way, there would be no mistakes.

"Go now and see to the woman," he ordered, "before she escapes. If the search of your castle was bungled, the rats may be running already."

"And the man?"

Pavel shrugged. "If you find him, make efforts to take him alive. Failing that, leave no trace of him for the authorities."

"I understand."

The Scot looked worried, and Andreiovitch was glad. Anxiety was motivational, unless it was allowed to run unchecked, evolving into absolute hysteria. MacAllister was still some distance from a breakdown, although the Russian would not have given odds on his contact's future stability.

Too much unaccustomed pressure could destroy a man, particularly if the man was weak in the beginning. The man who sat beside Pavel was unaccustomed to coping with life-or-death situations. MacAllister had not been reared on subterfuge, as had Andreiovitch, and he was not attuned to living in the shadows. Motivated by a lust for profit, he was not committed to the project, but belief was not required. Andreiovitch required subordinates, not converts. As long as the Scotsman did his job, he would survive.

Elimination of the enemy on-site must be his first priority. Before the spies could gather and transmit the information that they sought, they must be rooted out, eliminated. He would trust MacAllister to do the job, but only to a point.

He watched the Scotsman walk back to his Rolls and climb behind the wheel, a study in dejection. It had taken him some time to come around to the idea of working with Andreiovitch, for starters, and the recent troubles had not strengthened his resolve. Eliminating neighbors did not bother him so much, since he had never viewed the people of the town as equals. But the possibility of government investigators prowling in the area—and taking out his sentries in the process—clearly had MacAllister upset.

Andreiovitch refused to worry. He had dealt with hostile governments before, in the eternal game of cat-and-mouse that was international espionage, and he was fairly certain, from the evidence thus far available, that their enemies were not prepared to mount a major counterstroke in the Highlands. Not yet, at any rate. The time might come, but for the moment someone was engaged in the collection of intelligence, attempting to substantiate suspicions. When they had the information that they needed, they would move, but even then they would be cautious.

He wondered idly who the enemy was. The logical choice would be MI-5, or possibly SIS, but Andreiovitch could not rule out the possibility of intervention by a foreign service. The CIA would certainly be interested, if they knew what he was doing in Cairnaben. So might Interpol, or any one of several Western European agencies whose country had a stake in NATO. Any one of them might move against him if they felt the British were not taking proper steps, but his response depended in large part on who the opposition was and what they wanted.

Casually he wondered if the trouble in Cairnaben might have any possible connection to the recent Tartan Army debacle in Glasgow. Pavel had moved weapons to the Tartans on occasion, though the "army's" ideology was rather right of center. There were only vague reports from Glasgow so far, but he gathered that the Tartan hierarchy had been caught flat-footed and annihilated by a strike team that showed little interest in taking prisoners. Some rumors marked it off to feuding in the terrorist camp—the IRA and Red Brigades had both been mentioned—but it seemed more probable that covert extra-legal action had been taken by one of the major intelligence agencies. The fact that wholesale loss of life had been attended, and achieved, ruled out the more pacific of the secret services, but there were still a number of contenders in the field.

He gave it up, aware that guessing games were fruitless, unproductive. He would recognize the enemy when they were face-to-face. Until that time he was content to watch and wait, securing his own perimeters as best he could, leaving nothing to chance. Intensive preparation would prevent Andreiovitch from being taken by surprise.

They were at risk, but it was still a situation he could handle, something he could salvage. If MacAllister should prove unequal to the task, then Pavel would dispose of him and carry out the mission on his own. It was his brainchild, after all, and he would see it born, a healthy living thing, before he was recalled to Moscow and promotion at Dzerzhinsky Square.

He would not be stopped now.

He would destroy anyone who tried.

13

Mack Bolan parked his BMW in the lot at the Cairnaben Arms and entered through the lobby. It was lunchtime, and the aromas wafting from the kitchen instantly reminded him that he was hungry. Flipping a mental coin, he moved to the house phone and dialed Rachel's room number. She answered on the first ring, as if she had been waiting by the telephone.

"Hello?"

"I'm back," he said without preamble. "Have you eaten?"

"No." She sounded irritated. "Where the hell have you been?"

"I'll tell you all about it over lunch. Five minutes."

"Make it two."

She made it more like ninety seconds, and he wondered if it was the daylight streaming through the windows or the anger in her eyes that made her so attractive. She was dressed in clinging navy slacks that complemented her brightly colored blouse. Her hair fell loose around her shoulders, framing a face that needed little makeup to accentuate its natural appeal.

They took a table by the window, smiling through the usual amenities until the waitress vanished with their order. When they were alone, Rachel's eyes abruptly changed to chips of ice.

"You had me bloody worried."

"Sorry."

"Sorry? Is that all you have to say?"

"I ran into a little hitch."

"How's that?"

He told her all about the sentries at the castle, interrupted once by the arrival of their food. She listened raptly, and the anger in her face immediately changed to a look of genuine concern.

"MacAllister *is* hiding something, then," she said when he had finished.

The soldier nodded. "Unfortunately we have no idea *what* he's hiding," Bolan said, "unless you stumbled onto something at his office."

Rachel frowned and shook her head. "I wish I had. He's very cagey, that one. I've been thinking I should have a look inside his private files."

"Too risky," Bolan replied, watching Rachel tense immediately, grow angry at his words.

"I know my job," she told him, frost creeping into her tone.

"I don't doubt it," he answered. "But this time there's KGB involvement, sure as hell. That means illegals, working black, and they won't hesitate to take you out if you appear to jeopardize their mission."

"I'm aware of the risks."

"I wonder if you are." Bolan pushed his empty plate back, holding Rachel with his eyes. "When was the last time that you faced a serious interrogation?"

"I've been trained to cope with that." He heard uneasiness beneath the firm self-confidence in Rachel's voice.

"You can't be trained to 'cope' with chemical interrogation," Bolan said harshly. "Once you're hit with haloperidol, aminazin, or triftazin, you spill your guts in spite of any training. It's inevitable."

"You say."

"Right. I say. You haven't lived until you've had a hit of sulphazin. One dose induces incapacitating nausea and a raging fever for a period of seventy-two hours. Eventually, after weeks or months of that, you die, but in the meantime you tell everything you know and make up things you don't. Anything at all to make it stop."

"I'm a professional. I can take care of myself."

He smiled. "Of course, they might rely on more traditional techniques. Electrodes. Cattle prods. A wood-burning set from the corner five-and-dime."

"If you're trying to frighten me, you shan't succeed."

"I'm trying to wake you up. The Russians play for keeps, and no one—I repeat, *no one*—can beat professional interrogators at their game. They love their work, and you're already points behind before you start."

"You sound as if you've been there."

"Close enough." He did not wish to think about the screaming turkeys, stripped of their humanity, their souls laid bare. He had enough blood on his hands already, and he needed no reminder of the innocents who had been martyred in his everlasting war against the savages. It was enough that he should try his damnedest to protect Rachel from their enemies. And from herself.

"I'm sorry." Rachel did not sound precisely penitent, but rather thoughtful. When he met her eyes again, it seemed as if she were looking through him, searching for an answer she would never find.

"Forget it," Bolan told her gruffly. "It's old business." But the fighting man was touched by her concern, her caring. All the more reason to keep her safe from harm, if possible.

And that, of course, would be the rub. *If possible.*

"It wouldn't hurt to take a look around his office, after hours," she insisted, leaning toward him, lowering her voice, although the nearest pair of ears was on the far side of the room. "He must keep records of transactions with the Soviets, for inventory, if no other reason."

Bolan frowned. "We're spread too thin. I need to check out the castle more closely, and the cannery could stand a closer look. We can't do everything at once."

"I understand that, but—"

The waitress came to clear away their plates.

The lady tried again. "I understand—"

"Let's take a drive," he interrupted. "Somehow, I can't shake the feeling that the walls have ears."

"All right."

They took the BMW and drove north along the coast, passing MacAllister's cannery en route to nowhere in particular. Bolan drove with the windows open, enjoying the fresh salt air, the sunshine, Rachel's presence. He did not speak until they cleared the town and started inland, climbing, suddenly surrounded by the vastness of the moors.

"I hope your partner's on the mend."

"He'll be all right," she answered, softening a little. "Did I thank you? For helping him, I mean?"

"Not necessary."

"Thank you, all the same."

"Any time."

"I hope it won't become habitual."

He smiled. The woman was easy to talk to, easy to be with. He never ceased to marvel at the types who were attracted to the service of their governments. It took all kinds, but even so, the sheer variety was staggering. From cold-eyed killers with ice in their veins, to women who could stop your heart with one arresting glance. All pros. All working different angles of their own.

In Rachel's case, it would be queen and country, uppermost. She struck him as an old-school patriot who still believed that right made might and Good would win out over Evil in the end. It was not Bolan's place to disillusion her, and he would not begin to try. It was enough for her to understand that there were mortal risks involved in going up against MacAllister, against the KGB.

She understood, of course, in abstract terms. She knew that agents sometimes died in the line of duty, and her partner's brush with death had driven home the point, but it would not be real until she tasted combat on her own. Until she saw the grim results, up close and personal. It was not something you could brief another person on, and even graphic training films could only have so much effect. There was a smell to death, a feel about it, that would never be forgotten once experienced firsthand.

He hoped that Rachel would not have to learn the hard way, but the soldier was not giving any odds. They had been thrown together by coincidence, but now their fates were interwoven in their mutual pursuit of Shane MacAllister and his connection with the Soviets. Whatever happened in the next few hours, they would meet the threat head-on, together. But a part of Bolan still hoped he could spare the woman, shield her from the worst of it. Protect her.

How long since he had felt protective toward another human being? Bolan knew the gentle feelings had not died; they surfaced now and then at need, but they were seldom needed now. His everlasting war consumed the soldier's waking hours, filled his bloody dreams, and there was little time for gentleness or caring in between his clashes with the enemy.

He did not regard the gentler feelings as a weakness, but they could distract a warrior from his business at the crucial moment, and in doing so, could get him killed. Mack Bolan had not traveled halfway around the world to see his war go up in smoke. Not if the soldier had a thing to say about it.

Bolan flicked a glance at Rachel, found her watching him in silence. "Care to share your thoughts?"

"Just wondering."

"What?"

"Exactly who the hell you are."

"It's not important."

Glancing in the rearview, Bolan spied the tail. He had not noticed it before, but logic told him that their shadows must have been with them, discreetly, since they left Cairnaben. He was slipping, and the woman had distracted him.

The tail was a Renault, with two men visible inside. He would have to try to lose them, but the open country offered little opportunity for deft maneuvers or concealment. He'd have to take them out if he couldn't shake them.

"What's wrong?" Without a word between them, Rachel had picked up on Bolan's sudden tension, his reaction to their shadow.

"Hang on," he told her, standing on the BMW's accelerator, feeling power throb beneath the car's hood.

Somehow, MacAllister and company had made his car, and they were on him now. Or they were after Rachel, and her presence in the BMW had added Bolan to the target list. Whichever, Bolan knew it didn't matter as the hunter riding shotgun in the tail car cranked his window down and stuck his head out, angling for a shot with the long-barreled revolver he carried. Bolan jerked the wheel and spoiled his adversary's aim, the first round whining into empty space.

But they had called the tune, and he was with them. To the end of the line.

RACHEL HUNTER WAS TURNING in her seat to take a look at their pursuers when Bolan swerved the car hard left across the narrow road. The sharp report of pistol fire was swept away by their momentum, but she saw the gunner lining up a second shot as Bolan cut the wheel back to the right, accelerating rapidly. The second bullet missed as well, but Rachel knew their luck could not hold out forever.

Digging in her purse, she found the Walther automatic, flicked the safety off, and was about to try a shot at their pursuers when Bolan placed a strong hand on her shoulder and pulled her back into her seat.

"Not yet."

No sooner had he spoken than a bullet struck the BMW's bumper with a loud, metallic *clang*. The hunter was improving.

The road was winding upland, dips and curves obscuring the chase car, making it more dangerous for Bolan to proceed full-throttle, but he kept the pedal down, the engine straining. Even so, the hot Renault was gaining by degrees, the gunner craning from his window, hair blown back around his ruddy face. A pair of aviator's glasses spared his eyes the worst of it, but he was grimacing, his lips pulled back from gritted teeth, his nickel-plated weapon leveled for another shot.

The BMW hit a dip, and Rachel felt as if her heart had been propelled into her throat. The gunner missed again, his bullet whistling above them, lost somewhere out on the moors. Emerging from the highway trough, she saw him cursing, lining up his pistol for another try.

Impulsively she twisted in her seat, the Walther in her left hand, and leaned out through her open window. She could hear Bolan cursing, but he did not haul her back; his hands and mind were fully occupied with piloting their vehicle along the narrow, winding road.

The rush of wind was deafening in Rachel's ears. Her hair streamed out around her, whipped at her face. She squinted through her lashes, steadying her gun arm with her elbow planted on the windowsill, and waited for her chance. One heartbeat, and another, then the chase car topped a rise and seemed to hang suspended in her sights. She squeezed off two quick shots and saw the driver swerve, the gunner ducking back inside as if he had been stung.

Convinced that she had not hit either of them, fairly certain she had missed the car as well, Rachel still felt moderately proud. The bastards knew that they would fight, and if it did not give them pause, at least it might retard their progress for the next few moments, offer Belasko something in the nature of a chance to shake them off.

As if in answer to her thoughts, the enemy accelerated, closing. Rachel was amazed by their audacity, their daring in the face of danger. She had startled them, retaliating as she had, but it was not enough to scare them off.

In abstract terms she knew that she was capable of killing human beings, but the thought had not been foremost in her mind till yesterday. Belasko had been first to raise the question, doubting her ability to cope with killing situations if and when they should arise, and now she wondered if his skepticism had been justified. It was a relatively simple thing, when you were being chased, to take some flying potshots at the other car. You were aware that you might strike another human being, but the odds seemed reasonably slim. There seemed to be a greater expectation that you might shoot out a tire or blow the engine, as so often happened in the cinema.

Except that Rachel Hunter was not in a movie. Reality was here and now, surrounding her with images of sudden death, inglorious and very likely painful. For the first time in her work with MI-5, she understood that she might really have to kill another human being, shoot him dead before he had the opportunity to do the same to her.

The BMW took another hit, this one a solid *thump* against the trunk. She lunged back through the window, sighting quickly down the Walther's slide and squeezing off before her enemy could try to do a better job with number six. The autoloader bucked in Rachel's fist, and she was instantly rewarded as a frosty divot blossomed in the center of the chase car's windshield.

Neither of her adversaries had been injured, but the driver slowed, allowing the BMW time to pull ahead. She pegged another shot in their direction, cursing underneath her breath as it went wild.

"Don't waste your ammunition," Bolan said as Rachel wriggled back into her seat. "They're out of range."

"We can't outrun them, can we?"

"No."

He reached beneath the driver's seat with one hand, hauling out the largest pistol she had ever seen. It was constructed out of stainless steel and filled the big man's hand, the vented ribbing on its six-inch barrel adding to the weapon's seeming bulk.

It was an AutoMag. She recognized it from the weapons catalogs she had studied in her training course. She had never seen a real one, but there could be no room for mistake. She remembered that a single round could pierce an auto's engine block or disembowel a man at better than a hundred meters.

It was a weapon for professionals who had the time and strength to master pent-up thunder, tame it to the needs. In expert hands the silver cannon was a fine, precision killing tool. A wild shot from behind them snapped her consciousness back to the hard reality of animal survival, and she concentrated on their enemies.

The gunner popped a shot at the BMW, missing by a yard or more as Bolan swerved, then ducked in the car to hastily reload. Rachel seized the opportunity to return fire, squinting in the rush of wind and centering her sights on the driver's silhouette behind the cracked windshield. Blocking out the image of a living face, she was already squeezing off when Bolan hit a pothole in the road and spoiled her aim; the Walther's bullet peeled a strip of paint across the hood of the Renault, and then was gone.

"I nearly had him, damn it!"

"Never mind," he snapped. "We've got a blind curve coming up. I'm going to take them there."

"What do you mean?"

She had a sudden mental image of the BMW parked across the narrow road and waiting while the Renault bore down upon them, Belasko standing like a duelist with the silver AutoMag extended in his fist and roaring like a piece of field artillery. The hostile driver hunching down below the dashboard of his car and standing on the pedal, crushing Belasko, turning both their vehicles to twisted, flaming scrap.

And she was trapped inside.

For just an instant, Rachel's vision was so real that she could almost feel the heat of lapping flames, could almost smell the stench of burning oil and rubber. Coming back to reality she glanced sidelong at her companion and hoped he knew what he was doing.

Both their lives were riding on him, and if he fumbled they were as good as dead. The gunners on their tail would not be forced to shoot them down; it would be easier—and just as final—if they drove them off the road at eighty miles an hour. They could sit back and watch as their quarry crashed and burned.

She wondered, briefly, whether they were after Belasko or herself. It didn't matter in the long run, but she would have liked to know. She thought MacAllister had been completely taken in, but if he had seen through her cover story, then the bullets might be meant for her. They might not have pursued Mike Belasko from the ruined castle, after all.

It was a sobering idea, and Rachel was not used to failure, but there was at least a possibility that she had blown it. If she had revealed herself, then all of this was her fault, and if Belasko died, his blood would be on her hands.

It didn't matter, really, since she would be dead as well, but Rachel Hunter was uncomfortable with the thought of bungling a mission. Relatively new to MI-5, she might have had a long career ahead of her, but she could almost feel it slipping through her fingers. First, Harry had been injured by the Tartans, and now she had blown the most important job that had ever been her privilege to handle.

The hostile gunner had reloaded, and his first shot removed the outside mirror beside her with a flat crack of powdered glass. Rachel leaned out and triggered off a wasted shot that came nowhere within a yard of her intended target.

Behind her, Bolan grabbed a handful of her blouse and jerked her back inside the car. She heard a button pop and felt a sudden flash of anger at the tall American. How dared he—

"Get a grip!" he snapped. "We're going in!"

The blind curve was upon them, and she braced one hand against the dashboard, closed her eyes. Another moment, now. Another moment...

14

Jock McMahon fought the wheel of the Renault and felt his car shudder on the rutted, undulating highway. He was standing on the pedal, desperate not to lose the BMW now that contact had been made, but they were taking hits and he was getting nervous. That last one through the windshield had been goddamned lucky, and the wheelman wondered if his own luck might be running out.

Beside him, O'Connor was still taking potshots at the BMW, leaning out the window like a hound on holiday. He had already scored a hit or two, but they were minor, nothing that would bring the target vehicle to heel. It would require a great deal more to stop the big man and his female sidekick. Something like the Ingram submachine gun lying on the seat beside him—but first he had to find an opportunity to use the lethal little weapon. It was useless to him while the driver of the BMW kept on playing fox and hounds.

O'Connor popped another round off, and a hole appeared, as if by magic, in the BMW's trunk. All smiles, he crowed, "By God, I got the bugger!"

"Aye," McMahon answered sourly, "you killed his spare, all right."

"Leave off, Jock. If ye knew enough to hold the damned car steady for a moment—"

O'Connor's words were cut off as a bullet struck the hood of the Renault and ricocheted, cracking against the trim of

the windshield before it caromed into space. A streak of
shiny metal where the paint had stripped away was aimed
directly at McMahon, and the driver knew a few more
inches might have done the trick. If they had struck a dip
just then, he would be dead, and O'Connor with him, the
Renault all fused and twisted like a steel pretzel.

He would have just as soon abandoned the pursuit, but
that would mean defying Lord MacAllister, and Jock was
not prepared for that. Not yet. The Ingram on the seat beside him gave him courage, but it would be suicidal going up
against MacAllister and all the darling friends he had accumulated in the past twelve months or so.

McMahon could remember when he used to do a bit of
strong-arm for MacAllister, just keeping track of things and
beating down the union men, no major worries. Then, a
year or so ago, MacAllister had opened his negotiations with
the Russians, and the business had been going downhill ever
since, in Jock's opinion. Sure, they had more money now,
and then some, but the profits came with major strings attached. He had been forced to kill a man in Edinburgh—a
weasel-faced accountant who had stumbled onto something in the books and tried to put a price tag on his silence—but it was not murder in the line of duty that had
Jock McMahon worried.

It was the castle, and even though he did not know what
they were doing there—he did not *want* to know—he realized that people had been paying with their lives for tres-
passing. Three locals from Cairnaben that McMahon knew
of, one of them a lass still in her teens. Now he was locked
in hot pursuit across the moors with targets he had never
seen before, assigned to kill a woman whom he honestly
would rather have escorted to bed. Her male companion
looked like trouble, and while he was not originally on the
menu, they could not afford a witness. He would have to die

as well . . . assuming they could overtake him in the first place.

He wondered idly what the woman might have done to put a price tag on her head. Most likely she had been discovered snooping at the castle, but had managed to slip past the guards MacAllister had posted. That was no mean feat, especially if the freak had been on duty at the time. Just thinking of that overgrown monstrosity gave Jock the creeps, and he was doubly thankful that his duties seldom took him to the castle. He was not a superstitious man, nor squeamish, but the looks of that one made him want to cross himself and confess his sins to the local padre.

It was the freak, primarily, who kept the castle grounds secure. There was a team of roving gunners in the daytime, for appearances, but after dark the big boy carried out his work alone. McMahon knew, in general terms, what had become of recent prowlers on the castle grounds, and he could get along quite well without the details, thank you. He especially did not wish to think about what might have happened to the girl before she died . . . or after. It could make you sick, the things that people did for sport these days, and killing in the line of business was the very least of it.

The weasel-faced accountant had not been his first, but Jock McMahon took no pleasure in the act of killing. He was not like some that he could name, who thought of hunting people as a sport, like stalking deer or fishing in a mountain stream. Jock killed when it was necessary—when it paid—and while he lost no sleep over it afterward, it didn't race his motor, either.

This job, now, was getting very awkward. They had messed about too long, but they could not turn back, allowing witnesses to get away. There was no second chance, and Lord MacAllister had been specific in his orders that the woman must be killed, along with any other persons they might encounter in her company. McMahon did not have to understand the why and wherefore of it; he was paid to act, and not to analyze the orders he received. It was a system that had worked thus far, but now he saw it breaking down before his very eyes.

The driver of the BMW was a pro, no doubt about it. Slick and competent, he still might shake them if the woman got the radiator or a tire with a lucky shot. McMahon did not want to think about MacAllister's reaction if they let the buggers get away and wrecked the car besides.

"Close up, Jock," O'Connor shouted, leaning halfway out the window so that his words were fairly whipped away by wind. He braced the heavy Webley-Scott revolver in both hands and squeezed another round off at the BMW, but the shot went wild, and he slid back into his seat, cursing bitterly, beginning to reload.

If Jock could get near enough, their odds of scoring a hit would be improved. Ideally O'Connor would get lucky and kill the driver, but McMahon was not counting on a lucky break at this point in the game. He thought about the Ingram, wondered if it might help to simply hose down the BMW with automatic fire, but he would have to shoot left-handed, driving with his right, and it was just as likely he would waste the whole damned magazine for nothing.

Damn the highway, anyhow! He grimaced as the undercarriage of his car grated on the pavement, twanging noises emanating from the shock absorbers. No car had been meant to drive across the moors at such a speed, and Jock McMahon wondered if they were already losing oil. He did not fancy being stranded there with two illegal weapons in the car, or hiking back the dozen miles or so to face MacAllister in failure.

No, they would continue if it killed them . . . and he was not ruling out that possibility by any means. He did not fear MacAllister so much at this point as he feared the possibility of leaving witnesses to an attempted murder. If the law got after him for this, they might discover other cases where the murders had not been merely *attempted*, and although the gallows had been done away with, Jock could not abide the thought of life in prison. He had done his time, and it had been ample. He was never going back inside if he had anything to say about it. They would have to kill him first.

It troubled Jock McMahon that his thoughts kept coming back to death, especially his own. He was not naturally a fatalist—in fact it went against the grain to think for an extended period on any subject—but the possibility of personal disaster had been on his mind of late. It was Mac-Allister, of course, and all the foreign types he was associating with these days. They were enough to make your skin crawl, and you didn't have to be the sissy sort to feel a little bit uneasy in their company.

It was apparent to McMahon that his boss was dabbling in treason. That did not worry Jock McMahon in itself; he owed the country nothing but a hard time, anyway, considering what it had done for him—or *to* him—but he recognized the stakes involved and realized that agencies more ruthless than the Yard would be involved if things went sour.

Make that *when*, not *if*. From all appearances, things were already going sour, and McMahon was not certain they could plug the gap by taking out this woman and her driver. They might be too late, already, if the woman had gathered crucial information and relayed it to her contacts.

O'Connor leaned out, trying another shot, and quite by accident blew off the BMW's outside mirror on the passenger's side. If only he had waited for the woman to reveal herself again, she would be dead right now, but there was no use crying over wasted rounds.

Displaying a sudden surge of power, the BMW pulled away from them, accelerating toward a narrow curve two hundred meters farther on. McMahon ground his boot against the floorboards but he could not milk another ounce of power from the trembling Renault. The dashboard tach was red-lined now, the engine whining like a winded, wounded thing. If O'Connor and his Webley could not slow the bastard down, they were as good as finished. It was apparent that they could not overtake their quarry on the flats, and they would have no chance at all in higher country as the road began to wind and climb.

The woman took another shot at them, and Jock was easing off of the accelerator when the driver of the BMW yanked her back inside the car. The lead car was some fifty yards ahead, already drifting as it took the curve, and Jock McMahon knew that he might lose them if he allowed himself to falter. Bearing down on the Renault's accelerator, hands white-knuckled on the wheel, he pushed it to the limit as they hurtled toward the curve.

"Hang on!" he shouted, putting his companion out of mind immediately as he fought to keep them on the road.

THE BMW STARTED TO DRIFT as it came out of the curve, but Bolan fought the wheel and regained control. Beyond the turn, the road ran arrow straight for several hundred yards, and he knew that he would have to make his stand right here, right now, if he intended to succeed.

He hit the brakes and cranked the wheel hard left, bringing the BMW around in a 180-degree skid, tires smoking on the asphalt. Rachel gasped and braced herself against the dash with one hand, clinging to her automatic with the other. She was shaken, but apparently prepared for action as Bolan slid out from behind the wheel, the AutoMag in hand.

The BMW's doors were open wide and standing out like an elephant's ears, offering cover for Bolan and Rachel on their respective sides of the car. They watched and listened, knowing from the straining engine sounds beyond the nearest curve that they would not have long to wait. A glance at Rachel showed him that the woman from MI-5 was standing firm and carrying her weight.

The Renault exploded into view, its engine snarling, eating up the blacktop on a hard collision course with Bolan's vehicle. He sighted quickly down the barrel of the AutoMag, already squeezing off before the hostile driver had a chance to stabilize his wheels. The silver cannon roared, 240 grains of thunder sizzling downrange and ripping through the grill of the Renault in search of vital engine parts.

The chase car's hood blew back, obscuring the windshield, oily smoke erupting from the open engine compartment. Bolan put a second round dead center through the hissing radiator and was instantly rewarded by a gout of flame, more smoke, a harsh metallic clanging sound. The driver nearly lost it then, but he retained enough composure to apply the brakes, steering into the inevitable skid, the car screeching to a halt no more than twenty yards from where the BMW sat.

The doors on the Renault sprang open, figures scrambling out on either side. The passenger squeezed off two hasty rounds from his revolver, ducking under cover once again as Bolan answered with the AutoMag. His boattail bullet pierced the door and slammed it in the gunner's face, knocking him off balance, but before the Executioner could finish him, the driver surfaced with a submachine gun, rattling off an aimless burst of cover fire.

Across from Bolan, Rachel fired on the driver, punching two slugs through his door, their impact leaving shiny circles where the paint was chipped away. The driver pivoted toward Rachel and fired a burst that sprayed her legs with chips of asphalt, somehow managing to miss the car entirely.

Bolan had no decent angle on the driver, and he concentrated on the second gunner, hesitating as the enemy prepared to try another shot. He waited, letting the shooter make his move, reveal himself, before he slammed a rapid double-punch through his door. The boattails mushroomed, tumbling, but they still had force enough to lift the gunman off his haunches and propel him backward, boot heels skittering across the pavement as he fell. His feet were visible beneath the open door of the Renault, and Bolan watched the dying tremors ripple through his legs, the gunner's life evaporating right before his eyes.

One down, but there was still another left to go, and Bolan could not take the guy for granted yet by any means. His automatic weapon made him dangerous, regardless of his skill. When parabellum slugs were being sprayed around the countryside at 700 rounds per minute, anything might happen. The worst shot in the world could always get a lucky break when there was so much concentrated power in his hands, and Bolan never took an easy kill on faith. You had to work for each and every victory, no matter how deceptively simple the task might appear.

"I'm going in," he whispered to Rachel, praying that the hostile gunner would not hear him in the sudden, ringing silence. "Cover me."

He fed the AutoMag another magazine and counted down from five, erupting out of cover like a track star in the finals, running in a combat crouch, the silver cannon ready to receive all comers. He veered wide around the open door and was halfway to the chase car when movement on his left told Bolan that he had been spotted by the sole surviving gunner. Squeezing off a blind shot, knowing it was hopeless, Bolan saw the stubby Ingram tracking as he cleared the front of the Renault, already sliding into home beside the dead man on the blacktop.

Rachel started to fire, unloading everything she had, taking the shooter by surprise. One round hit home, but it was all she needed, punching through the gunner's cheeks from left to right, performing sloppy orthodontics in the interim. The wound would not be mortal in itself, but it was adequate to spoil the driver's aim. He staggered, holding down the Ingram's trigger as he fell, his bullets chewing up the inside of the car and missing Bolan by a foot or more.

The soldier poked his AutoMag above the level of the passenger's seat, squeezing off three rounds in rapid fire. Two of them found the mark, his human target slamming over backward to the pavement, emptying his Ingram toward the sky. Another heartbeat, and an eerie silence settled on the killing ground as Bolan scrambled to his feet to survey his fallen adversaries.

Both men were obviously dead. He searched the pockets of the nearest gunner quickly and came up empty. Whether he had been a working pro or simply carried no ID in daily life, the guy was clean.

He circled back around the car, and Rachel joined him on the driver's side. Her face was pale, and Bolan thought she looked a little queasy as she stood above the man she had helped to kill.

"You did all right," he told her, crouching to rifle through the dead man's pockets as he spoke.

Nothing.

"Do you recognize them?"

Rachel shook her head. "I've never seen them before."

Bolan straightened, frowning, circling back to check the glove compartment of the car. It had been registered to something called the Herron Trading Company, with offices in Edinburgh. He passed the registration slip to Rachel.

"Ten to one says a check will prove that Herron is a front for MacAllister Enterprises."

"So, what now?"

The soldier thought about it for a moment. Short of calling in a medium, they had no way of knowing who the chosen target might have been this afternoon. If it was *both* of them, then Shane MacAllister was thinking faster, putting all the pieces into place more rapidly than Bolan had expected. On the other hand, if only one of them was marked to die, the other simply targeted as a potential witness, then they still might have sufficient time to make an end run, find out what MacAllister was doing with the Soviets.

Bolan fought an urge to drive directly to the castle, arm himself and storm the battlements, eliminating sentries as they came. He would not let himself be pushed into a careless, losing action. He would have to wait for darkness, use the night to his advantage, and attempt to learn precisely what was going on before he brought the house down on their heads. Without an understanding of the game, the Executioner could not be sure that he had dealt with all the players. And until the roster was complete, he had no way of gauging victory or loss.

Long hours remained until nightfall and in the meantime Shane MacAllister was free to strengthen his security around the cannery and the castle. He would be prepared when Bolan came, forewarned by the elimination of his gunners, fighting to defend familiar ground. The odds were on his side, and Bolan knew that going in . . . but it would not prevent the Executioner from trying.

MacAllister was into something serious enough that he would murder to protect his secret, risk a daylight hit to close the gaps in his security. Presumably, if his assassins had succeeded in their mission, Bolan and the woman would have simply disappeared, or else they would have been cremated in an "accident" along the winding mountain road. In either case, MacAllister would hope to purchase time, prevent the word from leaking out and ruining whatever he had worked so diligently to achieve.

The riddle nagged at Bolan, made him angry and frustrated, but he had no time to waste. "We have to go," he growled, already moving toward the BMW. Rachel followed quickly, glancing back one last time at the bodies before she reached the car.

"What will you do about the bullet holes?" she asked.

"Ignore them," Bolan said distractedly. "They're all around the trunk, except for where they shot the mirror off. I'll back into a parking space and hope the shrubbery covers it."

"They nearly had us, didn't they?"

"Not good enough," he told her flatly. "Nearly doesn't make it when you play for keeps."

"Somehow I never realized that it would be like this. I mean, to kill a man. I thought I would feel sick.

He studied Rachel briefly, saw the color coming back into her cheeks. "Don't sweat it. You're alive. You won. If you feel bad about that, *then* I'd say there's something wrong."

He put the car in motion, circling around the crippled Renault, driving on the grassy shoulder as he passed by.

"What now?" Rachel asked.

"Now, we wait," he informed her, his eyes on the road. There was still an outside chance of backup gunners, though they should have showed themselves by now. He was convinced MacAllister had put all of his eggs inside a single basket this time, though the Scotsman might not make the same mistake a second time.

"Tonight?"

He shrugged. "Tonight I get a look inside the castle, one way or another."

"They'll be waiting."

"Probably."

She said no more, but he could feel her tension even at a distance. Keeping to herself, she might be laying out her arguments for taking a more active role in Bolan's play, or she might have been remembering the gunner's tattered face, the color of his blood where it had spilled upon the macadam.

The woman kept up a brave front, but he had a fair idea of what her soul was going through. Her killing had been line-of-duty, self-defense, but it was never easy first time out. There might be nightmares afterward, but he had every confidence that Rachel would survive with heart and mind intact. She had a well of hidden strength to draw upon, and she had scarcely tapped it.

He hoped that she could hold it all together for a few more hours. Night would bring a different kind of test for Rachel, and for Bolan. Mere reaction time and instinct would not cut it in the shadows when the chips were down and everything was riding on the line.

Tonight it would be two against MacAllister, his private army and the Soviets. Tonight, it would be do or die.

15

Harry Wilson felt a good deal better by the time he got to Inveraray on Loch Fyne. There had been moments on the drive from Glasgow when he thought that he might doze behind the wheel—or just pass out from bouts of dizziness—but he had managed this far, and according to his calculations, he was halfway to his destination. The rest would be no problem, once he had some food and drank some good, hot tea.

He found a place downtown, a kind of back street bar and grill that offered terrible burgers and passable ale. Both suited Wilson at the moment, and he wolfed two of the greasy sandwiches, aware that heartburn might be beneficial if it helped keep him awake while he was driving. The ale had gone directly to his head, and he followed it with strong, dark tea to cut the haze.

When he had finished, he took a walk around the block. He was not looking for a tail—although he checked, from force of habit—but rather was working off the alcohol, allowing his metabolism to assert itself. When Wilson reached Cairnaben, he would need all of his wits about him, and there would be no spare time in which to get his act together. If the enemy was waiting for him, he would have to go on instinct, and reaction time might make the crucial difference between survival and extinction.

He was carrying the VP-70 holstered in shoulder leather. He was still uncomfortable with its weight against his battered ribs, but it was reassuring all the same. The American-style "jackass rig" permitted him to carry two spare magazines beneath his right arm, tethered upside down for easy access, and the combination gave him fifty-five rounds, ready at his need. Cairnaben might not be that kind of situation, after all, but it was definitely better safe than sorry in the service, and the worry ones were seldom heard from afterward.

In any case, the VP-70 would have to see him through. There had been no time for collecting more sophisticated weapons in his rush to hit the highway out of Glasgow. Rachel might already be in trouble, and he wanted to be on the scene in case she needed him.

He had no doubts about her competence, not really, but she had not dealt with anything this heavy in the past. If he was right in his assumption that the Soviets were moving arms and ammunition through Cairnaben, the KGB would have enforcers on the scene, policing the security of their arrangement. Rachel had been trained in self-defense, and he had seen her work with rowdy adversaries, but the Russian murder teams were something else entirely. Taught to kill on sight, they were relentless, seemingly devoid of human feeling, human failings. Once presented with a contract, they would work until they filled the order or they died in the attempt, and if the latter circumstance occurred...well, there were always more to take the fallen comrades' places.

He had been up against the Russians twice before, and each time he was forced to kill. It had been in the line of duty, cut and dried, but he had nearly lost his life both times, and Wilson treated the KGB with the respect its men deserved. They might be godless Communists, sadistic bastards...call them what you might, but they were efficient to a fault, and they would kill you without thinking twice about it, in the time it took to blink your eyes.

If forced to judge, he would have said that Spetsnaz troopers were the worst, machinelike in their singleness of purpose, their obsession with the execution of their orders from Dzerzhinsky Square. One of their best had nearly finished him in '84 with a ballistic knife. He had surprised a prowler in the heart of a secure installation outside Birmingham, and was prepared to drop the net when his assailant flashed a blade. At twenty feet, the man from MI-5 had felt secure behind his Smith & Wesson .38, until he heard a loud metallic twang and felt the blade strike deep into his abdomen. He had been on the ground before he understood precisely what was happening, and then the prowler was upon him, springing like a jungle cat to follow up his first advantage. It had taken all six rounds to stop him, and Wilson had immediately lost his faith in .38s.

The VP-70 had been his answer, eighteen parabellum rounds inside the magazine, with one more in the chamber. If he could not do the job with nineteen rounds, plus two replacement magazines of eighteen rounds each then he deserved to lose it, and the bastards could do with him what they would.

Returning to his car, he walked around it once to check for signs of tampering, then slid behind the wheel. A life in service had begun to make him paranoid, but it was better than the obvious alternatives. He did not jump at shadows, but he liked to check them out damned thoroughly. It was a cheap insurance policy, and it had yet to fail him in the field.

He thought again about the tall American who had appeared from nowhere at the Tartan Army's stronghold in Glasgow. He was curious about the man, but there had been no time to run a check on his description through the files of MI-5. When time was of the essence, and security on phone lines marginal at best, an agent sometimes had to take his chances with a minimum of solid information, trusting in his instincts, playing it by ear. It was not something they taught in the academy, but Wilson knew from grim experience that training sessions had a very loose connection to the realities of the field. The rule book tried to cover hypotheticals in general terms, but if you tried to operate in absolute conformity to printed guidelines, you would never see retirement age. An operative in the field was forced to improvise, adapt and overcome from time to time.

Despite the fact that they had obviously meant to kill him, Wilson's beating by the Tartans had been relatively minor, all in all. It scarcely held a candle to the Spetsnaz blade that had so very nearly finished him, or the two occasions when he had been shot in line of duty. Cronies in the Firm had been referring to him as "the human target" for some time, and while he tried to laugh it off, there was a nagging apprehension in the back of Wilson's mind. Next time, he thought. Next time...

Except that there might never be a next time, unless he played his cards correctly, watched himself and kept on checking out those shadows. If he ran into a killing situation in Cairnaben, he would do whatever was required to save himself and Rachel from the enemy. It was the job of his superiors to sort it out and sweeten things with the authorities, if necessary, when the smoke cleared. In the meantime brute survival was the one prevailing law, and Wilson liked to see himself as a professional survivor.

Rachel was another matter. He would have to wait and see. Sometimes a violent confrontation made the difference. It could make or break an agent, bring out the survival instincts or destroy him on the spot, and there was no way of predicting how a killing situation might turn out beforehand. When the wet work was completed, you assessed your damage and then got the hell away with all deliberate speed.

He put the car in motion, northbound, Inveraray dwindling in his rearview mirror as the moorlands opened up

around him. He was climbing, entering the Highlands, glad
to leave the city smoke behind him for a while. He loved the
open countryside, could lose himself among the mountains
here . . . but the Highlands were infested at the moment by a
nest of vipers, and it was his job to root them out, destroy
them if he could.

If he should fail, that would not be the end of it. He knew
that Rachel would have been in touch with their control before she traveled to Cairnaben, and there was a decent
chance that she had filed reports since her arrival. He would
be going in alone, without support, but if he disappeared,
if both of them were lost, then MI-5 would pick up the trail
where he left off. There would be retribution, in the end, no
matter what the costs involved, but it would do him precious little good if he was dead.

Survival was the key. There was no point in pondering a
posthumous revenge against his enemies, beyond the fleet-
ing satisfaction that it offered. Given half a choice, he would
prefer to kill his enemies in person, rather than observing
their destruction from on high. Assuming that he *was* on
high.

The last thing Wilson needed on the eve of killing time
was morbid contemplation of the afterlife, or lack thereof.
He was not a religious man, and it was rather late to sprout
a sudden interest in the Scriptures. He knew that overcon-
fidence could be a killer in the field, but he might say the
same for *lack* of confidence. An operative who anticipated
failure might create a self-fulfilling prophecy and doom
himself before a shot was fired.

MACK BOLAN FOUND A PARKING SPACE that allowed him to
hide the damage to his rented BMW by backing in against a
stand of shrubbery. It would require an extraordinary interest in the vehicle for anyone to spot the bullet holes, and

he was thankful that the nameless gunman had been more or less consistent in his aim.

It was approaching two o'clock, long hours yet before dinner was served, and longer still before nightfall. There was little he could do in daylight, and until they knew precisely who the target of the recent hit had been, it was unsafe for either of them to go wandering around Cairnaben openly. When Rachel, sounding shaky, asked him up to her room for a drink, the Executioner could find no reason to object.

The suite was more or less a carbon copy of his own, though decorated in a different range of pastel shades. It faced the sea, two hundred yards westward, and from Rachel's windows he could see the Russian trawler riding silently at anchor by the pier.

"I would have thought they'd have gone by now," she said, discovering the object of his scrutiny. He took the water glass of whiskey that she offered, sipped it slowly.

"Maybe they still have some business here," he answered.

"Waiting?"

Bolan shrugged. It stood to reason, but he could not have suggested what the Soviets were waiting *for*. He was confident, though, that it would be connected with MacAllister, his castle, and the lurking sentries who patrolled its grounds.

"I feel I should apologize about today," Rachel said. Her voice was small and faraway.

"You did all right," he said, and meant it.

"I suspect I nearly got you killed."

"I'd say you saved my bacon." Turning from the window, Bolan saw that she was trembling, on the verge of tears.

"So much for staying calm and competent in crisis situations, hmm?"

"First time for everything," he said, and knew instinctively that Rachel was not looking forward to the next time.

"I'm sorry. You don't understand. I was completely terrified."

"Of course you were. You're not an idiot. The point is, you were terrified, not *petrified*. You did your job, and you're alive."

"It doesn't feel like living," she informed him.

"Think of the alternative."

"I've seen it."

"So, be glad it's them instead of you."

"I am," she replied. "That's the problem."

"That's no problem. That's survival."

"They were Shane MacAllister's, of course."

"Who else?"

She took a healthy slug of whiskey, set her glass on the nightstand, moved to stand beside him at the window, staring at the empty street below. "They might have killed us."

"But they didn't."

Bolan reached for her, and Rachel turned into his arms as if the move were preordained, rehearsed. He drew her close and kissed her deeply, felt her soft lips open at the probing of his tongue. They moved in lockstep toward the bed, their hands exploring, fumbling with clothing. Rachel made no protest as he slipped the buttons on her blouse and let it fall from her shoulders. She helped him with her bra, and Bolan bent to tease her rigid nipples with his tongue. She arched her back and clenched her fingers in his hair, to better press his lips against her yearning flesh.

Bolan found the zipper on her slacks and opened it, the garment sliding down her silken thighs to pool around her ankles. He hooked his fingers in the waistband of her filmy briefs and peeled them off, then cradled Rachel in his arms and laid her out across the queen-size bed. With mounting urgency, he shed his clothing, letting it lie where it fell as he cast each item aside. When he was naked, Bolan joined her on the bed, and Rachel slid her arms around his neck, her body molding tightly against his own.

He teased her with his fingertips and felt her tremble. Her own hand found his strength and stroked him hungrily, demandingly, until he knew that he could stand no more. He entered her with fluid ease, and Rachel locked her thighs around his waist, her ankles crossed behind his back.

The moment was too heated, too intense to last. Rachel stiffened, clung to Bolan as a drowning person might grasp a life preserver, desperately, her fingernails raking his back. Bolan felt the sensual breakers sweeping him away, his senses reeling as they strained together, gasping.

In the aftermath of their coupling, Bolan held her close and felt her heartbeat slowing gradually from the red-line tempo of a moment earlier. He also felt her silent tears against his chest.

"What's wrong?"

"It's nothing."

"Tell me."

Propped up on an elbow, making no attempt to hide herself, she faced him squarely. Cheeks still flushed with passion made a striking contrast to her eyes, the lashes damp with tears.

"I'm frightened," she stated.

"Mmm. I thought we'd been through that. It's normal."

"Not of being hurt or killed. Of *failing*. I don't know if I can pull it off."

"You're doing fine, so far."

She frowned. "Then why do you insist on leaving me behind tonight?"

"It's tactical," he told her, knowing his response was only partly true. "I need a lifeline, someone who will know exactly where I am, in case it blows up in my face."

Except that, if it blew up in his face, he would be dead, and Rachel knowing where he was would do him no damned good at all. She might be able to provide the boys at MI-5 with information on his death, for all the good that it would do. He was concerned about Rachel, worried for her safety, and there was another facet to the Executioner's concern as well. If he went into combat with a woman on his mind, he would be operating at reduced efficiency, endangering himself from the beginning. He would be vulnerable, open to mistakes and errors of judgment that could cost him everything . . . and he was not prepared to take that risk with so much riding on the line.

"There should be something more that I could do," she said, intruding on his morbid thoughts of death. "Mac-Allister—"

"Is obviously on alert," he finished for her, frowning. "By this time he knows his shooters blew it. If he doesn't double up security around his office, he's an idiot."

"I still think I could get inside."

The soldier's frown deepened. He could not give the woman orders, and unless he took her clothes away or locked her in a closet, there was no way he could stop her from doing anything she wanted.

"I'd advise against it," Bolan said at last. "He will have purged his files by now, if he's got any sense at all. Why risk your life for nothing?"

"I can't sit around here like a hausfrau, waiting for the news reports to see if you're alive or dead." There was a mounting irritation in her voice, and Bolan knew the color in her face was not entirely due to passion.

"The castle is a one-man job, and if I blow it I'd like to think there's someone out there who can send the cavalry."

"You ask a lot. I still don't know who your sponsors are, Michael. Why, for all I know, I might be fraternizing with the enemy."

He grinned. "If so, you've worked a minor miracle in international relations."

"*Minor* miracle?" She feigned offense. "What's the time?"

He stretched to see the bedside clock. An hour had elapsed since their return to the Cairnaben Arms. They still had ample time, and Bolan told her so.

"This time, I'd like to see about a *major* miracle," she said, her smile enticing.

"I just hope I'm up to it."

"It seems you are."

As she began to kiss her way along his abdomen, the soldier let his mind float free. There would be time enough, when they were finished, to consider ways of keeping Rachel safe at the hotel while he went out to face the savages. Another miracle could only help his case, could only help them both.

He could already feel the magic, and he offered up a silent prayer of thanks to gods unknown for granting unanticipated R & R when it was needed most. It was like finding an oasis in the middle of a burning desert, an uncharted island in the middle of an endless, hostile sea. The Executioner would not have called it love, or even lust. There was a primal need involved, beyond a shadow of a doubt, but it was more akin to raw survival than to any reproductive urge.

Sometimes a warrior—male or female—had to take the edge off, stand down from the ready mark and claim a private moment from the everlasting struggle. Sometimes hellfire had to wait while souls and soldiers convalesced, recuperated from the numbing shock of combat. It was not a weakness unless a fighting man—or woman—let it dominate the mind to the exclusion of all else.

The first priority was duty. It was his duty to discover what was happening around Cairnaben, with MacAllister and his associates from Moscow. The problem was that

Rachel also had a duty to perform, and she apparently was dedicated to completing her assignment on her own. He could not fault her there, but he was not prepared to risk her life when it was clearly safer for her on the sidelines. Safer for them both, in fact, since Rachel did not have the field experience required for playing hard ball in the majors. She had done all right that afternoon, but she might just as easily have stopped a bullet in the process.

The woman's seeming lack of a reaction to the shooting on the moors was superficial, Bolan knew that much without the benefit of psychiatric expertise. Inside, she would be feeling certain doubts, a measure of confusion that was unavoidable the first time out. If she was forced into another killing situation prematurely, there was no predicting her reaction. She might function like a pro, without a hitch, or she might freeze and lose her life to momentary indecision.

And if Rachel froze in combat, when the chips were down, she might not be the only casualty. The Executioner was not afraid of death per se, but neither did he fancy the idea of giving up his life because of someone else's failing.

There was time enough to sort out the problem before he made his move against MacAllister. For now, the soldier gave himself up to the sensation Rachel's movements were producing, picking up the pace to match her tempo with his own.

A major miracle of the first degree. The warrior closed his eyes and started counting stars.

16

After dinner, Rachel Hunter took her second shower of the day. The first, some hours earlier, had been designed to clear her head and cleanse her body. The second, more abbreviated shower was intended to remove all traced of the powders and perfume she had worn to dinner. When she finished, Rachel would be free of artificial fragrances that might alert a guard dog . . . or a clever sentry.

Stepping from the shower, toweling off, she could not wholly stop the images of Belasko returning to her mind. For just a moment Rachel felt herself beginning to weaken, but she killed the steamy mental video display before she could surrender absolutely. He was skillful, passionate, persuasive—all of that, and more—but she was still a trained professional, and she had work to do.

She had been forced to lie when he insisted that she wait for him at the hotel. She had resisted the suggestion strongly, for a time, until she saw that it was hopeless. Finally she had allowed herself to be "convinced" that she was better off allowing him to take the risks, while she remained behind and kept the home fires burning, waiting to assist in the event of an emergency. It had been easy, seeing through his arguments—if she was tucked away at the hotel, how could she offer him assistance in the case of an emergency?—but she had finally pretended to agree, with just enough disgruntled pouting, so she hoped, to finally convince him her reluctance had been overcome.

In point of fact, she meant to forge ahead with her original idea, examining the confidential files of Shane MacAllister. It was a risky business, amply demonstrated by the ambush on the highway earlier, but she was being trusted, paid by MI-5 to take such risks and get results.

The hollow feeling that had settled in her stomach at the ambush sight was gone, driven out by primal sex and private understanding that she had done nothing wrong. The gunmen who had tried to murder Belasko, tried to murder *her*, were enemies of everything that mattered to her. They were—had been—the enemies of law and order, queen and country, traitors to the very country that had raised them from the cradle. They had deserved to die.

Once more she saw the profile of her adversary as her bullet struck him, drilled him through one cheek. He had looked surprised, above all else, as if the wrathful hand of God had slapped him hard across the face, and then Belasko's Magnum rounds had finished it, erasing Rachel's enemy as if he were a typographical mistake in the script of life. When Rachel closed her eyes, she saw the man stretched out on the ground beside his car, the glassy eyes half open, focused on a point no living man could ever see.

Deliberately she wiped the image from her mind, allowing memories of Belasko and their recent encounter to replace the scenes of death. As Rachel began to dress, she still felt Belasko's hands upon her, urging her another step beyond the boundary lines of inhibition. Thinking of him made her ache, and finally Rachel had to blot those images again, deliberately focusing her full attention on the preparations for her mission.

Dressed in black, tight-fitting slacks and sweater, with a knitted stocking cap to hold her hair in place, and crepe-soled sneakers on her feet, she felt herself prepared to work undetected in the dark. It would have helped if she could cover her face and hands, but she had come away without the necessary paints, and she would have to improvise. With any luck, she might find a mud hole near MacAllister's.

As for equipment, Rachel meant to travel reasonably light. She wore a black nylon pistol belt, with high-rise holster for the Walther automatic on her hip and Velcro pouches for two extra magazines. A clip-on flashlight and another pouch containing special burglar's tools completed the ensemble. She had been trained at the MI-5 academy in picking locks and canceling alarms, but she had never tried it under pressure in the field. This time her life might very well depend on her dexterity.

If he was still on schedule, Belasko would be near the castle by this time, perhaps already starting his approach. She dared not waste another precious moment staring at her black-clad image in the mirror. It was time to act.

She slipped on a stylish trench coat to hide her outfit, tucked the stocking cap inside a roomy pocket and locked the door behind her as she left. The night clerk scarcely noticed as Rachel crossed the lobby and slipped out into the darkness of the poorly lighted street. She was alert to any sign of danger, conscious of the fact that Shane Mac-Allister could scarcely be expected to repent his earlier attempt upon her life. There was a decent chance that he would try again, with even more determination than the last time, and she did not mean to let him catch her unaware.

Feeling foolish, Rachel gave her vehicle a quick once-over with the flashlight, but found no signs of tampering that might have indicated booby traps or man-made "defects" likely to produce a crash. When she was confident that she could drive the car in safety, she slipped behind the wheel. The engine started on the first attempt, and Rachel wheeled out of the parking lot, running in the dark for two blocks with her lights out, watching for a tail. When she was reasonably certain that she was not being followed, Rachel flicked the headlights on and set her course for the offices of MacAllister Enterprises, Ltd.

It would be suicide, of course, to drive directly to her target. Even if MacAllister was not employing extraordinary measures at the office, she could not afford to let her car be seen. There was a chance, however slim, that she had not been on the killers' list that afternoon. For all she knew, their target might have been Mike Belasko, marked from his encounter with the sentries at the castle, and she might have merely been included as a witness. She might not be under any sort of scrutiny at all, and she could not afford to jeopardize her cover—if it still remained intact—with careless errors.

Rachel drove by MacAllister's office complex, noting a single vehicle parked to one side. Unless she missed her guess, it was the watchman's car, and she experienced a gleam of hope that only one man might have been detailed to watch the premises.

The open country was a problem. There were no convenient trees or gullies to conceal her car, no side roads winding off across the moors. Two hundred meters past her target, Rachel passed a lay-by on the other side and made her choice. She killed the headlights, swung her car around and doubled back. She turned into the lay-by, parking on the shoulder so that she was headed toward Cairnaben, digging for a pen and scrap of paper in the glove compartment. When the note was ready, Rachel left it on her windshield, tucked beneath a wiper blade. She took off her trench coat, stowed it in the trunk and pocketed her keys.

She was as ready as she would ever be. The more she thought about it, mulling over everything that might go wrong, the more uncertain she became. Aware that she was weakening, she pushed away the morbid thoughts and concentrated on her duty, moving through the darkness like a shadow, crossing to the far side of the road and homing in on MacAllister's establishment.

The complex was a sprawling single-story layout, and Rachel knew her way around the place, prepared by her previous visit. She would have no trouble finding Mac-Allister's office, provided she could get inside the building to begin with. Closing on the complex, Rachel slowed her pace and took more care to scan the dark terrain around the buildings, every sense alert to danger signals in the night. . There might be sentries she had not anticipated, guard dogs, even high-tech gear of one sort or another on the first line of defense. It seemed improbable, around Cairnaben, but she was acquainted with the new advances in security technology, so she took her time.

No sensors, nothing in the way of infrared detectors, and she knew there were no guards on duty as she reached the eastern wall, concealed herself in shrubbery and shadows there. The planter soil was soft and moist as Rachel smeared it generously on her face and the pale backs of her hands. Considering the neighborhood, MacAllister had trusted luck and skimped on floodlights, which was fine with Rachel. Writing off the front approach as an impossibility, she circled back around the complex to attempt an entry from the rear.

She would be totally exposed, a sitting target underneath the lights, while she was working on the lock, but there was no alternative. She had not come prepared with any gear for cutting glass, and if she tampered with the windows, working in the dark, she would be multiplying risks of touching off a burglar alarm inside the building. No, it was the door or nothing, and she knew that there was nothing for it but to forge ahead and try to be prepared for anything that happened afterward.

She scuttled forward, out of shadow and into light, her shoulders hunched and waiting for the bullet that would slam between them, snuff out her life like a candle flame. A quick glance through the inset window in the door showed no one in the corridor beyond, but that might not mean anything at all. As Rachel crouched before the lock, her picks in hand, she was completely vulnerable to attack from every side. The enemy could take her now, and there was little she could do about it.

Working with the tension bar and pick, she coaxed the tumblers, worried them until they finally surrendered, one by one. It took her several anxious moments, and she was perspiring heavily before she heard the telltale *click* of disengagement from the locking mechanism. Gently, cautiously, she turned the knob and pulled the door ajar.

The corridor beyond was long and dimly lighted, seemingly unguarded. Slipping through the opening, she checked the lock to verify that it would need no key for personnel departing from the complex, finally closing it tight behind her. Doorways opened off the corridor on either side, but she ignored them, homing on her destination. As she moved along the corridor toward MacAllister's office, she remained alert for any sound that might betray the presence of the watchman and help her place him in advance before he had an opportunity to take her by surprise.

And, halfway there, she found him.

Yellow light was spilling into the hallway through an open door. Rachel pressed herself against the wall and closed the gap on tiptoe, one hand resting on her holstered automatic pistol. If she had to, Rachel knew that she could kill, but she was praying all the while that it would not be necessary.

She heard voices, clearly filtered through a speaker system. Rachel recognized the sounds of television, a dramatic program filmed in the United States and broadcast weekly. If the guard was locked into a favorite program, she would have a maximum of twenty-seven minutes to herself, before he made another round of the facilities. Her problem was getting past the door itself.

She risked a glance inside and was relieved to find the watchman with his back turned toward the open door, his feet up on the desk beside his portable TV. He had a cup of tea in one hand and a sandwich in the other, full attention focused on the tiny screen. Deciding there was nothing to be gained by further stealth, Rachel moved across the open doorway in a single stride, aware that any sound would instantly betray her, bring the watchman to his feet with gun in hand.

But she was rolling now, and there was no mistake, no fumble. Rachel cleared the doorway easily, swept on along the corridor as if nothing could stop her now. Another moment and she stood outside Shane MacAllister's private office, tried the knob...and found it locked as well.

She bent to use the picks again, with even greater urgency this time. She was inside the hostile camp, engaged in criminal activity. The watchman only had to stick his head outside his door to see her crouching in the hallway and there would be no escape, short of killing, once he blocked the path of her retreat.

The office lock was not designed for real security, and Rachel had it open in a moment, careful to avoid unnecessary racket as she closed the door behind her. Working with her flashlight, sparingly at that, she made her way across the darkened room to MacAllister's filing cabinets, discovering to her chagrin that he had also locked the drawers.

A smaller lock this time, more delicate and time-consuming, but she finally had it. Glancing at her watch, she found that she had thirteen minutes left before the watchman's program ended, freeing him to make his rounds. Less than a quarter of an hour, and she realized that she had no idea of what, precisely, she was looking for.

The files were alphabetically arranged by names of companies and clients. Many of the firms were owned by Shane MacAllister, while others would be companies he did business with as a supplier or a customer. Whatever his covert activities, they would be cleverly disguised—no files in *R* for "Russia," or in *T* for "treason." Recognizing her mistake too late, she realized that she would have to scrutinize each file in turn, alert for anything that seemed to be amiss.

And what, exactly, would that be? Consignments from the Soviets would be an obvious example. Any contract dealings with a front group for the IRA, the Tartan Army, sundry other terrorists in Western Europe. Once again, the buggers would not be employing proper names, and Rachel cursed herself for being unprepared. The world of terrorism was a complex and chaotic realm, with front groups rising out of nowhere, overnight, to deal with a specific operation, instantly dismantled once their work was done. A few, like NORAID with the IRA, hung in for years, but most were built to self-destruct within a period of weeks or months, their business finished, principals dispersing like the jackals that they were.

The code name might be literally anything, the documents so cleverly disguised that Rachel would not recognize a fraud when she was looking at it, but she had no options now. Having come this far, she could not simply turn away and leave her mission unfulfilled. She would be forced to start with *A*, and work her way right through the files to *Z*, if she was granted time.

In fact, she had begun on *C*, with nothing yet to show for it, when Rachel's world fell in. She had expected warning from the guard, footfalls in the corridor, obligatory whistling or jangling of keys as he proceeded on his way, but there was nothing, absolutely nothing, to prepare her for the shock of actual discovery.

Well-oiled tumblers answered instantly and silently to the inserted key. The only warning came as Rachel heard the door begin to open, squeaking slightly on its hinges, and she was already turning from the files, one hand descending on her holstered pistol, when the bright fluorescents blazed to life and momentarily blinded her. When she could focus on her enemy, she was amazed to find MacAllister before her, gun in hand and smiling thinly. At his back, the startled-looking watchman was intent upon preparing his excuses, realizing it would be no use.

"Miss Scribner, I believe," the Scotsman purred, his tone all slick malevolence. "How nice of you to visit me again."

CAIRNABEN WAS perhaps two miles ahead, and Harry Wilson was relieved that he was almost finished with his journey. Not that he would be allowed to rest this evening, necessarily, but there was every reason to believe that he would have the opportunity to freshen up a bit and dine before he started scouring the town for Rachel Hunter. There was only one hotel, and it was virtually certain that she would be registered, though probably the name she used would be an alias.

He smiled. It was a minor challenge, but it never hurt to practice. Wilson knew her favorite pseudonyms, and wondered which, if any of them, Rachel would be using for the job at hand. Would she be Scribner? Maybank? Posner? He was points ahead from the beginning, since she had a tendency to use her real first name, and any unfamiliar Rachel on the register was due for closer scrutiny, but there was still a chance she might have tampered with tradition, changed both names this time.

Of course, the very season would be working on his side, the list of guests reduced by half or more from summer standards, making Wilson's choices that much easier. He would be looking for a youngish woman who had registered alone, attractive in her way. She would have caught the bellman's eye, and no mistake. If all else failed, a pound well spent would gather the information that he needed, put him on the track.

She would not be attempting to conceal herself from him, but neither would she be expecting reinforcements. If he managed to surprise her, which was likely, he could have a bit of fun and be instructive in the bargain. It would be a lark, and then they could get down to business, as a team. The way that it was meant to be.

He very nearly missed the darkened vehicle at the roadside. If he had not chanced to shift his gaze in that direction for an instant, Wilson might have passed it by, but there was something instantly familiar in the shadow shape. He braked, reversed until he reached the lay-by, and left his engine running as he moved to check the vehicle on foot, his VP-70 in hand.

And it was Rachel's car, the one she had been using on the Glasgow job. He recognized the license, and as he picked the note off her windshield, there could be no doubt about her penmanship. "Gone for gas," it read. "Returning soon."

He felt the old, familiar chill begin to worm its way along his spine, his hackles rising at the scent of danger. The gas gauge on Rachel's car was one of those that gave continuous readings, even with the engine off, and when he squinted, he could see her tank was still three-quarters full.

The note was a deception, but why? And meant for whom? Had Rachel penned the message voluntarily before abandoning the car, or had it been dictated by abductors? Wilson had no way of knowing, but he felt compelled to check out the immediate vicinity before proceeding into town, in case she was around and needed help.

He parked his car in front of hers, preventing her from pulling out if she returned and he should somehow miss her in the darkness. There was nothing to the rear, no buildings whatsoever for the better part of twelve kilometers, so he set off for Cairnaben, walking on the shoulder of the road, prepared to go to ground at any hint of danger.

Wilson's legs and back were stiff from driving, other portions of his body aching from the beating he had recently received, but the adrenaline was pumping now. As he walked he threaded the silencer onto the muzzle of his VP-70, prepared to answer any challenge without immediately giving up his own position. If his partner was in trouble with all that had already happened to him back in Glasgow, he was primed to kill, and he would do the job with pleasure.

There were buildings up ahead, and on the other side of the road. He crossed obliquely, moving in a crouch, keeping at a distance from the lights and watching out for guards. Two vehicles were parked outside what seemed to be an office complex, one of them a Rolls-Royce with the engine idling, its driver visible in silhouette behind the wheel. As he approached for a closer look, there was sudden movement in the doorway. Flattening himself along the verge, he watched two men as they conveyed a smaller man across the blacktop toward the Rolls. After a second glance Wilson caught his breath, immediately realizing his mistake.

The prisoner was not a man at all. It was a woman.

Rachel.

He was rising to his feet as she was shoved into the waiting car. Before he had a chance to aim his weapon, the limousine was rolling, and he knew that it would be no good to open fire, in any case. The limo might be armored, and if not, his rounds might splinter, striking Rachel rather than her captors.

"Damn!"

Retreating, heedless of the uniformed guard who was disappearing through the doorway of the complex, Wilson pounded back along the shoulder of the road to reach his waiting vehicle. He lunged at the ignition and put the car in motion. Leaving off the headlights, he stood on the accelerator, burning rubber in pursuit of the Rolls. His thoughts were spinning, a chaotic vortex that defied his efforts to extract a neat solution from the evidence of what he had observed.

He had no idea what this installation was or who the men were, why they were abducting Rachel, where they might be taking her. With any luck, the man from MI-5 might still be able to rescue her from their clutches. Failing that, if he arrived too late, he was prepared to punish them for any damage she suffered at their hands.

He placed the silenced automatic pistol on the empty seat beside him, close at hand in case he needed it at once. He still had half a tank of gas, and he hoped that it would be enough, because there would be no chance to refuel along the way. If he ran dry en route, then all was lost, and Rachel's blood would be upon his head, as much as on her killer's hands.

And Wilson had no doubt the men intended her to die. For all the questions crowded in his mind, he recognized the signs of an impending execution, what the Americans would call a one-way ride. The only hope that Rachel had was riding with him now, and he would take it all the way. To the end of the line.

17

He had expected tight security around the castle after dark, but he found no guards at all in evidence. It was a puzzle, and Mack Bolan, crouching in the shadows, tried to resolve the mystery before he chose a final course of action. It was ultimately useless; he could not resolve the riddle from the outside of the castle looking in, and Bolan knew that he would have to take the risks if he expected to uncover a solution.

He was dressed in midnight black, his face and hands obscured by camouflage cosmetics. The Beretta 93-R hung beneath his arm in leather harness, and the silver AutoMag rode Bolan's hip on military webbing. Nylon pouches on his belt held extra magazines for both side arms, but Bolan's head weapon for the strike was an Uzi 9 mm submachine gun, slung across one shoulder at the moment. Bandoleers of extra magazines for the Israeli stuttergun crossed Bolan's chest. His military rigging also carried several different types of hand grenades. The pockets of his blacksuit cleverly concealed stilettos and garrotes.

This time he was prepared for hellfire, and he cherished no illusions that the probe would be a soft one. If Mac-Allister had troops or arms in place, the soldier meant to know their number and their final destination. He was ready to destroy them on the spot, and he was not especially concerned by any odds against him.

It was good to know that Rachel was secure at the hotel. He had persuaded her, with difficulty, to forget about examining MacAllister's office and his private files. If they contained significant material, it would be cleverly disguised, requiring teams of special experts and accountants to unravel all the twists and turns. As for the Executioner, he did not have the time or patience to sit back and wait for auditors to make the trip for London...always granting that they had sufficient evidence to get a warrant from the courts.

There was a better, more direct approach, and he was making it tonight. Relieved of the distraction Rachel might have posed, he would be free to concentrate wholeheartedly upon his enemies and take them down.

His entry to the castle would require some thought, for openers. The simple breach he had utilized that morning would not work a second time. If Bolan's enemies were on alert, they would be watching for intruders there, and at the other points where stout retaining walls had crumbled over time. He would require an alternative approach, some avenue of entry overlooked by the defenders as improbable. If he could hold on to the slim advantage of surprise, it just might help to shave the odds a little, shift them slightly in his favor.

Bolan circled back along the stone perimeter of the keep, Beretta in hand, prepared to answer any challenge swiftly, silently. The tall grass whispered at him as he passed, then closed behind him like the waters of a living sea. Alert for any signs or sounds of human habitation, any hostile presence, Bolan reached the tower's base. A shadow in the deeper shadows of the night, he raised his eyes to scan the tower wall. The stone was old and crumbling, with many gaps where mortar had eroded over generations past. Some forty feet above him, midway to the summit of the tower, Bolan spied a window in the weather-beaten wall of stone.

He holstered the Beretta, repositioned the Uzi on its sling so that it hung across his back, and began to climb. The stone was slippery with moss in places, dry and rough in others. Bolan wore no gloves, and he was immediately sorry for the oversight as he inserted fingers in the stony crevices and felt unknown insects scuttling away from his exploratory touch.

The climb itself, while difficult, was not the soldier's major problem. He was totally exposed, climbing like a spider on a wall. If he was spotted by the sentries, he would be defenseless while they took their time and picked him off, a sitting target they could scarcely miss. In his position, there could be no swift ascension or retreat, no fighting back.

He scrabbled upward, inches at a time, his fingers torn and aching in the first few moments of his climb. The crevices were generally large enough for Bolan's fingertips, but too small for his feet, and he was forced to brace the inside edges of his shoe soles on the narrow lips of stone where mortar had been worn away by centuries of wind and rain. At some points, where the mortar was intact, he hung in place by fingertips alone, clinging to the castle wall with a determination that defied the force of gravity to drag him down. Each time the night wind brought a sound to Bolan's ears, he froze, preparing for the impact of a killing round that never came.

The window was a narrow aperture, approximately eighteen inches wide and two feet tall. He looped one arm across the sill and hung there, letting circulation gradually return to aching legs while he surveyed the bare interior of a restrictive, claustrophobic chamber with his penlight. Finally satisfied that no one waited for him in the shadows, Bolan worked the Uzi off his shoulder, lowered it inside. He jack-knifed through the window, twisting as he entered to accommodate the space available, his belt and holster dragging for a heartbeat, holding Bolan back until he eased them free.

In size, the chamber was approximately equal to a smallish service station rest room, obviously utilized in ancient times by guards in the event of an attack. From here, they could have showered arrows on the enemy below with greater accuracy than their fellows at the summit of the tower sixty feet above. The room was functional in its design, without a trace of creature comfort, but the placement of its single window would have allowed a bowman stationed there to fire upon his adversaries on the ground with virtual impunity. An open doorway granted access to the winding staircase that ascended through the center of the castle tower.

Bolan palmed the Beretta 93-R, easing off the safety as he stepped into the darkened stairwell. Silence. Darkness at his feet like the mouth of a bottomless pit. He descended slowly, listening on every second step, prepared to fire instinctively if he was challenged. Any ambush in the stairwell would find Bolan almost as exposed as he had been while scrambling up the wall. It would be difficult to miss a man-sized target, even in the dark, and Bolan knew that only swift reaction time would save him if he met the opposition unexpectedly.

He reached the bottom of the stairs, remaining in the shadows of the doorway as he scanned the courtyard, searching for his enemies. It took a moment, but he finally noted subtle movement on the far side of the compound, several yards from the breach that had afforded him access to the castle earlier that day. He smiled grimly, his first suspicion finally confirmed. They *had* been waiting for him, counting on him to be stupid enough to use the same approach the second time around.

Two men, from all appearances, and Bolan wondered if they were the same incompetents he had already dealt with once before. If so, they would be motivated by embarrassment and their employer to do better on the next occasion, but he could not believe they had been left to watch the shop alone. There would be others, certainly—the giant possibly among them—and he was engaged in scanning for the backup troops when he detected sounds of an approaching vehicle.

It stopped outside the ruined castle gates, beyond his line of sight, and Bolan listened as the doors were opened, subsequently closed again. Unable to decipher muffled voices, he was watching, waiting, when three figures cleared the gates. Two men in suits, a smaller, black-clad figure wedged between them, seemingly a captive. Guards materialized from the shadows, bearing arms and flashlights, heading off the latecomers in a hurry. Apprehension turned to sudden deference as flashlight beams revealed the faces of the new arrivals.

One of them was Shane MacAllister, grim-faced and brooding. The other flanker was apparently his bodyguard or driver, helping to support the captive's weight with burly arms. It was the central figure, centered in the glare of flashlights now, that riveted the Executioner's attention.

Rachel Hunter.

Bolan felt as if a fist had just been driven home beneath his heart. Was that a shadow or a bruise across the woman's cheek? Was she sedated? Semiconscious? Or had she been beaten senseless by her captors?

Grimacing, the soldier did not need ask himself where they had captured her. The lady's outfit said it all, and Bolan cursed himself for letting her deceive him into thinking she would buy a passive role. She had gone after MacAllister's files despite her promise, and the enemy had caught her at it. If there was an upside, it would have to be the fact that she was still alive.

As Bolan watched, the woman was conveyed across the castle grounds in lockstep, gunners bringing up the rear.

They reached a stony hut that was positioned near the center of the courtyard, and MacAllister called out to someone waiting inside. A door was opened, spilling cold fluorescent light into the yard before they disappeared inside and slammed the door.

Whatever he was looking for, it lay beyond that door...and underneath his feet. The soldier realized his error, searching for equipment in the courtyard and the tower of the castle. It would be impossible to guarantee security in either place, but every self-respecting castle came complete with cellars, dungeons catacombs—another world, constructed underground to serve as storage space and lodgings when the keep was under siege. Whatever Shane MacAllister was doing with the Russians, they were doing it beneath the surface of the earth, secure from overflights and prying eyes.

It would be Bolan's task to find a way inside the hidden chambers and finally discover what the Scottish laird and his Soviet accomplices were trying to achieve. If he could rescue Rachel Hunter in the process, so much the better. And if not...

Well, Bolan told himself, she had known the risks involved before she broke her word and tried to bag Mac-Allister alone. The Executioner would help her if he could, but in the end, his mission took priority. He would not leave his duty unfulfilled.

It was a bitter pill, but Bolan was prepared to swallow it and spend a lifetime living with the consequences, if it came to that. Rachel Hunter was a trained professional, and she would have to take her chances, just like any other agent in the field.

He was prepared to move, attempt a recon of the entrance to the underground, when sudden movement on his flank distracted Bolan. Near the breach where he had entered on his first reconnaissance, the sentries were in mo-

tion, closing in response to some apparent threat. He flicked
a glance in the direction of the silent darkened hut where
Rachel and MacAllister had disappeared, aware that she
might be approaching rough interrogation, even now. If
there was any hope for sparing her, he would be forced to act
at once.

And yet he could not tear his eyes away from the reaction of the sentries in the courtyard. Clearly, they had spotted someone, or imagined that they had, and they were
laying down an ambush near the open stretch of the wall.
Had someone followed Rachel from Cairnaben? And, if so,
who could it be?

The soldier had no choice. He could not leave armed
enemies and a prowling stranger on his flank. Whatever was
about to happen, he would have to check it out and neu-
tralize the hostile guns before he sought MacAllister and
Rachel in the underground.

Who else would he find waiting for him there? The Executioner could not be certain, but he was prepared to see
them all in hell, whomever they might be.

HARRY WILSON PULLED the dome light's tiny bulb and
dropped it in the empty seat beside him prior to opening the
driver's door. No point in flashing an unnecessary warning
to his enemies and giving them an opportunity to plan a hot
reception for him. He was operating on a tightrope as it was,
with little on his side except the slim advantage of surprise.

Maintaining contact with the Rolls had been no problem. He had simply tracked the taillights, hanging back a
quarter of a mile or so, and speeding up whenever his quarry
disappeared around a curve. All things considered, it had
not been much of a pursuit. Within ten minutes, more or
less, the limousine had left the highway altogether, winding
up a rugged driveway to the entrance of a ruined castle,

which was perched upon the high ground, overlooking the silent village of Cairnaben.

Wilson drove past, without his headlights on, trusting filtered rays of moonlight to guide him and keep him on the pavement. Three hundred meters farther on, he found a narrow cattle track and followed it away from the main road, parking his car at the base of a knoll, which—he hoped—would conceal it from sentries who might be patrolling the castle.

The VP-70 was heavy in his fist as he struck off across the moorland, homing on the castle ruins, with the single tower thrusting toward the navy-velvet sky. Rachel and her captors should be well inside by now, but Wilson dared not try to enter through the open castle gates. The entrance would be guarded, almost certainly, and he would be no use to Rachel if he let himself be captured going in.

There had to be another way, a viable alternative approach, and Wilson worked his way around the stone perimeter, examining the ancient wall for cracks and fissures. When he found the eight-foot breach, it was a gift from heaven, but he also knew the risks involved. Inside, he would be stalking predators on unfamiliar ground, outnumbered, probably outgunned. He had no way of knowing what his partner had uncovered, but her life was clearly on the line, and preservation of that life took top priority for Wilson at the moment. If it came to killing, he would act without a second thought, and let the Firm's custodial division clean up afterward. Provided, always, that the Firm could find some trace of them, for starters.

Suppose Rachel hadn't been in touch with London prior to striking off cross-country... In that case, they were literally on their own, without a hope of reinforcements or a chance of retribution if they bought it. While he had been working undercover with the Tartan Army, Wilson had reported only to his partner, and the lead on Russian weapons moving through Cairnaben had been passed to Rachel only after he was in the hospital. If she had taken off without advising their superiors....

He did not wish to think about the consequences. Wilson had been on his own before, though never quite by accident. He recognized the first, faint stirrings of anxiety, and knew he could control the feeling, channel nervous energy to action as the need arose. The agent's mind was on survival, for both himself and Rachel. Going in, he knew that he would not come out again without her, one way or another.

Wilson held the silenced automatic pistol ready as he scrambled through the breach in the retaining wall. He found himself inside a sort of dog run, with another wall directly opposite, this one in even worse repair. Beyond, the filtered moonlight offered him a glimpse of the castle courtyard, rubble-strewn, whole sections lost in shadow.

Hesitatingly, Wilson hedged this way and that, attempting to make out a larger portion of the courtyard. All clear, from what he could discern, although he heard the old, familiar warning signals sounding in his mind. He would be stepping out of peril into mortal danger when he crossed that ruined threshold, but he simply had no choice.

His finger was already tense around the automatic's trigger as he stepped across a pile of rubble, entering the courtyard proper. Wilson's VP-70 was strictly double-action, with a longer pull than average, but as a compensation, there was rarely any need to use the safety, and the weapon could be carried, cocked and locked, in perfect safety.

He felt the presence of his enemies before he saw them. They were closing on his flanks, two men, at least. They had been waiting for him in the shadows, clinging to the wall like geckos, scarcely breathing as they waited for him to decide whether to enter or retreat. It flashed through Wilson's mind that he might have surprised them by deciding to turn back, but as it was, surprise was their advantage. Still...there might be something he could do to save the situation from disaster.

Neither of his adversaries spoke. Their leveled weapons did the talking, compact Ingram submachine guns fitted with noise suppressors. Clearly the proprietor—whomever he might be—was interested in keeping up appearances. He did not want a raging firefight to disturb his sleeping neighbors in the village.

So be it.

Wilson hesitated, feigning indecision, tightening his finger on the trigger of his sidearm, shortening the final pull. The gunner on his right stepped forward, lowering the muzzle of his weapon for an instant, reaching for the gun in Harry's hand. It was the edge he needed, the survival margin, and the man from MI-5 was not about to let it slip away.

With blurring speed, Wilson kicked out to his left, his heel impacting on the muzzle of the second gunner's weapon, knocking it off target, staggering the startled sentry. Even as the kick struck home, he whipped around the silenced VP-70 and shot his starboard adversary squarely through the forehead.

Point-blank impact knocked the dead man backward, off his feet, before he had a chance to bring his weapon up and into target acquisition. His surviving cohort triggered off a burst as Wilson made his move, the stubby Ingram giving off a sound like canvas ripping. The rounds were wasted, crackling off through darkness, cleaving empty air.

Before the sentry could recover and improve his aim, a second parabellum mangler punched a blowhole through his sternum, ripping through the spastic muscle of his heart and flattening against the shoulder blade. He sat down, hard, a dazed expression on his face, the light of life already fading from his eyes as massive blood loss into the thoracic cavity began to empty out his lungs. Another moment and the gunner toppled over backward, trembling in the final throes of death.

The courtyard was as silent as a tomb. If anyone had overheard the brief exchange of lethal fire, the listener gave no sign. Moving swiftly, Wilson tucked the automatic in his waistband, stopping to grasp the nearest dead man by the ankles, dragging him back through the breach in the inner wall, stretching him out in the shadows, away from casual discovery. He went back for the second gunner, hesitating for a moment, listening, increasingly convinced that he had taken out the only guards on duty at the moment. He could not be sure, of course, but he had whittled down the odds, in any case. The final confrontation, when it came, might find him still outnumbered, but these two would not be fighting for the other side.

Before he left the corpses, Wilson searched them thoroughly, retrieving several loaded Ingram magazines. Whatever he was called upon to face from this point on, it would not hurt to have a little extra hardware on his side. God might not necessarily support the side with heavier artillery, but any warrior who passed up a chance to arm himself for combat was a bloody fool, deserving of the worst that came his way.

On his third time through the inner breach, Wilson picked up the Ingrams, selecting one and drawing out the other's partially depleted magazine. He tucked the half-clip in a pocket of his jacket with the rest, aware that every round might count in the approaching conflict with his nameless enemies.

He did not know the men who had abducted Rachel, probably would not have recognized them on the street, but he was totally prepared to kill them without a second thought. Her enemies were his, and Wilson understood that somehow, almost by coincidence, he had been placed in contact with the traitors he was searching for. It remained only for the man from MI-5 to face them down and see them brought to book.

He set the empty submachine gun down with care, avoiding any sound of steel on stone. As Wilson came erect, his ears pricked up, detecting muffled sound behind him, setting off alarm bells in his brain . . . but it was too late.

The cold steel muzzle of a weapon pressed against the flesh behind one ear, and Wilson felt his stomach rolling, threatening to spew his dinner up. A graveyard voice was whispering advice into his ear.

"No sudden moves. I'd hate to take your head off, Harry."

18

Rachel Hunter's head was swimming, throbbing, but she was aware of movement, muffled voices. Sickened by the latent smell and taste of chloroform, she fought to keep herself from gagging as the mists began to clear. A car, of course. At least she had survived this far.

Returning memory brought jumbled images to Rachel's mind. A sudden flare of lights in MacAllister's office. The gun in his hand, aimed directly at her face before she had an opportunity to reach her own. She recalled surrendering her weapon, standing with her hands against the wall while the uniformed security guard frisked her, his fingers probing here and there with more enthusiasm that was strictly necessary. MacAllister had covered her while the guard ran to fetch his driver, and the three of them had walked her to a waiting Rolls.

Before she had been settled in her seat, the driver had produced a wad of cotton wool and and pressed it tight across her nose and mouth. She had resisted, and held her breath as long as possible, until she felt as if her lungs would burst. Then the chemical was choking her, obliterating conscious thought and will. The ride might never have occurred...and, then again, it might have taken hours. Startled by the cold wind in her face, she had been struggling toward consciousness as she was lifted from the back seat of the Rolls, arms pinned on either side, feet dragging as she tried walk and found that she could not.

A hundred meters, a kilometer, she had no way of knowing how far they had traveled on foot, when suddenly a door was opened just in front of her and artificial light blazed through the darkness, dazzling her eyes. Her head began to throb immediately, and she lost it then, the contents of her stomach reappearing in a heated rush. She heard men cursing as it spattered some of them, and Rachel would have smiled if she had had the power. As it was, her facial muscles had begun to twitch involuntarily. Then there were the stairs, and she was forced to concentrate entirely on the art of staying balanced.

She had never seen a staircase quite so steep, with risers quite so tall. The steps were made of rough-hewn stone, and Rachel knew that if she fell, she would be injured, maybe killed. Someone beside her thrust a hand beneath her arm, supporting her, and Rachel thought that if the hand was pulled away, she might have plunged headlong to merciful oblivion. It would be oh, so simple to escape, provided that she did not mind the cost. Provided that she was prepared to sacrifice her life.

It was an option, and as the thought took shape, she knew that she was rapidly regaining total consciousness. She realized the nature of her plight, and while she did not recognize her prison instantly, she knew that she was at the mercy of her enemies. If she could not escape—and it appeared impossible at present—then her duty called on Rachel to prevent the opposition from obtaining any useful information. They had never dwelled upon this aspect of the problem during basic training, but it had been understood that drastic situations called for drastic measures. No one could withstand sophisticated, modern-day interrogation methods, and with failure preordained, it might be preferable to...

She pushed the morbid train of thought away and concentrated on negotiating the steps, bringing herself safely to

the lower level of what seemed to be a basement complex.
Tunnels tracked away in various directions, but the room
where Rachel stood, supported by her captors, was approximately forty feet in length and half as wide. Long trestle
tables split the room, technicians clad in spotless jumpsuits
busily assembling the parts of what appeared to be a heavy
dish antenna. Giant rolls of cable lay coiled in one corner of
the room, like sleeping serpents waiting to be fed.

She was propelled along a corridor etched out of living
rock. Her destination was a room no more than twelve feet
square. The central feature was a heavy wooden chair that
had been bolted to the floor. Stout leather straps, unbuck-
led at the moment, were affixed to arms and legs. Nearby,
a stainless-steel table of the sort employed by dentists and
physicians for their instruments stood vacant, waiting to be
utilized.

Released by the supporting hand, she tottered and nearly
fell before she found her balance, staying upright with an
effort. Staring at the chair and empty table, she felt ill again,
but there was nothing for her stomach to expel.

"You will remove your clothes."

"I beg your pardon?"

Shane MacAllister stepped forward, hooked his fingers in
the neckline of her sweater and immediately ripped it
downward to her waist. Her bra went with the torn material, exposing Rachel's breasts, and she could feel her nipples tighten as the cold air of the stony chamber reached her
flesh.

Behind her, MacAllister's driver seized the back of
Rachel's sweater, ripping it away and throwing her off balance. She went down on one knee, instinctively covering
herself with crossed arms, aware that she still wore the
sweater's ruined sleeves.

"You may remove the rest," MacAllister instructed her,
"or we shall do it for you."

"Aye, I'd like that," Donner growled, leering at her hungrily.

Discarding modesty, she struggled to her feet and peeled the useless sleeves from her arms like opera gloves. The men were watching her intently, but she sensed that Shane MacAllister shared little of his driver's lecherous intent. His eyes were mainly focused on her face as she began to peel the jeans and panties from her hips, and there was something. new behind those eyes. A trace of apprehension, even fear.

When she was naked, Rachel sat down in the chair as she was ordered, shivering involuntarily at contact with the cold, hard wood. She offered no resistance as her wrists and ankles were secured with the leather cuffs, her bonds drawn tight enough to slow the circulation in her hands and feet. The grinning driver stooped to run a hand between her open thighs, and he grunted, startled, as MacAllister stepped into push him back.

"Get out, for God's sake. If I need you, you'll be summoned."

"Aye." The big man licked his lips. "An' I'll be lookin' for'ard to it, sir."

When they were left alone, he knelt beside her, resting one hand on her naked thigh. "If I were you," he said, "I would consider all the consequences of refusing to cooperate. Your situation is a desperate one, my dear, and there is no escape. When my associate arrives, you would be well advised to tell him everything, without delay or pointless efforts to deceive. It's absolutely hopeless, after all."

"Go straight to hell."

The Scotsman's smile was wistful, sad. "I have, child. It was most instructive, as I'm sure you will agree, once you have seen it for yourself."

He left her then, securing the door behind him. Alone, she felt a sudden urge to weep, to scream and strain against her bonds, but she did none of that. There was a decent chance that she was being watched, and Rachel would not let her captors have the satisfaction. They might violate her body with their eyes, their hands and other instruments, they might destroy her mind . . . but they would never lay a finger on her soul. Whatever happened, Rachel meant to suffer—and, if necessary, die—with honor, courage, dignity. Before they broke her, she would find a way to end it; even bound and helpless, there were ways.

Alone and frightened, absolutely vulnerable, Rachel prayed that she would have the strength to face her coming trial. She felt a moment of regret for hesitating on the stairs, but it was quickly gone. Not yet. She was not finished yet, by any means. With the returning clarity of thought, she knew precisely where she was, and with that knowledge came a gleam of hope.

The castle. Nowhere else within an easy journey of Cairnaben village would such subterranean retreats be found. MacAllister had brought her to his ancient family home for questioning, and that meant Michael Belasko would be close at hand. If he had not been killed or captured, if the sentries had not driven away, then he would find her.

Up until the moment of her capture, she had not believed in miracles, but now she found herself with nowhere else to turn. If she believed, perhaps, salvation might be possible. Besides, the woman realized that she had nothing left to lose. When all was said and done, she had no options left.

"No sudden moves. I'd hate to take your head off, Harry."

Wilson forced a smile. "I'm none to fond of the idea myself," he answered, lowering the loaded Ingram submachine gun at his side, its muzzle pointed toward the rocky earth. How did the bastards know his name? How many of them were there *now*? Would he be able to eliminate a few of them, at least, before they cut him down?

The weapon's muzzle was withdrawn, surprising Wilson. "Turn around."

He followed orders, braced to risk it all and take a chance on bringing up the Ingram, when he recognized the American from Glasgow standing there before him, with a silenced automatic in his fist. He recognized the all-black outfit from their Glasgow meeting, and a sudden surge of sweet relief made Wilson shiver where he stood.

"Good Lord, you're quiet."

"When I have to be," the American replied, and cocked his head in the direction of the fallen guards. "You're not so bad yourself."

"I have my moments." Sobering, he flicked a glance around the darkened courtyard, seeking other enemies, some sign of Rachel. "I'm a bit surprised to find you here."

"I'd say the same. You bounce back pretty well."

"It all depends on motivation, actually. These buggers have my partner hidden on the grounds somewhere. I'd like to have her back, if possible."

"You're standing on her, more or less," the American informed him. "Dungeons, catacombs, whatever's going on here, it's been going on below ground, and for some time."

"The Soviets?"

"I wouldn't be surprised, but they've got locals backing up the effort."

It was Wilson's turn to glance back at the recent corpses. "So I see. I don't suppose you've got a plan, all nice and tidy?"

The big man was frowning in the shadows. "I've already marked one entrance to the underground," he said. "A place this size must have a dozen other access routes, but we don't have the time to scout them out. When all else fails, I find the front door sometimes works just fine."

"Right, then. And once we're in?"

The tall man shrugged. "Kill everything that moves, except the woman. Hope we're not too late."

He did not have to think about it twice. "Let's do it."

"Right. Let's do it."

Wilson hesitated, frowning. "It occurs to me that I don't know your name."

"That's right. You don't."

The man in black struck off across the open courtyard, Wilson trailing, studying his back. They took advantage of the shadows, moving stealthily, aware that premature encounters with the opposition might alert their enemies below ground, doom their enterprise before they had it fairly under way.

And who the hell *was* this American? He seemed to take the news of Rachel in his stride, and Wilson wondered if they might have been in contact. With a town Cairnaben's size and two people working on the same puzzle, it was entirely possible. And if they knew each other, might they not have been cooperating, working toward a common end? The American might well be here to rescue Rachel, which was fine with Wilson. He had seen the man in action once before, and knew that he was qualified in that regard. With Glasgow still emblazoned in his memory, the man from MI-5 could not have sought a better partner for the sort of work he had in mind.

Their destination seemed to be a sort of blockhouse on the far side of the courtyard and they were approximately halfway there when Wilson was distracted by a heavy shuffling sound off to his right. The American had also heard it; he was frozen in his tracks, the silenced automatic leveled in the general direction of a target neither man could see. They went to ground as one, and Wilson was immediately thankful for the fact that no one had apparently been hired to clean the castle courtyard in a century or so. Where walls of inner rooms had crumbled, stones lay piled in tall, untidy heaps, and these were perfect for concealment in the dark of night. Provided that they had not been seen before they had a chance to hide.

He held his breath and listened as the shuffling sound receded. Darting up to risk a glance, he saw a hulking shadow—humanoid in form, if not in size—just disappearing through the open doorway of a chamber several meters distant. As he watched, the man-shape faded into darkness, followed by a grating sound of stone on stone. When several moments passed and nothing more was seen of the behemoth, Wilson scrambled to his feet, the American beside him.

"Did you see that?"

Nodding, the big man immediately deviated from their former course, proceeding toward the portal where the human hulk had disappeared, with all deliberate speed. Bringing up the rear again, Wilson found himself almost literally jumping at shadows, wondering which patch of darkness might conceal another giant—or a simple man-sized enemy with automatic weapons, ready for the kill. They were on hostile ground, and it was not without surprises for the uninvited.

Standing in the doorway, peering into utter darkness, Wilson felt as if he were about to enter hell. There were no flames, of course, but deviation from the standard script served only to increase the terror of the place. His finger tightened on the trigger of his captured Ingram, ready to respond without a second thought if they were challenged from the Stygian shadows.

Boldly, the American produced a penlight and began to play its beam around the ruined chamber. They were totally alone, and Wilson was about to question his own sanity when both men spied the open pit before them in the center of the floor. A lid of heavy stone, disguised as flooring, had been dragged aside, resulting in the sound they had heard. The giant had not bothered to replace it, covering the hole, which might mean anything . . . or nothing. If he was returning soon, at least they ought to have a decent shot at him before he cleared the pit. If two of them, with automatic weapons, could not stop the hulk, then they had problems Wilson did not even wish to contemplate.

They stood above the pit, one man on either side, and took turns studying its depth. Cylindrical in shape, with metal rungs implanted in the rock on one side, it appeared to drop for ten or fifteen meters, though the distance was impossible to judge in these conditions. At the bottom, faintly, Wilson thought that he could see a gleaming of reflected light, as if the access tunnel opened, at its nadir, on a dimly lighted chamber—or a horizontal tunnel, leading in its turn to welcome light.

He glanced up from the pit to find the tall American intently watching him. He forced a smile. "So, now we have two entry points."

The man returned his graveyard smile without a trace of levity. "It seems a shame to waste one."

"Yes, indeed."

"You up for this one?"

Wilson held the crooked smile in place by force of will alone. "I'll see you down below," he said. "Don't miss the party, hmm?"

"Stay hard," the big man growled, retreating through the open doorway and disappearing into shadows seconds later. Wilson mulled over his parting words, then let them go. It was an apt enough expression, actually. The agent thought that he might have to be extremely hard from this point onward, creeping down into the stronghold of his unknown enemies.

The Ingram had no shoulder strap, and Wilson laid it beside the pit as he prepared to slither down, feet foremost, weight supported on his hand, then on his elbows, as his toes sought purchase on the metal ladder rungs. At last he had it, and he gripped the uppermost rung with his right hand, reclaiming the Ingram with his left, making doubly certain the safety was off before he lowered it, the silenced muzzle pointed down into the pit. If anyone came up below him, he simply had to hold the trigger down and hose them off the ladder—being careful, in the meantime, not to shoot his feet off or exhaust his magazine in one wild burst and thereby leave himself defenseless.

Cautiously descending, Wilson was painfully aware of his own vulnerability on the ladder. Hostile gunners merely had to hear or see him, poke a weapon up the spout and drop him with a single, well-placed burst. It would be perfectly effective, and assuming that the bullets did not kill him outright, he would certainly be finished by the fall.

It was precarious enough, without a running battle going on. Essentially one-handed at the moment, Wilson was compelled to trust his full weight on his legs whenever he released a rung above his head to grasp another roughly level with his waist. The move took practice, and he needed no reminder of the fact that he was working in the big leagues now, without a safety net.

He struggled with recurring images of huge, misshapen giants scrambling up the ladder just below him, reaching out for him with eager hands. Each time, he glanced between his feet and found the access tunnel empty, filtered lighting closer than it had been moments earlier. He wondered where the hulking figure had gone off to, suddenly concerned that he might be concealed in ambush just beyond the corner of the pit below. When Wilson scrambled off the ladder, he would be immediately vulnerable to surprise assault. He wondered if the human juggernaut had heard him, made his mind up to play spider, sitting in his web and waiting for the tasty insect to present itself.

He hesitated, frozen on the ladder by a mental image of the giant crouching just beyond his line of sight, prepared to spring. Six feet at least, no more than eight between his boot heels and the stony floor below. It would have been a simple drop in normal circumstances, but his circumstances now were far from normal. If he risked a free-fall, he was courting danger, facing any one of several calamities that might arise. Off target, he might strike the ladder on the wall, begin to tumble, wind up in a senseless heap. Off balance, he might sprain or break an ankle, leave himself a cripple in the tunnels, creeping like a snail until grim retribution overtook him. If he made a perfect drop, but accidentally wound up facing in the wrong direction ... well, he might as well have stayed in bed.

And there was nothing for it but to proceed. He could not double back, could not remain inanimate on the ladder while the American did everything within his power to rescue Rachel. If the enemy was waiting for him down below, then he—or they—was in for a surprise.

Teeth gritted and as silent as a cat, he made the drop.

MAJOR PAVEL ANDREIOVITCH was not amused. All things considered, it was bad enough that the infernal woman had penetrated MacAllister's office in the first place. That alone betrayed a glaring lack of adequate security; her capture had, by all accounts, been accidental, mere coincidence. Instead of dealing with her on the spot, the Scotsman had seen fit to bring her to the castle for interrogation. He was "certain" that the Rolls had not been followed from his office, but he had not searched the woman for directional transmitters, microphones or any other such devices.

As Pavel finished picking through her clothing, savoring the female scent that clung to every garment, he was satisfied, at least, that she had not been wired before embarking on her fishing expedition. Granted, there was still the possibility of surgical implants, but the Western powers seldom bothered with such outré methods, and he saw no evidence of recent scars on any portion of the body that was totally revealed to him, ten feet away, bound upright in a wooden chair.

She was a lovely woman. Given time, he might have taken some amusement from her body, passed it off as part of the interrogation process, but his full attention was demanded elsewhere at the moment. They were near completion of the hookup. A few more hours should see it done, and he was needed everywhere at once, it seemed. Construction teams could not proceed without his supervision; engineers were anxious for their calculations to be double-checked, off-loading the responsibility in case of error. He was used to the routine, but he would still be glad when all of this was finished and the listening devices were in operation.

The plan had been a masterstroke, conditional upon discovery of the precise location they needed, and he had not failed his masters in Dzerzhinsky Square. Within a week, at most, Castle MacAllister would be transformed into a mammoth directional microphone, receiving radio, TV and telephone transmissions from all corners of the British Isles along with major parts of western Europe, scrambling or unscrambling them and then beaming them by satellite to waiting ears in Moscow. When the post was fully operational, strategic NATO forces, British troops and visiting Americans would have no secrets left. The KGB would literally have an ear inside the hostile camp, and every day in operation would be worth a fortune in the form of raw intelligence received.

Andreiovitch was generally conversant with the principles involved, but he was still amazed by the capacity of modern information-gathering devices. Five years earlier it would have struck him as preposterous that any single installation could simultaneously receive, record and digest every radio and television broadcast in the British Isles and northern France, with time and energy to spare for scanning telephone circuits in Britain, Scotland, Ireland—north as well as south—and Wales. The latter feat still staggered him, but Pavel understood that certain major trunk lines had been infiltrated and tapped with miniature devices that recorded numbers, conversations, everything, and fired the whole lot back to dishes at Cairnaben at the speed of light. If he was interested, the major could tap into conversations of a minister in Cornwall or a randy housewife in Belfast. The vast majority of it was useless, certainly, but you could never tell when something interesting might arise, some bit of crucial information might be cataloged and filed for future reference.

The "tap-proof" lines of Britain's secret services had been a problem, but the vast majority of their sensitive communications were carried out by radio or mobile phones in any case, the scrambled messages available for snatching from the airwaves. All in all, the system came as near to perfection as the major could expect, and the KGB had paid a fortune for equipment, transportation, installation and imposition of security procedures. Not that Moscow missed the rubles, far from it, but there would be literal hell to pay if the project fell apart at this stage, prior to paying off on the investment. In a year, even six months, if Pavel's operation was exposed, he would be free of blame, content to point out all the raw intelligence that had been gathered in the meantime, but for hostile operatives to learn his secret now, this soon, was unimaginable.

It was imperative, therefore, that he should pick the female agent's brain and learn her secrets with all possible dispatch. There were a number of competing agencies who might have sponsored her, but he would know the name of her employers by the time the sun came up, and there was still a chance she had transmitted nothing back to her superiors. If so, she would be simply made to disappear, and Pavel would be rid of her forever. In the future he would keep a closer eye on MacAllister, make certain that the Scotsman did not jeopardize their operation through an act of simple carelessness.

For all his clumsiness in crucial matters, Shane Mac-Allister was learning. Forcing the woman to undress herself had been a classic strategy of the interrogator's art, beginning the ordeal with a surrender, lowering the subject's self-esteem. A man, by contrast, should be forcibly disrobed by others, planting seeds of impotence within the subject's mind before offending instruments were ever put in touch with yielding flesh. If an interrogator could achieve the proper psychological advantage at the outset of a session, he was that much closer to the goal of ultimate success.

This woman, Pavel thought, might be a problem. She was frightened, but there was strength beneath the soft exterior. She held her head erect, did not avert her eyes in shame as he examined her. Of course, she had no reason to be ashamed of her body, but neither was there any of the usual embarrassment beyond a flush that tinged her cheeks and made her that much more attractive. Startled to discover that he was responding to her physically, the major cleared his throat and moved to stand behind her, where she could not see the swell of his erection through his slacks. It angered him, this weakness in himself, but rather than berating her in angry tones, he kept his voice reserved, soft-spoken, filled with quiet menace.

"You find yourself in a precarious position," Pavel said, delighted with the turn of phrase. "You are completely vulnerable, and your life is forfeit now, if I desire it. At the very least, you may expect severe discomfort. At worst..."

He let the sentence trail away, and left the very worst to her imagination. She was silent, sitting rigid with her eyes fixed on the wall in front of her. For all of the response she offered, Pavel might as well have been addressing his remarks to those surrounding walls of stone.

"I wish to know your name, the names of your employers," he informed her, standing close behind her now and fairly whispering. "There maybe time for you to spare yourself the worst, before it is too late."

She spoke then, offering the major a suggestion that, while physically impossible, was graphic and unique enough to make him smile. He had initially been worried that she might give up without the semblance of a fight, but now he knew that he would not be disappointed. They would have to break her, and, although the outcome was inevitable, there was infinite variety in the response of human subjects as they suffered catastrophic pain.

He ran his fingertips along her naked shoulder, smiling as she shuddered, tried without success to flinch from him. He cupped one breast, delighted with its weight, the velvet texture of her skin, the helpless tears of rage that sprang into her eyes. Suddenly, without warning, his teasing fingers turned to claws as Pavel caught her nipple, twisting cruelly, digging deeply with his fingernails until she arched her back and screamed.

"An appetizer," he informed her, cooing. "No one hears you. No one cares. Your soul belongs to me."

It was, he thought, the perfect gift for the man who had everything.

19

Wilson lost his footing, spoiled a perfect two-point landing and went down on one knee. He held the Ingram steady though, and felt a little foolish as the empty horizontal tunnel mocked his various precautions. Light was clearly visible some forty meters distant, and he saw that there was no one waiting to intercept him in the tunnel. Scrambling to his feet, he kept his finger on the submachine gun's trigger, just in case, and set off through the tunnel, following the light.

He took it slowly, hesitating every other stride and listening for sounds of enemies approaching. He was acting paranoid, but in the circumstances, his behavior struck him as entirely reasonable. Someone *would* be out to get him if they knew he was inside their stronghold. Two of them had tried already, and their lives had been the price of failure.

He had covered half the distance of the tunnel when he started picking up snatches of muffled conversation drawing closer, growing more distinct. Two voices, minimum, their message indecipherable, accompanied now by sounds of footsteps ringing on the floor of stone. The sounds were emanating dead ahead from the intersecting tunnel, and Wilson knew that he was trapped—nowhere to run to, nowhere to hide. If they passed by, continued on along the other passageway, there was a chance that they might miss him in the shadows. If they chose his tunnel though, he would be out of options, forced to cut them down and pray that there were only two, instead of half a dozen armed and ready for a firefight. As the numbers escalated, his chances of survival diminished, and he knew the odds were already stacked in favor of the house.

Flattening himself against the wall, he held the Ingram ready, with its muzzle pointed toward the slice of intersecting tunnel that was visible from his position. If the new arrivals passed him by, he would allow them to live. If one of them should notice him, or if they attempted to traverse the passageway that sheltered him, he would be forced to kill them on the spot as swiftly and efficiently as possible.

Two men in crisp, white coveralls and hard hats suddenly appeared, proceeding along the intersecting tunnel, tracking right to left and disappearing in perhaps two seconds' time. They did not glance in his direction, keeping up their patter as they passed him by, and Wilson knew at once why he had been unable to discern their words before.

The men were speaking Russian.

He had found them, then, the rumored Soviets, but Wilson knew instinctively that they were not involved in running arms. At least, he realized, smuggling of hardware to assorted terrorists was not their chief activity, the reason for their presence underneath an ancient Scottish ruin near Cairnaben. From their outfits he would guess they were technicians, engineers perhaps. They were installing or constructing something underground, secure from prying eyes. The new dimensions of the game, its elevated stakes, struck Wilson like a fist to the jaw, but there was no time left for speculation, no spare time for pondering the possibilities.

The ultimate solution to the riddle lay before him. All he had to do was follow the technicians, be discreet, and they would lead him to the object of his quest. Once there...then what? Destroy the project. Except that Wilson could not plan effectively until he saw his target, could not formulate his strategy without at least a cursory examination of the battlefield. His reaction to a large computer, say, would be entirely different form his tactics if the Soviets were setting up an ammunition dump or training center for the sleeper agents. Circumstances altered cases, and the man from MI-5 was not prepared to bungle his assignment through impetuosity.

But what of Rachel? If it had not been for her, he certainly would not have found his enemies so quickly—and he might never have found them at all. His first intent upon descending to the underground had been to rescue her, destroy her captors, but he had not realized that he was dealing with the Soviets. The Firm would doubtless urge him to pursue his mission, sacrifice the individual who had become expendable, pursue the Russians to a satisfactory conclusion of his task. It all made sense, except that Wilson could not bring himself to turn his back on Rachel.

She was his partner, after all, but there was more to it than that. In spite of Wilson's background, all the training he had received and his experiences in the field, some trace of chivalry remained. It mattered to him that a woman was in danger, possibly subjected to interrogation by the Soviets, and Wilson was embarrassed by the notion that he might more easily have turned his back upon a man. It made no difference, finally, since he might not be able to relieve her, but Wilson recognized the weakness in himself, and he was not ashamed.

Somewhere along the line, from college through his training with the Firm, and the field assignments that had hardened him and taught him how to kill his fellow man, he had retained a vestige of humanity. If that was weakness, he was willing to accept the diagnosis, live with it, because the "weakness" was what inevitably separated Wilson and his fellows from their heartless enemies. As it was, too many members of the firm resembled agents of the opposition, their single-minded dedication to the game obscuring the goals that all of them ostensibly espoused. If you became the enemy in order to defeat the enemy, your victory was lost, and Wilson was relieved to note that he had not yet crossed that line.

He risked a glance in each direction, up and down the intersecting tunnel, found it empty. On his right, from whence the two technicians had appeared, a sharp right-angle turn was visible no more than thirty feet away. To Wilson's left, the tunnel curved away and out of sight, illuminated by a string of naked bulbs suspended from the ceiling, hung at intervals roughly fifteen feet apart.

He chose the left, for in that general direction lay the center of the courtyard and the castle proper. If they had not tunneled out beyond the keep's perimeter, their efforts and equipment would be concentrated in the area within the castle walls. Whatever might be waiting for him underground, it would be waiting for him there. And so, he thought, might Rachel.

It was worth a try. And if he failed there was still the tall American, whomever he might be.

He set off down the tunnel at a cautious pace, still pausing every dozen strides or so to listen for the sounds of hot pursuit. He was prepared to fire in self-defense each time the passage curved beyond his line of sight, although he realized that he was actually safer, less exposed, in portions of the tunnel where the enemy might also find concealment. Somewhere, up ahead, he heard more voices, faint with distance, growing louder by the moment.

Soon.

His internal alarm bells went off in his mind, alerting him to danger, but he had no choice. Retreat was not an option. For the sake of Wilson's mission, for his partner, he must find out what the Soviets were doing and defeat them. Failing that, he would create as much confusion as he could, inflict as much damage as possible, buying time, allowing

MI-5 to trace him, finish off the work he had begun. In time, the firm was bound to trace him once his vehicle was found and reported to the local constable. When word got back to London, they would flood the area with agents, leave no stone unturned until the mystery was solved.

And in the meantime, Wilson might be dead.

He pushed the morbid thought out of his mind and concentrated on the tunnel. It was curving once again, and Wilson hesitated, listening. The sounds of voices and machinery were closer now; if the technicians had been speaking English, he probably could have eavesdropped on a decent portion of their conversation.

No time like the present. Wilson edged around the corner...and was struck a stunning blow across the face. He felt the Ingram twisted from his grasp by superstrong hands; it clattered on the floor as it was cast aside by his assailant. Fingers closed around his throat and he was lifted off his feet, his eyes still bleary from the backhand that had dazed him. Someone, something, hoisted Wilson like a rag doll, shook him violently and hurled him back against the stony wall.

His lungs were emptied by the impact, and he slithered to the floor, gasping for breath. His eyes swam into focus on a pair of legs that were like tree trunks swathed in denim, planted just in front him. The giant's boots were something on the order of a size eighteen, with hobnailed soles. The man from MI-5 was teetering along the razor's edge of consciousness, but in the seconds left to him before he lost it all, he studied his attacker. Massive chest and shoulders, long gorilla arms and hands like American baseball gloves. The head was small, in overall proportion to the giant's body, but the face was worst of all, a runnelled mass of scar tissue, pale and twisted, from which a pair of squinting evil eyes surveyed the world with unadulterated malice. Mutilated lips peeled back from yellow crooked teeth; the nostrils were two portholes in a countenance apparently devoid of a nose.

It was the visage of a demon, mounted on the body of a giant, and the combination was enough to make his blood run cold. The agent struggled to his feet, aware that the behemoth stood between him and the Ingram, cutting off his access to the submachine gun. There was still the VP-70, however, and although it seemed a bit like hunting tigers with a slingshot, it was worth a try. The freak was big, no doubt about it, but he was not armor-plated.

Wilson scrambled to his feet, ignoring protests from his aching head, his back and legs. He was already reaching for the silenced automatic when his adversary snarled and rushed him, massive hands outstretched and reaching for his throat.

MACALLISTER WAS NERVOUS, growing more so by the moment. Pacing did not seem to help, so he lit a cigarette, attempting to relax. Without success. The matter rested with Andreiovitch from this point on, but he had seen the Russian's eyes and read the danger waiting for him there. Andreiovitch was furious about his handling of the woman, and the fact that he had brought her to the castle. Not that there was any viable alternative; he had no other place to keep a hostage, and to kill her outright would have been extremely perilous without some knowledge of her background, her employers.

Even now, there might be other agents working to destroy him, bring him down. It was not the potential for embarrassment that worried him; despite the pose he maintained, there was no vestige of the vaunted family honor in his heart. The clan MacAllister would die with him, and it made little difference in the long run whether it should pass away in glory or humiliation. No, self-interest had been the guiding force behind his actions, from the moment he had formed his compact with Andreiovitch until the present day. In every move he made, each word he spoke in public or in private, Shane MacAllister was looking out for Number One.

It had been difficult of late to guard himself against misfortune, with the Russian pushing him from day to day. Andreiovitch cared little, if at all, for those he used; the major from Dzerzhinsky Square would gladly sacrifice his pawns as necessary to achieve the culmination of his grand design. Thus far, MacAllister had been a necessary cog in the machine, but that machine was very near completion now, and he could sense that he was verging on expendability. Within the next few days—perhaps, within the next few hours—Andreiovitch might come to feel that he could do without MacAllister, select a puppet to replace him in the scheme of things. In such a case, his life expectancy was nil.

He smoked and wondered how the Russian would arrange for his demise. An auto accident, perhaps? A "fall" at home? Or would he simply disappear, with phony paper trails implying debts and obligations that had driven him from the country? It would be simple for Andreiovitch to plant the evidence, especially with access to his private files. The ripples generated by his disappearance would be swiftly smoothed away by his replacement at the helm of Mac-Allister Enterprises, someone personally groomed by the KGB, no doubt already waiting in the wings for such a circumstance to clear the path.

When he was plagued by such distressing thoughts, MacAllister began to lay plans for survival, charting out scenarios in which he was triumphant, quicker and more clever than the Soviets. He might be dreaming, playing games with self-deception, trying to out-think Andreiovitch before the circumstance arose in fact. Disturbingly, he seldom triumphed even in his fantasies; it was a measure of the Russian's power, his dominance, that he had pared the

Scotsman's minimal self-confidence still further, to the point that it was virtually nonexistent.

He could still go public, there was always that, but it was tantamount to suicide. If he was not eliminated by the Russians, he would certainly be jailed. Protective custody was still imprisonment, and he was not prepared to make that sacrifice. Not yet, while there was still a chance for him to cut and run.

Andreiovitch would be preoccupied with his interrogation of the woman for the next few hours, at least. She was a tough one, that, and it would take some time to break her down. She had no hope of holding out forever, no one could accomplish that these days, but she would make it last awhile and give the Soviet a workout, even so. Meanwhile, if he could slip away, achieve a fair head start, he might be able to escape the Russian's clutches.

For a while.

MacAllister had no illusions that his life would be the same, that he would be at liberty in any true sense of the word. He would be forced to hide forever, fully conscious of the fact that there was nowhere truly safe from KGB reprisals. Still, it would be living, of a sort, and it was preferable to the alternatives.

All was settled then, except for stoking up his courage . . . which had lately been in short supply. The sheer mechanics of the move would be no problem. He did not have faith in banks, and most of his existing cash reserve was in a wall safe at his home. A pit stop on the way to Edinburgh or Glasgow, money in a suitcase, clothes enough to carry him while he was on the road, and he could catch a flight for God knew where before the Russian got around to missing him. It would be close, but it could be done.

He would be forced to kill his driver, silence him forever to prevent a leak that might betray him later, but he did not mind. The man was an annoyance at the best of times, his baser appetites entirely dominating conscious thought. He would have doubtless raped the woman if MacAllister had not prevented him, and then there would have been unholy hell to pay. Andreiovitch would not take kindly to an oaf like Donner tampering with prisoners before interrogation, and his anger would have certainly descended on Mac-Allister as well.

No problem then, when it came time to pull the trigger on his overpaid and underqualified chauffeur. The man had scarcely pulled his own considerable weight for some time now, and he would not be missed by anyone who mattered in the world. For some—his teenage wife included—Donner's death would doubtless come as a relief.

When the time arrived, MacAllister would have no qualms about disposing of his lecherous employee. He would think of it as his one last public service, a beneficent farewell gesture to the people of his homeland. Once the deed had been accomplished, once his flight was under way, he would no longer *have* a homeland. He would be a nomad, with his exile self-imposed for reasons of security, survival. If his trail was not obscure enough, the Soviets would sniff it out and make his life a short-lived hell on earth. MacAllister's future depended on his own ability to make himself inconspicuous, something that had never been a strong point in the past.

But he would learn, and quickly, for survival was the strongest instinct of them all. He stubbed out his cigarette, slipping one hand in the pocket of his overcoat to feel the reassuring outline of the pistol that he carried there. Eight rounds, more than enough for Donner, but it would not do if he was forced to tackle overwhelming odds inside the castle. His evacuation must seem normal, commonplace. If he aroused Andreiovitch's suspicion, he was as good as dead.

The key was acting normal. It was not unusual for him to leave the castle quickly, after an abbreviated visit, and the circumstances of this evening would serve to validate his personal expression of concern for the security of home and office. No one would consider it peculiar if he rushed away to check his home, his business. In fact, they might consider it bizarre if he did not.

A part of him was interested in finding out precisely who the woman was, and who she worked for, but to gain that knowledge, he would have to stick around until Andreiovitch had finished his interrogation. Such a move would cancel any later pleas of urgency, and might arouse the very suspicions he was trying to avoid. Besides, the prisoner was Pavel's business now; the Scotsman washed his hands of her and wished her well.

He owed her something, in a backward sort of way. If she had not invaded his office and been caught in the act, he would be searching for another plan, another means of breaking free. Andreiovitch would not have been distracted by his human toy, and ultimate escape might well have been impossible. But he was not concerned with might-have-beens. His opportunity was *now*, and he was grasping for it with both hands, determined that it should not slip away.

His driver was relaxing in a straight-backed wooden chair outside of the interrogation room. The room was nearly soundproof, but the grin on Donner's loutish face revealed the fact that he had captured bits and pieces of the grim activities proceeding just beyond the heavy door. MacAllister imagined him in adolescence, tearing wings off flies.

"We're leaving," he informed the wheelman.

"Now?"

"That's right. Come on."

A look of disappointment played across the driver's face, but Donner was not fool enough to jeopardize an easy job by arguing with his employer over something so trivial. Next time, perhaps, the Russian might allow him to participate.

With Donner leading, they were roughly halfway to the stairs and separated from the exit by an angle of the corridor when they were shaken by the sudden crack of an explosion. Nothing catastrophic, roughly the equivalent of large-bore pistol fire, but it was an explosion all the same. And it had emanated from the general direction of the exit, his connection with the outside world and freedom.

Frozen in his tracks, MacAllister was scanning options when his driver showed an unexpected flash of raw initiative. "I'll check that," Donner told him, groping for the licensed pistol that he carried in a shoulder holster. "Warn the major."

It occurred to Shane MacAllister that he was taking orders from a mere subordinate, but he did not protest. It was the best solution in a rapidly degenerating situation. The stairs and access door were not the only exits from the underground, and MacAllister knew them all—including some that had been added by the Russians very recently.

He did not know the cause or source of the explosion, and he did not care. It mattered nothing to him if the castle was demolished, blasted into rubble that would serve the Russians as a giant bier. It mattered not at all . . . as long as *he* got out alive.

And there was still a chance that he could do precisely that. Andreiovitch would have to cope with the apparent breach of site security, a possible invasion by the unknown enemy, and by the time he put things right—assuming that he could—MacAllister would have the long head start he needed to ensure his getaway.

Coincidence was marvelous that way.

MACK BOLAN TRIED THE DOOR and, as expected, found it locked. He was confronted with an urgent choice: gain entry this way, by whatever means available, and damn the racket that he made, or spend the time required to find another means of access to the underground. With Wilson on his way to contact with the enemy already, Bolan knew that it was no damn choice at all.

The Executioner had come prepared with C-4 plastique and assorted detonator fuses, just in case he was required to bring the house down, and he used a portion of the high explosive now, molding a wad the size of a walnut against the exterior locking mechanism. Picking out a fifteen-second fuse, he set it, primed it and retreated to the nearest pile of rubble, slipping under cover with perhaps a heartbeat left to spare.

He was forsaking the advantage of surprise, but in the circumstances, there was precious little choice. When time was of the essence, stealth sometimes became a liability, and Bolan knew enough to put his faith in fire and thunder at such times. With any luck at all, the man from MI-5 would be his secret hole card, striking from an unexpected quarter while defenders of the compound rallied to repulse their obvious assailant.

Sudden thunder rocked the courtyard, and the Executioner was on his feet before the echoes died away, the Uzi submachine gun in his hands. The locking mechanism of the heavy door had been demolished by the plastic charge, and Bolan hit the center panel with a flying kick that slammed the door full back against the blockhouse wall. He followed through, a crouching figure in the dust and smoke, eyes narrowed in the face of glaring artificial light. He found a staircase just inside, descending steeply to a netherworld beneath his feet.

The blast, though relatively small and muffled by the thickness of the door, had obviously drawn attention in the cellars down below. He heard excited voices, indistinct with distance, baffled by the intervening walls of stone, and in another moment Bolan recognized the sound of boot heels drumming stone. His adversary was approaching, rather than retreating in a search for reinforcements, and the soldier started down to meet him, full attention focused on the landing at the bottom of the stairs. If Bolan got there first, he would command the corridor; if he allowed his enemies to get there first, he would be nothing but a sitting target on the stairs.

It very nearly proved to be a tie. No sooner had he cleared the stairs than one of the defenders showed himself. The first man on the scene was stocky, seemingly uncomfortable in his business suit. His meaty fist was wrapped around a four-inch Smith & Wesson Combat Magnum, and at sight of Bolan, he responded with a speed surprising in a man his size. The gunner hit a combat crouch and snapped up his gun, his free hand rising to support the weapon, seeking target acquisition. There was death and cold determination in his eyes.

The gunner was already squeezing off when Bolan hit him with a blazing figure eight, the parabellum manglers ripping through his vest and jacket, crimson geysers spouting forth from ragged entry wounds. The impact toppled his assailant, sent the flaccid body sailing on a slick of blood. The Magnum's muzzle blast was like a thunderclap inside a phone booth, and the stray round flattened harmlessly against the ceiling.

It was in the fan, and Bolan knew that there was no point trying to be subtle. It was conceivable that some of those below ground might not know they had a problem yet, but the alarm would spread before he had a chance to reach his destination, which was in the center of the maze. He needed time to pinpoint what the Soviets were doing, time to wreak whatever havoc might be possible, more time to locate Rachel Hunter, if she was alive. No, scratch that; he would have to find the woman, either way, if only to convince himself that there was nothing he could do.

And he was running out of time.

How many precious moments left before he met a team of riflemen in this or that restrictive corridor? How many heartbeats left before a bullet took him down?

It didn't matter. While he lived, he had a job to do, and Bolan would not let himself be paralyzed by doubt or indecision. Harry Wilson was his secret hole card, and between them, they might still surprise the savages who hid their dirty work in underground burrows. The rats were in for a surprise, all right, and if they walked away from it victorious, at least they would be conscious of the fact that opposition still existed.

And a few of them, at least, would never walk away.

20

Harry Wilson ducked beneath the massive, groping hands and struck out with his own clenched fist, his knuckles slamming into contact with the giant's groin. The big man grunted, staggered, one hand pawing at his wounded genitals, but he recovered swiftly, shrugging off the pain much as a dog might shake off clinging drops of water. Wilson tried to dodge around him, take advantage of the moment, but he was not quick enough. An open palm exploded in his face and sent him reeling back against the wall.

With brightly colored pinwheels dancing on his inner eyelids, Wilson tried again. This time he feinted to the right, dodged left with all the speed he still retained, and aimed a snap kick at the giant's knee. His adversary saw it coming and turned to take the glancing blow on one muscular thigh, responding with a backhand swipe that almost missed its target.

Almost.

As it was, the callused fingertips caught Wilson's cheek and snapped his head around with stunning force. He struck a different wall this time and slithered to his knees, reflecting that full contact with a blow like that could easily have snapped his neck. His body ached from head to toe, his prior injuries responding to the latest stimulus with savage glee. His stomach churned, and Wilson thought that he might vomit any moment, but he fought to keep it down.

The situation was becoming desperate, and he was still no closer to the Ingram submachine gun that had been wrenched from his grasp at the beginning of the contest. Groping underneath his jacket, he found the silenced VP-70 and hauled it clear, his finger tightening around the trigger eagerly before he had a chance to find his hulking target. He was squeezing off when his assailant sidestepped, dodging with a smooth agility unusual for one his size. The man from MI-5 was compensating when those giant fingers closed around his gun hand, twisted sharply, and he was again disarmed.

He heard the automatic clatter on the stones somewhere behind his adversary, but he could not see it, had not time to track the fallen weapon as two Herculean arms encircled him, squeezing the air from his lungs. He was airborne again, feet dangling in space, his rib cage trapped within a crushing vise, arms pinned against his sides. He felt as if his spine might snap, but Wilson thought that it would be a toss-up; it was every bit as likely that his ribs would snap and puncture vital organs first, before the vertebrae could crack and fray his spinal cord. Hobson's choice, but there was little he could do. His feet thumped ineffectually against the giant's legs, but he was swiftly losing power in his legs, unable to deliver kicks with any sort of accuracy or force.

Up close, the giant's face was even worse than Wilson had imagined, scarred by fire perhaps, with help from amateurish surgeons. Livid scars from relatively fresh incisions seamed the twisted mass of twisted flesh, as though a shaky hand had tried to reconstruct the ruined face without a clue as to directions or procedures. As it was, the not-so-helpful hand had turned a withered, melted countenance into a sort of abstract checkerboard, from which the piggy eyes stared out with dark malevolence. But there was something strange about those eyes. . . .

Another squeeze, and Wilson's stomach was compressed against his adversary's ribs. He felt the remnants of his evening meal returning and made no effort to contain the urge this time. Revolted by his adversary's fetid breath, he opened wide and aimed directly for the monster's eyes.

The impact was immediate, dramatic. Wilson tried to brace himself for impact with the floor as he was suddenly released, the giant flinching back away from him, snarling. Sprawling on the stony floor, he saw the gargoyle clawing at his splattered face, fresh vomit streaming down his shirt-front, puddling around his outsized boots. There was no time to waste, and Wilson scrambled on his hands and knees to reach the nearest weapon, which coincidentally turned out to be the Ingram submachine gun.

Gasping as his fingers closed around the weapon's pistol grip, he turned to find the human juggernaut still tearing at his face and bellowing in rage. As Wilson watched, dumbfounded, savage fingers ripped the flesh of nose and cheeks away, brute rage obscuring pain and common sense. A six-inch strip of ragged flesh was cast aside...and Wilson noticed that the gaping wound produced no blood.

Another tug, and half the ruined face was gone, revealing other flesh instead of blood and muscle underneath. He understood at last; the giant had been fitted for a latex mask, as if his size alone had not been adequate for frightening away unwanted visitors. Beneath the layer of rubber was a dull but rather ordinary face, still flecked with vomit and contorted by a snarl of rage.

This time he did not wait for the behemoth to attack. Before his enemy could take a single giant step, he swung the Ingram into target acquisition, held the trigger down and hosed the man with a stream of automatic fire. It took the stuttergun a second and a half to empty its load, and at the present range, no more than half a dozen parabellums missed their mark. He did not have to count the holes to know the giant was a dead man, simply waiting to fall down.

But he would *not* fall down. Instead he took a shuffling, sidelong step, one hand outstretched to brace himself against the wall. Misjudging the distance, he stumbled, groping for support, his face colliding with the rough-hewn stone. The giant's legs betrayed him, and he collapsed, a prehistoric monster finally surrendering to long-postponed extinction.

Harry Wilson staggered to his feet, resting for a precious moment with his back against the wall. He fed another magazine into the Ingram, then retrieved his automatic pistol, fighting off a wave of dizziness and nausea that struck him as he bent to pick it up. He was alive, and he had work to do. The countless aches and pains would have to wait their turn; he had no time to deal with them just now.

Three down, and if the inner guards were all like Wilson's last assailant, he was finished. He could not survive another bout of hand-to-hand against Goliath, and his finite store of ammunition might not be sufficient if they came at him en masse. He did not want to think of dying in the tunnels, needlessly, before he had a chance to help his partner, but he could no more control the outcome of events than he could stop the planets from proceeding on their predetermined course. And yet—

He nearly missed the sound of the explosion, muffled as it was by distance and the intervening walls of stone, but there was no mistaking the report of submachine-gun fire that followed, punctuated by the thunder of a large-bore handgun.

Wilson shook his head to clear it, and struck off down the tunnel, following the sounds of battle. Someone had surprised the American...or had it been the other way around? Whichever, there could be no question of surprise from this point forward. If the warriors of the underground were not alerted yet, they would be in the next few moments, and they would be fanning out to hunt down the invaders of their stronghold.

SHE TREMBLED ON THE KNIFE-EDGE of a scream, aware of every nerve and muscle in her straining body, totally unable to control their functions. Kneeling on the floor in front of her, the Russian gave the handle of his portable electric generator three more turns, and current crackled through the alligator clips attached to Rachel's nipple and the inside of her upper thigh.

She would not scream, *would not*, and when the sound escaped her lips in spite of everything, it had a disembodied quality, as if it might have come from somewhere else. Her supple torso, slick with perspiration, shuddered with a final spasm, then relaxed, the surging flow of current terminated as abruptly as it had begun. Her sweat would give the clips a better contact, but she scarcely cared at this point. Suffering had reached its peak, in Rachel's mind, a point beyond which nothing could be any worse.

Her captor gave the generator's crank a few more lazy turns, and Rachel knew at once that she was wrong. It could get *so much* worse, beyond imagining, until her lips were drawn back in a rictus of agony, the breathless whining from her throat more animal than human in its sound.

Relief. Her head fell forward, sweaty chin on sweaty chest, eyes closed against the light that had become a mere extension of her suffering. She was experiencing difficulty breathing, and she wondered if the voltage might not stop her heart or paralyze her lungs before she broke. It was a prospect she found repulsive and appealing, all at once.

"I must congratulate you on your stamina," the Russian told her. She could feel his mocking smile, and had no need to see his face. "Another woman—many *men*—would be a mental wreck by this time, babbling anything and everything to save themselves."

"Bastard." Rachel's throat was parched; her mouth was filled with dusty cotton wool. "Nothing to tell."

"A pity." There was disappointment in the Russian's voice, and then he spun the crank with relish, keeping it in motion while she danced and strained against the leather straps that held her in her chair, her eyes rolled back, teeth clenched involuntarily by spasms in her jaw. A stench of burning meat filled her nostrils, and in one small corner of her mind she realized the smell was emanating from herself. When they were finished with her, Rachel wondered if they might devour her body like a giant Christmas turkey, cooked to order on a spit.

The pain evaporated, spastic muscles taking longer to relax with each new application of the current. This time, when her eyes swam into focus, Rachel was surprised to find the Russian gone. She turned her head, a major undertaking in the circumstances, and discovered that the door was open, her interrogator peering out into the corridor beyond. A cool draft played across her skin and cooled the burning sensation in her breast, her thigh.

The Russian was not speaking; rather, he was watching, listening. For what? There was a ringing in her ears, and Rachel shook her head to clear them, instantly regretting it as lightning bolts of pain fanned out across her temples, lancing her eyes. She ground her teeth together, waiting for the sudden, blinding agony to pass.

Outside her cell, from somewhere in the distance, came sounds of gunfire. Automatic weapons and at least one pistol, minishock waves buffeting around inside the tunnel network, echoing until one burst became a raging firefight, all sense of direction lost.

Her captor closed the door behind him, moved to stand in front of her, immaculate despite his recent labors. "It appears that I have no more need of you," he said. "Your comrades have arrived in person."

Comrades? He was talking gibberish. She had no allies in this place. There was no one to set her free, unless...

Her groggy mind made the connection. Belasko! Could it be? Could he have found her, after all?

The Russian stopped to wrap the insulated wires around his hand, and he was smiling as he ripped them free with sudden, savage force. He left her bleeding, but she merely whimpered, lacking strength or energy enough to scream. She felt warm blood begin to mingle with her sticky perspiration, dripping from her breast to paint vague patterns on her thighs.

"I should destroy you now." The Russian had an automatic pistol in his hand, and Rachel waited for the impact of the bullet that would flatten after drilling through her forehead, coring out her brain before it punched a larger exit wound in back. The bastard was a cool professional who had undoubtedly performed this task before. She prayed he would not botch it now.

"I should destroy you," he repeated. "But there really is no need. Your friends will soon be dead, and then I will return to finish our discussion."

Rachel caught a bitter sob before it could escape, and bit it off. She would not shame herself by showing further weakness to this man... this animal. He held the power to destroy her like an insect, rape her body and her mind, but he could not invade her soul unless she let him. She would not invite him in by acting vulnerable, even in her last extremity. She would present him with a mask of stony hatred to the end, and he would draw no satisfaction from his work tonight.

She watched him go, his mocking smile in place, too weakened by the pain she had experienced to even curse him. Had he been working over her for minutes? Hours? Days? She had no sense of time; eternity had focused in her breast and in her leg, where biting alligator clamps and sizzling electric current had become the alpha and omega of her universe. A few more moments and she might have told him everything, but Rachel sensed that it would not have been enough.

The bastard liked his work, that much was clear, but it did not seem to be a sexual enjoyment. Instead the Russian seemed to find a sort of intellectual release in plundering a fellow human being, lowering his victim to the level of a cringing animal. No matter what he did to her from this point on, the lady was determined that he would not have the satisfaction of reducing her to subhumanity.

The door snicked shut behind him, and she was alone. Rachel listened to the distant, muffled gunfire for a moment, gathering her strength to strain against her bonds. The heavy leather chafed her wrists and ankles, drawing blood, but Rachel kept on twisting, tugging, till she felt the strap around her left wrist start to weaken, giving her more slack. A little more, and she could work her hand free, if she held her thumb just so . . .

It came, and for a moment she was startled, staring foolishly and wiggling her fingers, like an infant in the crib discovering its body for the first time. Tears of sweet relief spilled down her cheeks to join the blood and perspiration on her chest.

One hand. It was a start. She used it to attack the binding on her other wrist, and in another moment, that hand, too, was free. Outside, the gunfire was becoming louder, closer, and she knew that there was no more time to waste. The Russian might return at any moment, or dispatch a gunman from what seemed to be his sizable contingent. Anyone at all, to finish off the job.

When she bent forward, reaching for the straps that held her ankles fast, the muscles of her abdomen cried out in protest. Grimacing, she put the pain behind her, walled it up inside a corner of her mind for later examination at leisure.

There was no leisure now; just urgency, the haste of life and death.

One ankle free, and then the other. Trembling, she rose from the chair, one hand remaining on the arm, ensuring that she would not topple like a scarecrow with its broomstick suddenly removed. Her legs felt lifeless, weak, and she was trembling inside. She wondered about permanent damage, then as quickly walled that thought off, to be handled in conjunction with the pain. Later.

Rachel scanned the room for clothes. She had undressed here, how many lifetimes earlier? If she could find her clothing, fine; if not, she was prepared to leave, in any case, and do the best she could with what she had. The notion struck her as hilarious, and she began to giggle, recognizing the symptoms of incipient hysteria but powerless to dam the tide of laughter welling up inside her. A naked woman, bruised and bleeding, running through the middle of a firefight, suddenly struck Rachel as the funniest thing she had ever heard of. It was really *too* delightful.

Sobering with effort, she began to search the room again. Her bra and sweater had been shredded. They were useless now, but Rachel found her jeans and panties, sneakers and stockings, crumpled all together in a corner near the door. She donned the wonderfully familiar garments eagerly, already feeling better as she finished lacing up her running shoes. She still was naked to the waist, but it would have to do for now. It did not seem to matter half as much, and in a flash of understanding, Rachel thought back to a psychological report commissioned by the Firm some years before. Beneath the layers of techno jargon lay some fairly basic findings; one of them contended, not surprisingly, that modern men and women felt less vulnerable clothed than nude. When forced to make a choice of garments, either sex was prone to cover the genitalia before all else. In short, when faced with danger situations, men and women both felt better with their pants on.

Brilliant.

Someone had been slick enough to screw the Firm on that one, when they could have asked around the office and discovered much the same. She *did* feel better with her pants on, less exposed, less vulnerable, and if several dozen strangers had a chance to see her boobs before she found a shirt or jacket, well, it was a hassle she could live with.

More important than a jacket, at the moment, was the problem of a weapon. She had been disarmed by Shane MacAllister before they left his office, and her tiny cell contained no object she could convert to an offensive or defensive tool. She would be forced to take her chances empty-handed, but with any luck she might be able to acquire a weapon on the way.

The way to *where*?

It struck her that she had no real idea of where she was. She reckoned that it might have been a basement of the castle, from the rugged walls and simple architecture, but that told her little in itself, assuming that she was correct. Her normally acute sense of direction was not functioning at par—she had been semiconscious on arrival—and while Rachel understood that she would have to find a set of stairs, she had no inkling as to where she should begin.

At the beginning, certainly.

The longest journey started with a single step, and never mind that she was groggy, naked to the waist, still bleeding from a lacerated nipple, aching where her slacks rubbed against the other cuts and burns. It was a simple fact of life that if she did not move, and soon, she would be killed. It was an unacceptable alternative.

And so, she moved.

MACK BOLAN STEPPED across the fallen gunman's body, leaving footprints in the blood slick that had spread beneath him, flattening himself against the wall. He listened for the sound of footsteps, paramilitary gear or weapons, but the corridor was momentarily silent. Bolan risked a glance around the corner, found himself alone, and knew that there never be a better time to get himself in gear.

He took the corner in a rush and covered fifteen yards before he heard the opposition coming, nervous voices calling back and forth across the corridor, no doubt preparing strategy. He could not say for sure, of course, because the troops were speaking Russian.

Beautiful. They would be either KGB or Spetsnaz, possibly the worst of both. A project of this sort, on foreign soil, with high potential risk, demanded an elite contingent standing by in case of problems with the game plan. Bolan qualified as something of a hitch, no doubt about it, and he knew the troops would be intent on putting him away with minimal expenditure of energy. A simple kill and mop-up operation, nothing that they had not done before. Except that none of them had ever tangled with the Executioner.

He chose his ground, midway between two elbows in the corridor where a pair of recessed doorways faced each other, granting him at least some measure of concealment from his enemies. He chose the doorway on his left and found it locked, as he had half expected. No time now to reconsider, as he heard the pounding boot heels drawing nearer, eating up the stony floor.

He thought of Wilson, wondered what had happened to him. If he was still alive, there was a chance that he would find the woman and bring her safely out of there, while Bolan kept the shock troops busy. There was still the matter of discovering the Russian scheme that had been furthered by MacAllister and nurtured in the cellars of his castle, but the soldier knew that he would have to deal with one thing at a time.

Bolan unclipped a thermite grenade from his web belt and yanked the pin, holding the safety spoon down as he waited, listening, gauging the distance of his enemies, their speed. He started counting down from ten; at five, he let the spoon fly free, initiating detonation sequence for the fat incendiary can. On three, he reached around the corner, pitched it underhand and heard it clatter on the stone, uprange. As it began to roll, the clomping footsteps faltered, turned to scuffling, milling sounds. First one voice, then another, shouted the alarm.

Too late.

From hiding, Bolan watched a fireball blossom in the corridor, its superheated shock wave rolling up and down the hall. Hurtling coals of thermite filled the air, adhering instantly to solid surfaces like stone or flesh and burning through to find their core.

Around the corner, men began to scream and thrash about, attempting to extinguish flames that fed upon their clothing and ate into their flesh, their mission and their weapons momentarily forgotten.

He emerged from cover in a combat crouch, the Uzi tracking, stuttering its words of death before he even took the time to count his enemies. No less than four of them were down and writhing on the floor in flames, while six or seven others milled around and slapped at burning pieces of thermite that had fastened to their arms, their legs, their chests, their scalps and faces. Bolan raked them left to right and back again, imparting mercy rounds to those still writhing on the floor. It took perhaps ten seconds over all, and then he was alone with the smoldering dead.

Or so he thought.

He fed another magazine into the Uzi's pistol grip and snapped the bolt back, chambering a live one. On his right, the other door creaked open, and an oval face with spectacles and a receding hairline plugged the gap. Moist eyes took in a portion of the carnage in the hallway, what little color there was draining from the pasty cheeks. The man gasped at the sight of Bolan, and the heavy door was closing when Bolan threw himself against it, toppling the soft technician type unceremoniously on his butt.

Three other men in white lab coats were gaping at him, frozen at their duty stations around the room. They had been working on assorted pieces of high-tech equipment when the firefight interrupted them; a couple of the men still had tools in hand when Bolan burst upon the scene. The warrior made no claims to scientific genius, but he recognized the main components of the setup easily enough. Computer relays, dish antennas prepped for installation, state of the art high-speed transceivers, miles of insulated cable.

He was looking at a disassembled listening post, and given the location of the castle, Bolan did not have to think too long or hard about precisely what the Russians would be picking up with their antennas and transceivers. NATO operations in the British Isles would be an open book, revealed in ways that even supermodern satellite surveillance could not emulate, and western Europe was conceivably within their reach. There would be other capabilities, no doubt, but Bolan had already seen enough. He had already seen the bright red lever on the wall that would initiate the sequence for a fiery self-destruct.

The four technicians were illegals, and he could have killed them on the spot, but Bolan stood aside and let them leave instead. The odds were fairly high that they would never leave the underground in any case, and he had ample work to do without expending time and energy on noncombatant personnel.

When they were gone, he spent a moment studying the self-destruct switch with its built-in timer. He could give himself a maximum of twenty minutes, or as little as a minute and a half. He split the difference, set the clock for fifteen minutes, then threw the switch. It was a rudimentary arrangement, simple but effective. Once the switch was thrown, there seemed to be no means of canceling the doomsday order short of tracking down the hidden charges one by one and defusing them before the clock ran out.

He wired a frag grenade up to the laboratory door—a little something extra to delay a rescue party, if it came to that—and saw that he had used up ninety precious seconds. He was literally running out of time, and there was still so much to do. He must find Rachel, Harry Wilson, and do his best to see them clear before the place went up. In the process, if he found MacAllister or any of his comrades, Bolan meant to deal with them as swiftly and efficiently as possible.

But he was running out of time. No more than thirteen minutes till doomsday, and if he was still inside the tunnel complex when the clock ran down . . .

The soldier concentrated on his search. It served no purpose to anticipate the worst. He knew the cost already; he had known it well before he threw the switch and sealed their fate.

If he was in the tunnels when the clock ran down, then it was over. But it would not have been in vain. He would have done his duty, carried everlasting war back to the savages and rammed it down their whining throats. It was the best that he could hope for.

It was what the soldier's war was all about.

21

Shane MacAllister was terrified. His plans, such as they were, had all gone up in smoke before his very eyes. Somehow the secret cellars of his castle had become a battleground, with Soviet commandos and their unknown enemies exchanging fire on every side, stray bullets whining overhead and ricocheting from the ancient walls. At least the Russians recognized him, and he thought they would not cut him down deliberately without an order from Andreiovitch, but some of them were firing aimlessly at shadows, clearly stunned and frightened by the suddenness with which their small, clandestine world had started to disintegrate.

It was the woman's fault, of course. The armed invaders would be her compatriots—the SAS, perhaps, or even Royal Marines. It scarcely mattered; his hazardous survival scheme was scuttled from the moment when the first blast shook the corridor. Unless...

He knew another way out. There was a chance that it might not be covered yet, particularly if the raiders were engaged in battling the Russians in the cellars. If MacAllister could reach his secret exit and make it to the surface, he was halfway home. The Rolls-Royce might be under guard by now or physically disabled, but the Scotsman was prepared to walk if necessary. In a relatively short time, he could reach his home on foot, acquire another vehicle, clean out his safe and be away to parts unknown.

The death or capture of Andreiovitch and his commandos was a blessing in disguise. The Russians would not talk to the authorities, assuming they survived the raid. Andreiovitch was cloaked in diplomatic immunity, and his associates would be content to wait for an exchange of prisoners at some time in the future. Granted that Andreiovitch might not be held in jail for long, but any time at all would grant MacAllister the head start he required. And there was still the possibility that Pavel might be killed, a silver lining for the brooding storm clouds that had rained on MacAllister's parade.

A sudden, jarring note intruded on his thoughts. Suppose the exit was discovered? What if he was spotted as he tried to leave the grounds? Unarmed but for a pistol, obviously guilty by his very presence in the cellars, linked with the subversives by his title to the ruined keep, MacAllister would need some strong insurance to protect himself, assuming that he ever made it to the surface world again. Some strong insurance like the woman.

It was brilliant notion, born of desperation, but still brilliant nonetheless. Assuming that the raiders were associates of Pavel's prisoner, they would not fire upon her, risk her life to bag a man whose only proved crime was renting property to some illegal aliens. What could they prove against him, after all, if Pavel and the others kept their mouths shut? There would be no leak from Donner, Shane had realized that much the instant that a submachine gun opened fire and put the driver's handgun out of action. Donner was a bit of history by now, good riddance, and he would not be relating any of the things he had seen or heard these past few months.

The woman would be his shield and his salvation from the enemy. With a specific destination now, MacAllister picked up his pace, still cautious in his haste. It would not do to stop a bullet at this point, not when he had the means to save himself and make a clean escape. It tickled him to think of Pavel sitting in a government detention cell while things were sorted out, unable to relay the orders that would doom MacAllister before he got away. The Russian's ultimate release would come too late to keep MacAllister from winging off on any one of several bogus passports he possessed. More time—a great deal more—would be required for the KGB to pick up his trail, and by the time they broke his first identity, he would be working on another, moving toward a third, constantly in motion till he found the perfect isolated spot to settle down.

It might be years before they found him, if they ever did. Too far beyond tomorrow to concern him at the moment. MacAllister's concerns were more immediate, more pressing, and they centered on the person of the woman Pavel had been interrogating when the roof fell in.

Supposing he had killed her? Choking on a sudden spasm of anxiety, MacAllister refused to entertain the thought. She was alive, and she was waiting for him, unaware of the important role she would play in his salvation. After he was finished with her, after she had seen him safely through the hostile lines...well, he would worry over that one when the time came. There would be no time to take her, as he would have liked, but in the end, she would have served him better on her feet than she could ever have done on her back. He would be merciful and swift when it was time for her to die.

Another thirty meters, maybe less. He was beginning to experience the first small stirrings of excitement, picturing the woman, naked, bound and waiting in the straight-backed chair. If there had only been more time...

Andreiovitch appeared from nowhere, striding purposefully along the corridor with gun in hand. MacAllister almost collided with the Russian, lurching awkwardly to one side in an effort to avert the impact, feeling all the color drain from his face. The Russian's eyes were riveted on his, and they were burning now.

"You led them here," he growled. "You've ruined everything."

"I was not followed. I—"

"You clumsy idiot! You are too foolish to exist."

MacAllister could see it coming, and he was surprised by the immediacy of his own reaction. Stepping back a pace, until his shoulders nudged the wall, he was already digging for his pistol that was tucked inside the waistband of his slacks when Pavel smiled at him and coolly shot him in the chest.

Again.

The world was tilting, sliding, and his fingers could not seem to find the pistol. Incredibly there was no pain as rubber legs began to buckle underneath him. He was numb, unfeeling, as he slithered down the rough-hewn stone toward the floor. A part of his free-floating mind was conscious of the fact that both his legs were folded under him at awkward, painful angles, but he could not feel them. He was dying, and he was surprised to find it did not hurt a bit.

Above him, Pavel held the pistol steady. Leveled at his face, the cold, unblinking eye was already staring through him to the pulsing center of his brain, the point where it would place another bullet, blotting out all consciousness along with pain.

"Goodbye," the Russian said.

And fired.

THE LAB TECHNICIAN HAD BEEN SHOT three times at point-blank range. The entry wounds were clustered in his upper chest, and they had bled profusely. It was worse in back, if that was possible, where ragged exit wounds had drenched the once-white smock with sticky blood from shoulder blades to hemline.

Rachel Hunter grimaced as she stripped the dead man of his laboratory coat. She felt an urge to vomit as the fabric plastered to her naked flesh in front and back, but she'd had enough of running through the corridors half-nude, with soldiers alternately gawking or trying to drop her in her tracks. At least the smock would cover her, and with its bloodstains, Rachel might be able to play dead in an emergency.

She nearly laughed aloud at that idea. If she was not already caught in an emergency, she never would be and she did not understand the definition of the word. On every side, the din of automatic weapons echoed in the labyrinthine corridors, accompanied by the screech and whine of ricocheting rounds. The lab technician was the first dead man that she had seen so far, but Rachel would have bet that there were others, with many more to come.

There was no weapon on the body, in his belt or in his pockets, and she left him, moving cautiously along the corridor without a destination firm in mind. She wanted *out*, but Rachel had no way of telling where the exits were or how she could find one. It was strictly trial and error, with the odds against her all the way. She might be killed, by friend or foe, before she found a way out of the nightmare tunnels and found a way to the surface world above.

If Belasko found her first—if he was even looking for her—he might easily mistake her for a member of the opposition in her stolen bloody lab coat. For an instant she was tempted to disrobe again, but the idea of moving naked through the tunnels made her cringe. She had no way of knowing it was Belasko who had crashed the Russian's hideaway. It might as easily be someone else, from MI-5 or SIS or God knew who. They might not know her, clothed or otherwise, and there were still the Russian gunmen to contend with, trigger-happy buggers dueling with the shadows, shooting anything and everything that moved.

As if in answer to a silent prayer, she turned a corner and nearly fell across the prostrate body of a man in uniform. Two others lay nearby in awkward attitudes of death, blood pooled around their bodies, eyes locked open, staring at eternity in awe. Their AK-47s lay abandoned on the floor, and Rachel scooped one up, instinctively checking the safety and clearing the chamber, making certain the weapon was ready to fire. Swallowing her squeamishness, she rolled over the nearest body, rifling the pouches on the bloody web belt for extra magazines, stuffing them into the pockets of her own equally bloody smock. When she had gathered all the surplus ammunition she could comfortably carry, she put the killing ground behind her, seeking safer ground.

But there was no safer ground inside the labyrinth. She knew that all too well, but Rachel could not give up trying. If they took her now, at least she had a means of fighting back, and if she found the Russian officer who had interrogated her...

Throughout her life, she could remember countless references to people "seeing red" in moments of extreme anger. Now she was surprised to learn that it was more than just a mere expression. At the thought of her tormentor, Rachel's vision blurred for something like the space of half a heartbeat, and her mental image of the Russian was, in fact, tinged with a bloody crimson.

She would kill him, no questions asked, if she was given half a chance. There would be no remorse, unless she missed the bastard, let him get away. And if he killed her in the process, at least she would have tried.

But she was losing sight of her priorities. Survival was the key. Above all else, if she survived, there would be time to track the Russian down, see justice done. If she escaped the tunnels, she would have all the time in the world.

There was a chance that Michael Belasko might get to the Russian first. She would have paid to see that match, and she would not have bet against the tall American, regardless of the odds. Once having seen the man in action, she thought there might be nothing he could not accomplish, with determination and the proper hardware.

Suddenly she missed him terribly, an empty feeling in her stomach bringing back the nausea and dizziness again. She hesitated, shoulders pressed against the stony wall, and fought the feelings down. If she could not control herself right here, right now, then she was finished. There would be no second chance with her interrogator, no escape, no freedom. No survival. If she could not take herself in hand, she was as good as dead.

With new determination, Rachel set off down the tunnel, closing in on a point where two shafts forked in opposite directions. Hanging back, she moved on tiptoes, listening intently for the slightest sound that might betray a lurking enemy. It would be death to let them take her by surprise.

No sound. No movement. Rachel steeled herself and took a firmer grip on her assault rifle, stepping out boldly into the intersecting corridor.

She was face-to-face with a ghost, and he was leveling a pistol at her face.

"Good God! Are you all right?"

She gaped at Harry Wilson, stunned by his appearance in the middle of the maze when he was theoretically asleep in a hospital in Glasgow.

"Harry?"

Lowering the pistol, Wilson smiled. "You're right the first time." He was staring at the bloodstains splashed across her breast. "I take it that's not yours?"

"I'm fine," she told him, giddy with relief. "What are you doing here?"

He was about to answer when a loud explosion rocked the corridor around them. "No time, love," he answered. "Got to run."

"Which way?"

He cocked a thumb across one shoulder, toward the corridor behind him. "Follow me. It isn't far."

A burst of gunfire, closer, but she placed a hand on Harry's arm, delaying him. "Are you alone?"

He frowned and shook his head. "The Yank who save my arse in Glasgow's somewhere on the premises. I couldn't tell you where, though."

"The two of you? Nobody else?"

The boyish grin was back. "We didn't have a lot of candidates to choose from, I'm afraid. It was a hasty sort of operation."

Rachel kissed his cheek impetuously, stepping quickly back to wipe at her eyes with a sleeve of her smock. "All right. Let's go."

Behind them, sounds of combat were approaching, drawing nearer. Rachel gripped her automatic rifle tightly and followed Harry as he struck off down the corridor. Mike Belasko might be fighting for his life back there, and Rachel felt a sudden urge to double back and help him, stand beside him to the end. Of course, it was a foolish thought; she had no way of knowing where he was, or whether he was even still alive.

The thought of Belasko, dead, struck Rachel hard. Her breath was burning in her throat, and tears were in her eyes, but still she followed Harry toward the exit. Toward the night above, and freedom.

There was nothing she could do for Michael now, except survive herself, and wreak grim vengeance on his enemies if he did not. It was the best that she could hope for... and it seemed to Rachel Hunter that it was not nearly good enough.

THE SPETSNAZ TROOPERS had been shot from ambush, bodies set afire by thermite, left to burn. Their stench was nearly overpowering, but it was nothing that he had not smelled before. Andreiovitch surveyed the twisted corpses with a sense of mounting apprehension, not because they had been killed, not for the grisly manner of their deaths, but rather for the timing and location of their fall. He had already found two lab technicians, dropped by automatic fire from one side or the other, indicating that the members of the crew had either fled or been evicted from their workroom. Now, the shriveled, blackened bodies of his soldiers reconfirmed the worst, that everything he had worked for was in jeopardy.

Thus far, he had not even glimpsed the enemy, could not have guessed his number or his name. *Someone* had penetrated their security, undoubtedly by following MacAllister when he had seized the woman, but it bothered Pavel not to know precisely what and whom he was confronting. Long accustomed to controlling every situation, he was not in a position to dictate terms. Not helpless by any means, but neither was he in control.

He hated it.

His masters in Dzerzhinsky Square would not be satisfied with anything except success. Andreiovitch knew that, and he was conscious of the fact that failure would be catastrophic for his own career. Expenditures of time and money had been authorized on Pavel's word that he could get the job done, bring the project to fruition. He had been so close, so very close . . . but now he saw the victory about to slip between his fingers, and he felt as helpless as a child.

If two of the technicians had been killed, that left at least eight others wandering around the complex somewhere, waiting to be organized again. More than enough to do the job, assuming that Andreiovitch could finally eliminate his enemies and restore the kind of order that was necessary for success.

The Russian laughed aloud, the harsh sound ringing in the corridor. It was ridiculous, of course, to think that they could still proceed. No matter who their enemies might be, no matter who emerged victorious from the engagement, they were finished in Cairnaben. It would be impossible to hide the evidence of such a battle from the local peasants; Pavel would have been surprised if some, at least, had not already heard the echoes of explosions, the automatic-weapons fire. The raiding force would certainly be acting under orders, and superiors would know precisely where they were. If they should fail, or simply disappear, there would be others sent to find them, others after those, and so on, through eternity.

His scheme was ruined, but the Russian knew that there were still obligatory steps to take, procedures to be followed. His commandos carried no ID; they would not let themselves be taken prisoner, and Spetsnaz service records would be permanently closed to British lawmen. There would be suspicion, questions, some embarrassment for Moscow, but no lasting damage . . . if he got rid of the evidence in time.

He could not let the raiders capture any of the made-in-Moscow listening equipment. That would be a major error, and he had already planned against it, taking steps to guarantee that nothing would be left for confiscation by an enemy, if one should find them out. The charges were in place, the mechanism waiting to be primed, and he would still have ample time to make his get away, to clear the scene before he could be spotted and identified.

But first he had to get inside the lab.

Behind him, somewhere in the winding maze of corridors, another burst of automatic fire erupted, sounding closer than the last. Thus far he had not seen their enemies, had no idea where they might be, but from the sound of it, they were engaging Pavel's troopers in a struggle to the death. The man from KGB could not afford to wait and see which way the final outcome went, especially since his plans were doomed in either case. The sooner he destroyed the evidence, the better for himself. From that point on, Andreiovitch could concentrate on getting out, on making good his ultimate escape.

But where was he to go?

A lifetime in the service of his country was about to end. He saw that clearly and he recognized the fact that he could not go back to Moscow in disgrace. They would be looking for examples, scapegoats, and he did not plan to spend his golden years exploring all the wonders of the Gulag. He would be fortunate to escape with life imprisonment, once the old men in Moscow finished arguing about his failure. There were even worse alternatives: the hospitals, where minds were scrambled and reduced to jelly in the name of "psychotherapy"; the Lubyanka, Moscow's grim bastille, where few emerged at all, and none unscathed; the firing squads and "accidents"" that had, of late, claimed several fallen Party favorites.

It was extremely fortunate, Andreiovitch decided, that he was a man with foresight. He had laid up secret cash reserves in Switzerland and the Bahamas, taking out insurance for his most uncertain future. He had passports in a wide variety of names, which traveled with him everywhere, courtesy of KGB's documents division. Four of the identities were not on file with Moscow, and he thought that they should be enough to see him through the coming months, until the hot pursuit began to cool a bit.

Not that he would ever be entirely safe. In retrospect, however, life in hiding, looking back across one's shoulder, was a damned sight preferable to the obvious alternative. If Pavel ran—*when* Pavel ran—he would be running for his life, and there would be no turning back.

He thought about his wife—the bitch—and their two whining brats in Moscow. He had married the daughter of a Party minister, and thereby helped his own career. Their marriage had not been precisely loveless—not at the beginning, anyway—but Sophia was a child of privilege, self-indulgent, spoiled. If anything, she had grown worse with age, and Pavel would not miss her in the least. As for the children, they were easily her equals when it came to pouting, throwing temper tantrums, sulking when their every wish was not immediately granted.

Pavel smiled. Good riddance to them all.

He tried the laboratory door and found it locked. Andreiovitch removed a key ring from his pocket, found the proper key, inserted it and turned the lock. The door swung inward on its well-oiled hinges, but he was surprised to hear a small, metallic *snick*, as a second latching mechanism disengaged. Something pinged against the floor, and Pavel glanced down at his feet, unable, for a moment, to believe what he was seeing.

A grenade. It had been secured to the jamb with electrical tape. The safety spoon was nearby, a useless twist of metal lying on the floor.

There were perhaps three seconds left, and Pavel saw the pin, secured to the door with wire. It dangled like the brass ring on a carousel in which the bonus prize was death.

The Russian tried to turn and run.

The world exploded in his face.

No more than seven minutes were left, and the Executioner was running out of options. He had found the grim interrogation room, complete with tools in place, but there had been no sign of Rachel. He had roamed the corridors with purpose, sectoring the place and taking down a dozen of the Spetsnaz troopers in the process, but he was no closer to the woman than he had been at the outset. Worse, there was no sign of Harry Wilson, either, and he had begun to think that all of them might still be running through the maze, like laboratory rats, when time ran out.

He had no way of knowing how the charges had been laid, or in what quantity. There would be adequate amounts of high explosive to destroy the listening devices, wipe out every trace of Soviet involvement in the operation, and it figured there would be strategic charges planted here and there throughout the tunnel network to ensure that excavators would be looking at a long, hard job.

There would be enough, no matter how you sliced it, to eradicate all personnel inside the tunnels. Which made the soldier's mission that much more imperative. There were two allies to be found before he cleared the killing grounds, and so far he had run in circles. If he did not find them soon and get them out of there, it would be too damned late and too damned bad.

Ahead of him and around a corner of the tunnel, Bolan heard a sudden hammering of automatic weapons. Frozen in his tracks, he listened, waiting for another sharp exchange—and heard the ripping-canvas sound so characteristic of a silenced Ingram submachine gun, nearly overpowered by the bark of AK-47 automatic rifles.

Wilson!

Bolan took the corner in a sprint, homing on the sounds of combat, slowing only when he realized that one more corner, one more turn, would put him in the middle of the killing ground. He risked a glance around the tunnel's bend and found himself behind a group of Spetsnaz. They were firing downrange toward a recessed doorway where their targets were apparently concealed. Another squad of riflemen was stationed at the far end of the corridor, pinning down their prey in an effective cross fire.

As he watched, the man from MI-5 ducked out of cover long enough to snap a burst in the direction of his starboard enemies, retreating as the AK-47s roared in concert. Bolan knew the guy could not hold out much longer. *None* of them had much time left, and he was wasting precious seconds, even as the thought took shape inside his mind.

He edged around the corner, tightening his finger on the Uzi's trigger, feeling no compunction as he raked the Spetsnaz gunners from behind. The parabellum manglers swept their line from left to right and back again, their bodies jerking, dancing with the impact. At the far end of the corridor, their startled comrades scattered fire that gained momentum by the heartbeat.

Sudden, ringing silence fell across the claustrophobic battleground, immediately broken by a woman's voice. "Is that you, Michael?"

"Here," he answered, working loose a frag grenade from his web belt. "Keep your heads down!"

Bolan yanked the pin and let the spoon fly, leaning far enough around the corner for a solid overhand delivery. A couple of the Spetsnaz gunners opened up the moment he showed himself, their probing rounds impacting on the stony wall and showering his face with jagged slivers, drawing blood. He saw the high-explosive egg bounce once, then wobble on its way along the floor, directly toward the nest of crouching riflemen.

A clap of heavy-metal thunder deafened Bolan, and he burst from cover in a combat crouch, his Uzi roaring at full throttle. Sudden movement erupted in the corridor, between the soldier and his targets as Wilson and Rachel joined the rush, their weapons rattling in counterpoint. Their enemies were rising, scattering, returning fire...and they were falling as concentrated bursts of autofire ripped through their ranks and toppled them like bowling pins.

Together, three survivors stood among the dead, reloading superheated weapons, conscious of the fact that they were not home free by any means. Rachel wore a smock that had been torn by bullets, soaked with blood, and none of it apparently her own. Two buttons had been ripped away, and it was obvious that she was wearing nothing underneath. As for her partner, he resembled someone who had gone a dozen rounds with Rocky Balboa and had fought the slugger to a draw. Amazingly, both of them smiled.

The soldier checked his watch and said, "Two minutes. We're on self-destruct. This place is going up."

"This way!" barked Wilson, moving off along the corridor at double time. They followed him through twists and turns, the numbers falling in their wake, and Bolan hoped their self-appointed guide knew where he was going. If not, they would find a rather different destination, and they would all be there together when the smoke cleared.

They raced past the twisted body of a giant, which was sprawled in the middle of a narrow hallway, lifeblood leaking from at least two dozen wounds. Bolan had a momentary flashback to that morning and the hulking form that had attempted to pursue his car as Bolan left the castle, all bets off now that the brute had been withdrawn from play. No time for questions, answers, anything beyond the animal reflex of flight.

They reached a ladder and scrambled upward toward a dark rectangle flecked with distant stars. Rachel first, with Wilson on her heels, and Bolan made it three, scrambling through the hatch with less than half a minute left to spare. They raced across the courtyard, Rachel stumbling, about to fall, when both men caught her underneath her arms and hauled her, struggling, to the eastern breach. They were staggering downslope when, suddenly, the earth began to buck and heave beneath their feet.

Together, arm-in-arm, they turned to watch the castle fall. At first the earth appeared to ripple, loose stones toppling from the ancient walls, and then a gout of smoke and flame erupted from the center of the courtyard, shock waves battering their ears, rocking them back on their heels. A chain reaction of explosions was occurring underground, expelling clouds of smoke and chunks of stone in varied sizes, some as large as compact cars. A secondary blast ripped through the single standing tower at its base, and Bolan watched as the ancient spire began to telescope, collapsing in upon itself, a mushroom cloud of dust appearing in its place.

And lights were being turned on below them, in Cairnaben. The village was awake, and soon the curious would start to wind their way across the moorland, following the sounds, the firelight from the ruins.

Bolan felt the others watching him. Waiting.

"Seen enough?"

"And then some," Rachel told him, grimacing.

"I think we'll soon have company," said Wilson, nodding toward the village. "I recommend we not be here when they arrive."

"I second that."

They moved downslope, through fire-lit darkness, toward their waiting cars. Behind them, Shane MacAllister's ancestral home was burning like a funeral pyre, a fiery monument to avarice. It was a cleansing fire, and Bolan hoped that it would be enough.

For now, his job was finished. With the sunrise, other targets would present themselves, demanding his attention, but the remnants of the night were his, to do with as he pleased. Good comrades and the knowledge of a job well done were all he needed at the moment.

And tomorrow would take care of itself.

Nile Barrabas and the Soldiers of Barrabas are the

SOBs

by Jack Hild

Nile Barrabas is a nervy son of a bitch who was the last American soldier out of Vietnam and the first man into a new kind of action. His warriors, called the Soldiers of Barrabas, have one very simple ambition: to do what the Marines can't or won't do. Join the Barrabas blitz! Each book hits new heights—this is brawling at its best!

"Nile Barrabas is one tough SOB himself. . . . A wealth of detail. . . . SOBs does the job!"
—*West Coast Review of Books*

GOLD EAGLE

Available wherever paperbacks are sold.

SOBs-1

JAMES AXLER

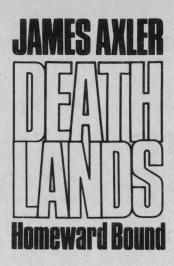

DEATH LANDS

Homeward Bound

In the Deathlands,
honor and fair play are words of the past.
Vengeance is a word to live by . . .

Throughout his travels he encountered mankind at its worst. But nothing could be more vile than the remnants of Ryan's own family—brutal murderers who indulge their every whim.

Now his journey has come full circle. Ryan Cawdor is about to go home.

You don't know what NONSTOP HIGH-VOLTAGE ACTION is until you've read your 4 FREE GOLD EAGLE NOVELS

TAKE 'EM NOW

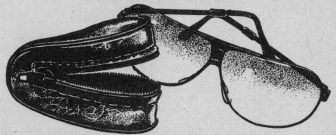

FOLDING SUNGLASSES FROM GOLD EAGLE

Mean up your act with these tough, street-smart shades. Practical, too, because they fold 3 times into a handy, zip-up polyurethane pouch that fits neatly into your pocket. Rugged metal frame. Scratch-resistant acrylic lenses. Best of all, they can be yours for only $6.99.

MAIL YOUR ORDER TODAY.

Send your name, address, and zip code, along with a check or money order for just $6.99 + .75¢ for postage and handling (for a total of $7.74) payable to Gold Eagle Reader Service. (New York and Iowa residents please add applicable sales tax.)

Remove from pouch...

unfold once...

Gold Eagle Reader Service
901 Fuhrmann Blvd.
P.O. Box 1396
Buffalo, N.Y. 14240-1396

unfold twice...

and they're ready to wear.

GES-1A

Offer not available in Canada.